Jennifer flicked him once with her tongue and then lay back on the bed. The sheet had been flung away. She narrowed her eyes at him. "What are you waiting for? Get out of those clothes."

As John Eagle, Expeditor, took in her rising breasts and taut nipples, he felt he would soon reach the high point of a most enjoyable adventure.

HAVE YOU READ ALL THE JOHN EAGLE—EXPEDITOR BOOKS?

SILVERSKULL

PAUL EDWARDS

PYRAMID BOOKS ▲ NEW YORK

CHAPTER 1

Sir Rodney Hamilton had a secret. A shameful secret, he supposed, though he did not think it fair that a man should be held accountable for thoughts he could not control. Still and all, incest was the one terrible taboo which no man might break with impunity, so he strove mightily to suppress his sexual thoughts about Jennifer.

In truth he loved his daughter dearly—she was the one aspect of life he did love, other than money and power—and he had known for a long time that she did not love him. He often wondered, in rare moments of depression and introspection, if Jennifer suspected his thoughts about her. Women were intuitive about such matters, so he'd always heard, but certainly her mother—he had difficulty recalling her name—had not intuited that Rod Hamilton would seduce her, take their daughter and leave without marriage. Berenice; that was her name. Berenice had been a very beautiful and very stupid woman. He still sent her a pittance, but he had not seen or spoken with her since Jennifer's birth twenty-two years ago.

At the moment Sir Rodney, who had bought his way onto the Honours List five years ago, was in Tokyo on unpleasant business. He was withdrawing his support, both in money and prestige, from a Japanese shipbuilding consortium. Japanese inflation was rampant, nearing thirty percent, and the deal was no longer viable.

Mr. Hediki Noguchi, his host for the weekend, was Chairman of the Board for the consortium. He smiled sadly when Sir Rodney informed him of his decision to withdraw and cut his losses. Noguchi, one of the few Japanese whom Sir Rodney had actually found inscrutable, did not mention the matter again until after the *kabuki* that evening. They had attended the

Kabuki-za, at Mimara-Bashi, and were being chauffered to Noguchi's home in one of the wealthier suburbs.

While they were caught in traffic on the Ginza, the Japanese gave Sir Rodney a penetrating stare and asked, "You never mention your own affairs, Rod. You seem to know everything about everybody else, but nobody knows much about you. I don't, and we've been business friends for ten years. How *is* it going with you in this wild, depressed world today?"

Sir Rodney stared at the lighted display windows of the Matsuzakaya department store, at shapely plastic mannequins wearing miniskirts. He shrugged, lit a dollar cigar and gave his Japanese acquaintance—Sir Rodney did not have friends—a cool stare.

"The world is full of fools, Hediki. At least I never have any trouble finding them. These are hard times for most, but very good times for some; a few, with money and brains, who know how to take advantage. I think it will come to mass starvation, breadlines, then war, but out of that a clever man can make as many fortunes as he chooses."

Noguchi's smile was wry. "I have heard that before, Rod, and I suppose it can be done. But one needs enormous amounts of money to begin with. Cash. My, our, cash flow has slowed to a trickle. With no new springs in view. Speaking of that, I was wondering . . ."

Sir Rodney noted the change of tone, a hint of supplication, a dignified wheedle, and he abruptly changed the subject. He had no intention of bailing out the consortium. Even had he been able to afford it. He was near to ruin himself, though until now he had covered so well that no one suspected. Nor must they. His own cash flow was all but gone, though so far the international banks with whom he dealt were quiet and cooperative. No pressure. How long this would endure depended, as Sir Rodney well knew, on how soon he could come up with a huge amount of cash or prime collateral.

Time mattered. Sir Rodney glanced at his watch as the Bentley purred past the Shinjuku Gardens. Ten past eleven, Tokyo time. He nodded to himself. Less than twenty-four hours now and it would begin. In Venezuela. The scheme, the plan he had so carefully fabricated to lift himself out of the mire of bankruptcy. Comparative bankruptcy, he supposed, for at the moment he could have retired with a few million. But that was not his way. He was only fifty-one. To retire with a few million, to be on the shelf, to lose his vast power, would be the same to him as death to a lesser man. No way, he thought with a grim smile, was he going to do that. Not with the greatest opportunity of a lifetime staring him in the face. A certainty of cleaning up as he had never cleaned up before. The United States would come back strong; all the intuition and financial logic that had made him a millionaire told him this. He felt it in his bones. And he could come back with it. All he needed was a hundred million or so to sock into the now-depressed American market. The old axiom still held—buy cheap and sell dear. He needed millions enough to buy big and hold on until the market began to bull. He could end up owning a tenth of the United States.

Noguchi interrupted his thoughts. "How is your head these days, Rod? The silver plate never bothers you?"

Sir Rodney was not sensitive about his silver dome. He took off his hat and swept his fingers over the polished silver plate that was the top of his skull. The remark was, he supposed, Noguchi's mild way of getting back at him for the financial snub. A subtle implication that the silver plate in some way made Sir Rodney a cripple.

Sir Rodney smiled at his companion. Let the little bastard have his revenge, if that was what it was. He said, truthfully, "I have mild headaches now and then. Nothing much. The doctors give me pills to control them. And, as I've told you before, Hediki, a silver plate in your skull is a hundred percent better than the alternative. There are far worse fates."

Hediki Noguchi nodded and stared out at the affluent suburb through which they were driving. He had given up what little hope he had ever had that Hamilton would bail out the consortium. The Englishman was a cold fish, a hard man with an enormous ego, and he had not come to Tokyo with any intention of helping. Quite the opposite. Noguchi had his spies and he knew that while in Tokyo Sir Rodney had been casting

7

around for bargains, looking for companies on their uppers which he could buy in for a fraction of their real worth. It was some small comfort to the Japanese that, so far as his informants knew, the Englishman had up until now failed.

"You will be going back to London tomorrow, then?"

Sir Rodney nodded. "Yes. I'm booked on an early flight."

They drove for a time in silence, each man busy with his own thoughts. Noguchi wondered how he was going to tell his eldest son that he was all but broke. Sir Rodney wondered how matters were going in Venezuela. He hated delegation and his great worry was that the thing would be bungled. He detested having to depend on others, but in this case it was absolutely necessary. There was absolutely no way in which he could perform this deed himself. Not that he objected to violence. He had committed some, been a witness to more and his youth had been a wild one. He had driven racing cars—a nasty crash was responsible for the silver plate—and there had been a period of smuggling. Rodney Hamilton had been both lucky and clever, much more so than some of his companions who were now dead or still serving long terms.

The Bentley turned into the drive leading to Noguchi's Western-style mansion. Sir Rodney had been a house guest for the past four days.

"How is your lovely daughter?" Noguchi inquired, as the car swung under the porte cochere. "She is quite grown up, I suppose."

"Twenty-two on her last birthday," said Hamilton. His tone was brusque. He did not much like thinking about Jennifer. Sexual fantasies came unbidden and, when he was alone and let his thoughts flow untrammeled, when he was brutally honest with himself, he clearly saw his own daughter as a sex object. No one, not one of the many people he had wronged or cheated, could have invented a more exquisite torture. The more so because he was almost certain that Jennifer knew. There were times, or so he imagined, when she looked at him with clear and candid eyes and, he could have sworn, saw through him. Or was it his own guilt that

8

made him imagine the contempt and revulsion in her gaze?

"I hardly ever see her," he told Noguchi. "She's of age now, and independent, and she makes the most of it. Paris today, New York tomorrow, London or Beirut or Hong Kong the next. She goes where the sun and her friends are. She's had homes and apartments all over the world."

Mrs. Noguchi had retired for the night. A servant brought them cigars and brandy in the library and was dismissed. Noguchi said, "I do not criticize, you understand, but I think it is not a good life for a young lady. There is no certain young man? A husband-to-be?"

"There are plenty of young men." Sir Rodney's laugh was dry. "Believe me, Hediki, there is no shortage of young men."

He did not like thinking about that. Jennifer, the daughter he loved, the infant, the child and the adolescent he had watched as she grew up, the young lady he had worshiped, for whom he had worked, to whom he had given so much . . . it was agony to think of her wasting herself on those stupid young clowns. Bending over for them, spreading her legs, even taking their parts into her mouth . . . He had read that fellatio was very big with the young these days.

Such thoughts drove him to frenzy. Jennifer knew that and, hating him as he was sure she did, she must enjoy love making just a bit more than others. Screwing all over the world. He knew he would read more social notes, society pages, wherein the latest man would be named. Hardly a week passed when Jennifer Hamilton was not mentioned in the columns.

Sir Rodney gulped his brandy, an excellent brand and year, and said a rather hasty goodnight. If he lingered Noguchi would summon up the courage to try to talk business again, would even come as near to begging as he could, and tonight Hamilton did not want to hear that. Ordinarily he enjoyed watching men beg, but not tonight.

Noguchi, recognizing the inevitable, said, "I may not see you in the morning, Sir Rodney."

The formal Sir Rodney! Hamilton concealed a smile.

Noguchi had accepted the facts and would be of no further bother. Too bad, of course, but the world of high finance, of high stakes, of real wheeling and dealing, was no place for the weak or the unlucky.

"I must get an early start for Osaka," Noguchi continued. "And from there on to San Francisco and New York. I have connections and still some small hopes. I am only sorry, very sorry, that we cannot come to an agreement. If you should change your mind . . ."

"I won't," said the Englishman as he went to the door. "I am sorry, Hediki, but I just don't see anything in it for me. Not in what you showed me—and I gather that there is nothing else?"

The little Japanese shook his head. "No. There is nothing else. The statements I showed you are accurate in every detail. We have three supertankers on the way, half completed, and without help we cannot finish them."

"Hard," said Sir Rodney. "Hard indeed. Perhaps this is just not your day, Hediki."

He paused at a table and pointed at a leaf desk calendar, then picked it up and showed it to Noguchi. With gratuitous cruelty he said, not smiling, "It certainly isn't your day, Hediki. I had forgotten the date, but you see . . ."

December 7.

In his room Sir Rodney undressed and got into his pajamas. After cleaning his teeth, fine, strong, white teeth, he took a tin of what looked like shoe polish from his suitcase. It was not shoe polish. It was silver polish and was made by a small firm in the west of England, near Bristol. The firm had been making Marlow's Marvelous silver polish for over a century. It was expensive and used by discriminating servants in all the great homes of England.

Sir Rodney had only a fringe of hair, reddish with patches of white at his temples and over the ears. He brushed it aside so that the entire crown of his head was exposed, a gleaming silver tonsure that protected the brain beneath. This was a nightly ritual with him. He daubed polish on a soft cloth and began to polish the silver skull. Polish and buff—polish and buff.

Sir Rodney smiled at himself as he worked before

the mirror. At fifty-one he was not an unhandsome man. In no way pretty, in some ways coarse, but handsome enough for all that. He had very little fat on him and the hard drinking of his younger days had not marred his cheeks or nose. As a rule he shaved twice a day to keep the white bristles from showing. He got enough exercise, kept his weight down to two hundred—only five pounds over his racing weight and he had the shoulders and thick muscular waist of a good fullback. He had fought a good deal in his day, fought dirty, and, as he finished polishing his silver skull and moved toward the bed, he thought that now, if all went well in Venezuela, he would be fighting dirtier than he ever had before. And for bigger stakes.

Sir Rodney never had difficulty in falling asleep. No matter how many men he had ruined on any particular day, a few deep breaths, usually, a tuning-out process, and he snored . . .

Not so tonight. He managed not to think of Jennifer, not to fantasize about her—images he would never dare drag into the daylight.

The Venezuelan scheme had to work. It had to. When it worked, he would be off the hook for all time. To be the richest man in the world, a mover and shaker such as the world had not seen before. Hunt was dead and Getty was old; big families didn't count. Hughes was all but retired. The time was right for a new man to seize the world stage. To show the little people how it was done.

Sleep was slow in coming. Sir Rodney regretted that he could not command it. He rubbed his silver skull, smiled to himself and thought, with a wry and truthful humor which he occasionally allowed himself in private, that the Venezuela thing had better come off. Otherwise he was stone cold dead in the market.

He had made too many enemies. Too many of them hungered for revenge. As long as he possessed great sums of money, and the power that went with it, he was reasonably safe. But let him fail, let him fall, and they would be on him like wolves after a lamb.

He had a tiger by the tail, though—and he couldn't let go.

As he waited for sleep, he named them in his head—

11

a dozen, two dozen men who would be happy to see him go under, who would be happy to play a part in putting him down. More than that, of course, but he couldn't remember *all* the people he had harmed.

One thing he did know—if they ever got him down, they would kick him to death.

CHAPTER 2

Joe Garm was one of the last of his kind, an adventurer and soldier of fortune, less than a gentleman and more than a common mercenary, one of those men who cannot breathe in the strict confines of society, who arrive at outlawry by choice.

Joe was pushing sixty, but he had kept himself in shape. His bulldog face was a bit wattled about the chops and he was white at the temples, but the rest of him was lean and hard and mean. His father had worked in the stockyards in Chicago, his mother died when he was a child, and Joe had dropped out of school and enlisted in the Marines at seventeen. By the time he got back to Chicago, years later, his father was buried beside his mother. Joe Garm did not bother to seek out the cemetery. When you were dead, you were dead and that was the end of it.

On this soft, rainy, misty night in Caracas, Joe Garm waited with his two men at the overlook. It was a place for lovers, a spot from which to view the harbor. Far off to his left, the lights of the Simón Bolívar Center gleamed, their warning beacons blinking red, and car lights drew gauzy patterns on the Plaza. The overlook was deserted. Garm lit a cigarette, and from the lighter flame sneaked a look at his watch. Half an hour before Conchita was due with the de Ojeda kid.

Garm studied the harbor lights without interest. the overlook, surrounded by a small park with benches and a drinking fountain, was on the seaward side of a superhighway linking the suburb of La Guaira to the city proper. It was not a night for traveling and the traffic was light. To his right, as he flicked his cigarette away, he saw the lights of a cable car as it began the long ascent from Macuto to the Hotel Humboldt on its 7,000-foot perch atop Mt. Avila.

Garm spat. Scenery. Venezuela was lousy with it. He hated it. Scenery was something that got in the way when you were running. Scenery could exhaust you, kill you, especially if you were carrying heavy things like guns or maybe barrels or boxes of whatever was bringing the best price at the time. He would take flat country anytime, flat country with plenty of water and maybe a ridge or two to give you cover if they were chasing you.

Ramon and Enrique, his helpers for the night, were sitting on a bench. They smoked a lot, talking in low tones, and Garm thought they were holding hands now and then. That was nothing to him. He didn't mind queers as long as they did their jobs and kept out of his way. He didn't really need these two punks; he could have done the job alone, but the Big Man was paying for it and the Big Man didn't want to take any chances—and what the Big Man said went double, in spades. None of it mattered anyway, not the way he'd planned it.

Enrique, the older of the two, left the bench and approached Garm. From long habit, by second nature, Garm shifted the .45 in his belt so that it was positioned for a cross-handed draw. Garm was old-fashioned. A lot of people sneered at the old Colt .45 automatic, but Garm had grown up with it; he liked and trusted it. As much as he mistrusted holsters and side draws.

Enrique had a whiny voice. "How much longer, *compañero?*"

Garm shrugged, careful to take a step away from the men. They were local muscle, recruited from the Caracas underworld through a connection. Knife men. Garm had insisted on that. No guns. The idea was to snatch young Carlos de Ojeda, not kill him, and gunsels had a way of being trigger happy if any little trifle went wrong. Garm was old enough to think that way—in terms of gunsels. Joe was long out of fashion, but he

13

knew how to do his job and had nothing but contempt for amateurs.

"Twenty, twenty-five minutes, maybe. What difference does it make? You're getting paid for the time."

The man giggled. Garm thought he sounded like some silly cunt. But he had the word of a connection he almost trusted that these two were good knife men. He had seen the knives, six-inch switchblades, and they should do. To terrorize young de Ojeda into non-resistance. Garm's orders were not to harm de Ojeda unless absolutely necessary and certainly not to kill him. To this end, and for this reason only, Garm was working with the two punks. They would provide just enough muscle and terror to cow the kid into utter submission.

"*Ramon tiene un raton,*" said Enrique. He giggled again.

Garm shrugged. "So he's got a hangover. So what? You want me to hold his head?"

The giggle climbed into a little shriek of laughter. Enrique pulled a flat bottle of rum from his hip pocket. "No, no, *señor*. Just the permission to take a drink. Just one drink or perhaps two. His head is very bad. Last night, and this morning, Ramon was *muy ebrio.*"

Garm had forbidden any drinking until the job was done. But he nodded and said curtly, "One drink. No more. You guys bungle this and I'll kick your asses up between your shoulders. You sure you got it straight now, what you're to do?"

The man did not giggle. He did not like the threat and showed it. It had been many years since Joe Garm worried about what punks like this liked. He said, "Well?"

Enrique shrugged. "I know. We both know. It is nothing. We wait until the girl arrives with the man. We remain hidden. She is a *puta* and she will suck his cock. While this is being done we appear and show them knives to their throats. Not a difficult thing, *señor*. Easy. It will be done correctly. Trust us."

Garm nodded. "Okay. Better get back in those trees for cover. They'll be here anytime. I'll be over there." He pointed across the parking space to a clump of tall coconut palms laced with vines and wild orchids.

Garm glanced at the sky. It was dark and moonless; the rainy season had lasted longer than usual this year, but the low clouds reflected enough light from the glare of Caracas in the valley. The rain was a persistent gentle weeping, soft and warm on his face. He lit a cigarette and moved it back and forth three times. "When you see this, go in. Not before." He gave a grunting laugh. "Give her time to work him over a little, to get it all in her mouth and lull him. You should be able to take him without a scratch."

Enrique scratched his crotch. "But if he resists, *señor?* If he fights back, attacks us?"

Garm spat in disgust. "Grab him. Hold him. Even you two ought to be able to handle a nothing like Carlos de Ojeda. He'll be caught off guard and anyway he can't weigh more than a hundred and fifty. Do I have to tell you everything, for God's sake! I thought you two were pros."

Enrique nodded hastily. "We are, *señor.* Not to concern yourself. We will do it correctly. But Ramon and I were wondering—"

"Wondering what?"

"The *puta, señor,* the woman. We were wondering if, afterward, after we have done the job, we could have her."

Garm was amused. "You mean rape her or pay her?" Not that it mattered. He had his own plans for Conchita.

Enrique's giggle was back. "Perhaps both, *señor.*"

Garm glanced at his watch again, puffing his cigarette into a coal to get enough light. Five minutes. The schedule wasn't all that tight, because the woman had to talk the kid into driving out here, but they might as well get set. He motioned the man away.

"We'll see about that. Now take Ramon and get back out of sight. No noise. Wait until you see my cigarette move and then for Christ's sake do it right."

Garm retreated into the palms and waited. Rain wept down through the fronds. A spate of traffic, nine or ten cars, whizzed past on the highway. Insect noises were muted by the dank soft air. Orchids rustled in a whisper of breeze off the ocean, a breeze that carried with it just a hint of oil smell from Lake Maracaibo.

15

Two hundred miles the breeze had traveled and still there was the smell of oil.

Oil.

It figured big in this deal. Garm knew that. The world was thirsting for it, some countries were dying for lack of it, and it had to be somehow tied into the Big Man's plans. Garm didn't know much. He had only a small part of the total picture, operating on a need-to-know basis, and that was okay with him. As the thing moved along, step by step, gaining impetus, his view would broaden. Not that it mattered. He was content to do his jobs, as they arose, and take his pay in cash. Half a million. It was his last big chance and he knew it. He could retire somewhere, he hadn't fixed on a spot yet, where they didn't know him and he didn't know them. He would keep it that way. Keep to himself, not mix, live his declining years in luxury with no scuffling to make a buck to survive. Every poor bastard dreamed of that and very few got it. What they mostly got was a cell or a bullet in the head.

Ten minutes passed. Garm began to wonder if Conchita had made the pickup. That was the weakest part of his plan. The poop he had on young Carlos indicated that the kid was a no good young prick, a drunk and a pot head alternately, a wastrel and spendthrift and all the rest of it. Booted out of the university last year. Not an unusual picture—the scared son of an important man. You could never depend on a kid like that. Not even to show up in his usual haunts and allow himself to be picked up by an eighteen year old *puta* who had a reputation for giving.

Another possible hitch was that once the girl picked him up she had to talk him into driving to the overlook. The kid might not go for it. Garm had coached the girl on that point.

"Give him a lot of shit about liking the wind in your hair, wanting to get out of those smelly, smoky dumps. If he's not drunk already, get some booze into him. That should help. Promise him the best head he's ever had, but you want to do it in the car, outside. No deal otherwise. No motels, and you won't go to his apartment." He showed her a thick wad of *bolivars*. "Get him there within a hour, either way, and this is yours."

16

Half an hour. Garm began to have doubts, to think up an alternate plan. The trouble with deals like this was that so many things could go wrong. Any god-damned little trifle could fuck you up. Well, not to worry too much. He had been allotted a week for the job and he had only been in Venezuela four days. Still plenty of time. If it came to it, he would do the job another way, by himself, though that meant exposure and he was trying to keep a low profile. He could . . .

A car was approaching from the direction of Caracas, its powerful lights shafting down over the lookout as it went into a curve and slowed. Garm stepped farther back into the palms. The engine sounded powerful and expensive. Could be.

The car slowed more to make the sharp turn into a blacktopped lane leading down to the overlook. Head-lights swept over the little park, the rain-polished blacktop, the white retaining fence. Garm nodded. Looked like the car, all right. He'd tailed the kid and the car for most of a day, familiarizing himself with both. The car was a 1974 Maserati Marek. Just for the hell of it, Garm had checked out the price. Twenty thousand.

Now, as he watched the car stop, its nose to the fence, and saw the lights go off, his mouth twisted in disgust. Give the fucking no good kids toys like this to play with, give them everything their stupid hearts and pointy heads desired, and then wonder why they weren't worth the powder and shot to blow them to hell. Spoiled young cocksuckers.

One of the car windows was down and he caught a rapid flutter of Spanish as the girl said something. A car whined past on the highway above and for a moment its lights caught the Maserati. Through the long slant of the glassback Garm saw them. Two heads. Still erect. She hadn't started on him yet.

Garm turned his back and opened his light trench-coat. He knelt and put his head down on his chest, pulled the loose coat around him and lit a cigarette. Two puffs to draw it into life, then he shielded it with his palm.

Clenching his hand lightly, keeping the butt out of sight in his palm, he left the trees and walked carefully and slowly toward the car. No talking now. He walked featherlight on the blacktop to within twenty feet of the car. The low clouds cast enough light for him to make out the single head reclining against the headrest of the driving seat. A faint gobbling noise came to him. Garm grinned. She was doing her part. Going down on him. Guaranteed to distract. Garm found that his own cock was reacting, was semi-hard, and that pleased him. He'd been having a little trouble lately—he was shoving sixty, damn it—but it wasn't all death down there. He moved a step or two closer and waited. He had instructed the girl to string it out, to pinch off the kid with her fingers if he started to come too soon. The ideal time to go in was just as the kid orgasmed.

Garm counted to sixty. Let's go. He raised the glowing cigarette high over his head, penciling it back and forth in the soft mist.

Enrique and Ramon came running softly from the trees, on tiptoe in basketball shoes, switchblades in hand.

Joe Garm took the .45 from his belt and notched off the safety. He turned to study the highway above. No cars at the moment. No oncoming lights. Okay. He approached the car.

Ramon was at the far side talking softly to the girl. He had her by the hair with his switchblade at her throat. They had agreed on this, the girl and Garm, that she would show surprise and terror, protect herself in the unlikely event that matters went wrong.

Carlos de Ojeda wore his hair almost to his shoulders. Enrique had a fistful of it and was yanking the boy's head brutally out of the car window. His knife point was shoving into the soft flesh of the kid's throat.

"*Bastardo,*" said Enrique. "One sound, one move from you, and I slit your fucking throat."

Carlos de Ojeda made a gargling sound. He was paralyzed with terror. Garm said, "Easy does it. Don't cut him. Haul him out of there. Take care of him first, then do the girl."

Conchita was weeping. Garm smiled. Good acting, or she was really scared. Wondering what she had gotten herself into. He'd told her only that they meant to rob de Ojeda.

Enrique let go of the boy's hair and, his knife still at the throat, reached in to unlatch the door. Ojeda tumbled out. Enrique caught him, threw him roughly to the blacktop and kicked him.

"None of that," Garm grated. Poor punks getting even with rich punks was not part of the plan. He wanted young Carlos as unscathed as possible.

From his pocket Garm took a wide roll of tape. He tossed it to Enrique. "His mouth first, then his wrists and ankles. Use a lot and make it tight."

The girl, between sobs, let out a choked falsetto scream. Garm looked across the car at Ramon. "Shut her up."

Garm kept watching the highway. No lights yet. He flicked his lighter to see the time. Half an hour before the police patrol was due. Sometimes they checked the overlook, sometimes not, but he had been thorough in his homework. So far so good. Another two or three minutes and it would be over.

Ramon had his hand over the girl's mouth. His other hand was down the front of her dress. Enrique was kneeling by the supine Carlos. He had just finished taping the young man's ankles. He tore the tape and looked up at Garm with a grin and giggle.

"Like a chicken for the market. Now what we—"

Garm shot him in the head with the Colt .45. Before Enrique bounced on the blacktop Garm had turned and fired into the car, across the front seat, once into the girl's head and once into Ramon's chest. The heavy bullet knocked Ramon back, but he did not fall at once. He kept walking backward, spinning and slipping, slapping at his chest and screaming but not falling.

Garm ran around the car and shot Ramon again, this time in the head. Ramon fell to the blacktop with a pulpy thud, face down. Garm bent and fired again into the back of his head.

The girl's head was lolling out the window. The left side of her head was all but gone; blood trickled from her ears and nose and mouth. Garm shoved the .45 into her ear and pulled the trigger. The cannon-like *blam-blam-blamming* of the .45 did not bother him.

He had never thought much of silencers and a .45 pistol needed a very special attachment for that.

He walked around the car. Enrique had not moved since he hit the blacktop, but Garm put another slug into his head just to make sure. He thrust the .45 back in his belt and looked at the de Ojeda kid. The boy— he was twenty-three but a boy to Garm—was staring at him with wide eyes that obviously did not comprehend what they had just seen.

Garm, careful to stay out of blood, walked to de Ojeda and stooped. He said, "You hear me? You can understand?"

A faint nod.

Garm slapped the kid's cheek lightly. "Okay, then. You saw it. You give me one bit of trouble, just one tiny bit, and you get the same thing. Got it?"

Again a nod.

Garm glanced up at the highway. A car was coming. He stood, not moving, until the car swished past, its lights high over them as it took the curve.

Garm waited until the car's purr died away. Now there was only the night and the mist and the insect noises. He picked the de Ojeda kid up as easily as he might a doll, swung him over his shoulder and carried him to where a rented Buick waited at the far end of the blacktop. A Buick that would never be returned and that Garm had rented with false papers.

Garm opened the trunk and tossed de Ojeda in. Air holes, one sixteenth of an inch, had been drilled inconspicuously into the trunk. Garm slammed the top down, locked the trunk, wheeled the Buick around in a tight circle and drove up the lane leading to the highway. No car lights were visible from either direction. He turned onto the highway and drove east toward Macuto.

CHAPTER 3

Sir Rodney Hamilton maintained a suite of offices on the top floor of the Graphic Building. He had other offices as well, occupying the fifth and sixth floors of the Hamilton Building in the city, where he played the role of multimillionaire and top drawer financier. For skullduggery he preferred the *Graphic* offices. He owned a controlling interest in the tabloid, which had been losing money the past year, and now and then did an editorial on a subject that interested him. This was not often. Sir Rodney was at times a coarse man, certainly he was an unforgiving and lethal man, but he was not vulgar. Which was, perhaps, why the *Graphic* was losing money. It attempted to match certain other papers, such as the *News of the World*, in vulgarity and so far was coming off a bad second.

London was dank and cold this morning. Sir Rodney left his house in St. John's Wood at eight and was driven to his office in the small Mercedes. Sir Rodney preferred small cars for the London traffic. The Mercedes was diesel engined and, insofar as Sir Rodney was concerned, there was no shortage of fuel. For the world perhaps, but not for him. He expected another oil embargo, a real crunch this time—the OPEC countries were just beginning to feel their oats—and in fact was counting on it. To make a few hundred million. A basic rule of his was—if you can't whip them, join them.

It all remained to be seen. He wondered, as he ascended in the lift, if Joe Garm's cable had arrived yet.

He made his way through outer offices crowded with busy workers. Now and again he nodded and spoke—he did not know many of the lesser people he employed—and came to his own sanctum. It was small and spare—no sumptuous furnishings here—and had tall windows overlooking Ludgate Circus. His private secretary, Cynthia Vorhees, was just coming out of his office. She was a tall blonde girl with magnificent legs, and they had a private agreement.

"Good morning, Sir Rodney." She had a thin, rather pointed nose over a mobile and voluptuous mouth.

"Morning, Cyn. Is there a cable for me?"

She smiled. Her teeth were good. "Just came in. I put it on your desk."

"Fine. Good."

As he edged around her she smiled again and said, "Will there be anything else just now? Will you need me for the next few minutes?"

This was their code for are you in the mood this morning. Cynthia was always available, on the desk or sofa or on her knees. It was unnecessary to lock the door; none of the employees dared enter when the red light was on, and for her services Cynthia received an extra fifty pounds weekly. She had been with Sir Rodney for two years now and was apparently satisfied. His demands were not inordinate, but when the urge struck him, he required immediate service.

He said, "Nothing for a time, Cyn."

The cable was on top of a stack of mail. He ripped it open and read: *Operation successful—am opening negotiations immediately—Garm*

The cable had been filed in Caracas slightly before midnight the previous day.

Sir Rodney lit a long cigar and wandered over to stare out one of the tall windows. A nasty London day with fog due to set in before long. He nodded and smiled to himself. If matters continued to go well, and why not with a man like Garm running things, he would be on the island in a couple of days, in tropic sunshine, out of this drizzling shit. He had never cared for London in the winter.

Joe Garm, A nasty bit of work, Sir Rodney thought. He smiled again. Garm was almost as nasty as himself. Maybe nastier, though he doubted that. Hamilton had no illusions about himself. As pious and hypocritical as he might appear in public, in private he faced himself. If he had an adage by which he lived it was: "Lie, if you must, to everyone in the world, but don't lie to yourself."

He buzzed the intercom and asked Cynthia to come in. She entered with a tentative smile, ready for work or sex, and for a moment he was tempted. It had been a while. He contented himself by patting her excellent ass and said, "Work this morning, Cyn. Just work."

With no change of expression she took her chair, an instant and efficient secretary, pad and pencil ready.

Sir Rodney considered for a moment. He had given Joe Garm fifty thousand going in, as front money, with another fifty to come as soon as Garm committed himself and had the balloon off the ground. True that he had only Garm's cable in evidence that the job was ongoing, but in a strange way, almost on hunch, he trusted Garm. And his own judgment of men. Garm knew who Sir Rodney was and he did not think Garm would dare fool around with him. And this was Garm's last chance, his final one big opportunity to avoid an impoverished old age. Besides, he had Ian Thomas' word for it that Garm was a professional hard case who would do anything, literally anything, if the price was right. Half a million dollars, Sir Rodney thought as he dictated to Cynthia, was just right for a man of Garm's character. Garm was a lowbrow and a hoodlum, to be sure, but such men were necessary in this world.

He dictated as he always did, sketchily and hurriedly, leaving Cynthia to fill in the spaces. Which his secretary did handily, being as good at her job as she was with her mouth or vagina. She seldom asked him to repeat anything, though Sir Rodney had a habit of mumbling words around his cigar.

"A check for fifty thousand dollars made out to Robert Brune, account number 392478. Include a line asking immediate acknowledgement of the deposit upon inquiry."

Garm was sure to cable the bank for confirmation.

Cynthia wrote and paused, pencil in air, "Which account do you want that drawn on?"

Sir Rodney pondered for a moment. He had accounts all over the world, in New York, London, Switzerland, Mexico City, Singapore. He had one in Caracas which he used only occasionally, when he was in residence at his island, La Blanca, off the Venezuelan coast. Lumping all the accounts, using one here and one there, gave him a free floating slush fund of better than a million.

It was, at this particular moment, just about all the cash he could raise without selling assets at a horrendous loss. This he had no intention of doing.

Cynthia was waiting. He took a small red notebook from his inner pocket and consulted it. A scrawled private code.

"New York," he told her. "Chase Manhattan. My private account. You've got the checks, of course."

Cynthia nodded. She had a desk full of various large checkbooks. She put checks through the machine on demand and he signed them and she never questioned or wondered. These were no concern of hers. Cynthia was one of those rare women without curiosity. She loved her job, was happy in it and only hoped it would last forever. Already she had banked a bundle and she hoped for more.

She was still waiting. Sir Rodney said, "That's it for now. Get it off immediately, please."

"Where shall I send it?"

"I didn't tell you, did I!" He patted his forehead. "Getting absent-minded in my dotage. Send it to Swiss Credit, the Paradeplatz, Zurich."

She finished and, after lingering for a moment to be absolutely sure her other services were not required, headed for the door. As she reached it Sir Rodney snapped his fingers.

"I damned near forgot. Call down to the city room and ask Ian Thomas to come see me. As soon as he can make it."

While he waited for Ian Thomas, Sir Rodney unlocked a desk drawer and took out a brown packet securely strapped around with scotch tape. He slashed the tape with a paper knife and revealed a six-inch stack of crisp new five-pound notes. He riffled through them, thinking it was a pity one had to pay so much for silence when there were other more efficient and economical ways. But this was too close to home. London was his nest and he dare not foul it.

Not that Ian Thomas was a bad sort, or much of a menace. Hamilton rather liked the man. It was Thomas who had put him onto Joe Garm in the first place.

Ian, who was a first class newspaperman despite his ratty appearance, was the *Graphic's* top foreign correspondent and knew Joe Garm from way back. When Garm had been a mercenary in Africa, fighting in various small wars, Ian Thomas had interviewed him several times. Both men were heavy drinkers; Thomas, both off and on the job, and Garm when there was nothing else to do. They had become friends of sorts, more out of boredom than anything else, and when the wars were over had kept in infrequent touch.

When Ian Thomas entered, scruffy and tweedy and smelling of drink, Sir Rodney was seated at his desk with his feet on it. As Ian came in, Hamilton pressed the button activating the red light. He waved at a small bar in one corner.

"Morning, Ian. Care for a drink?"

Thomas, who had spent a lot of time in the States, on occasion affected the American idiom.

He nodded. "A little snifter wouldn't hurt. Hair of the dog that bit me. Brother, did he bite me last night!"

Sir Rodney laughed. "Don't try that with me, Ian. I can smell you from here. You've already met the dog this morning."

Ian Thomas was a slight man, going bald and with a badly pocked face from juvenile acne. He had known Rod Hamilton, in a slight way, for years, long before his knighthood, and had never been in awe of him. He'd been covering sports when Hamilton had his racing accident and, though he had not covered that particular story, he knew all about it and the marvelous surgery, and marvelous luck, that had saved Hamilton's life. When drunk, which was frequently, Ian Thomas sometimes called Hamilton Old Silverskull.

He did now as, with an impudent grin, he headed for the bar. "You're right, of course. Hi, ho, Silverskull. Nice of you to offer me a blast but I have to wonder why. Am I being fired, eased out with alcohol?"

Unconsciously Sir Rodney raised a hand to stroke his glistening crown. He smoothed the hair around the silver plate, then said, "I got in touch with the Mr. Garm you told me about. I think I can use him. In fact he may turn out to be quite valuable to me. I want to show my thanks."

Thomas paused, glass and bottle in hand, appearing for the first time to notice the pile of five-pound notes. "I'm happy that you and Joe are happy together. It was a small favor, putting you in touch, but I don't mind being rewarded if you insist."

"I do insist."

Thomas swallowed his drink, grimaced, said "Ahhhhh," and approached the desk, his eyes on the stack of money. With a well-manicured finger, Sir Rodney pushed the stack toward him.

"Two thousand pounds, Ian. No tax if you don't want to report it. Up to you."

Thomas was disbelieving, unsure, but he could not disguise the greed he felt. He stared at Sir Rodney. "Two thousand pounds. Just like that. For introducing you to Joe Garm?"

He had not in fact introduced them. After hearing Hamilton describe a certain type of man, and listening to a story he did not believe, Thomas had come up with some old postcards from Garm. One of the return addresses had given Sir Rodney a lead. Even then he'd had to employ a private detective agency to track Garm down, this latter fact remaining unknown to Thomas.

Sir Rodney pushed the money at Thomas again. "I mean it. For services rendered. And for one more thing—an absolute blank spot in your mind. You never knew Joe Garm, he was never mentioned between us, you know nothing about anything having to do with Garm—in the past, in the future, now and forever."

Ian Thomas' thin mouth quirked in a cynical grin. "Like that, eh? Dirty work, I bet. Who knows what you big time financiers get up to. Not me, for sure. Don't know and don't want to know. Never, never in this world."

Sir Rodney watched as Thomas stuffed the money into his various pockets. He chuckled. "I'd get it to the bank as soon as possible, Ian. It makes that suit look even lumpier. I've always wondered about that—do you actually sleep in your clothes?"

"From time to time," said Thomas airily as he put away the last of the notes. "That all you had to say to me, Silverskull?"

A last effort to retain part of his pride and independence, Sir Rodney thought. Well, why not. Everybody had an ego, though few could afford to cater to it as Hamilton did. They hadn't the cash or the cast iron guts.

"One other thing," he said. "Old Carruthers is going to retire soon. He's overdue now, but I've kept him on because I haven't found the replacement I want."

Carruthers was the managing editor of the *Graphic*.

Ian Thomas grinned and nodded. "I get the message. It is perfectly clear. And do you know what? I feel the worst damned case of amnesia coming on."

When he'd gone Sir Rodney spoke to Cynthia over the intercom.

"Book passage for me on BOAC for Caracas. Tomorrow, late afternoon or evening. And get a cable off to La Blanca. To the housekeeper and Captain Vitale."

He dictated briefly over the box. The housekeeper was to ready the villa for residence and Captain Vitale was to begin readying *Nautilus II* for sea.

Most tycoons had yachts. Sir Rodney Hamilton had his own private submarine.

CHAPTER 4

The helicopter flapped down on a deserted beach twenty miles east of Macuto. Garm kicked sand over the red flare and carried the kid to the chopper. The pilot, a dark-skinned man wearing a leather jacket and a baseball cap, beamed a flashlight at Garm for a moment.

"What's the word?"

"Roughneck," said Garm, thinking that armies were all the same, even in these fly-by-night banana and oil republics. You had to have a password.

"Get him in," snapped the pilot. "We're close to jungle here and they patrol it pretty good." His English was fair enough, though heavily accented. There was a smell of fresh paint about the chopper and Garm figured the Venezuelan Air Force insignia had been painted over. He had already guessed at that angle—the Air Force and the Army, some of them anyway, were in on this.

Garm tossed the de Ojeda kid into the chopper like a bag of coffee. "I need five minutes," he told the pilot.

The man grinned nervously. "Make it three, *compañero*. I only borrowed this crate for a little time, *sí?* I got to get it back and cleaned up."

There was an Air Force base to the east, near Higuerote. Garm grunted at the pilot and ran back to the Buick. He had helped make a few revolutions in his time. Not that he liked the way this one was shaping up. Too many amateurs to suit his taste. A lot of them were looking to get stood up against a wall. He shrugged and got to work. No skin off his ass. He had half a million to earn.

He wiped the Buick down, just in case—he had touched nothing back at the overlook—and splashed gasoline over it, sloshing it heavily on the upholstery. He tossed a match and leaped back from the flare and sear of the flame.

As they swung away in the rainy dark air, Garm looked back at the burning car, a scarlet beacon on the beach. That would bring the cops and the curious. The area was fairly desolate, but there were villas scattered up and down this strip of the Caribbean. They called it the Gold Coast. A lot of monied people lived here. And on the offshore islands. People who could afford to pay for privacy.

La Blanca lay thirty miles out. Garm had never seen it, but the Big Man had described it and one of the first things Garm did on arriving in Caracas was procure a dozen Army ordinance maps. He knew that La Blanca was roughly square, three miles by three miles, rugged and hilly and stony. Not much cover and very little water. There was one good natural harbor on the seaward side and it was here that the submarine pen had been built. Garm shook his head at that. Not much impressed him. He had seeen it all. But a man with his own private submarine did impress him. He looked forward to seeing it.

They were over La Blanca in twenty minutes; he

could not see anything except the dimly lit pad. The pilot set down lightly within the low watt blinkers and turned to Garm. "Get him out fast."

Garm leaped from the chopper, dragged the bound body to the tarmac, shouldered him and stood aside as the chopper whirled and gusted upward. It careened away into the wind, running without lights.

Three men came out of the shadows and approached Garm. He stood over the kid and loosened the .45 in his belt. Not that he expected trouble—the orders should have come through by now—but this was going to be a tricky deal all the way.

Two of the men wore coveralls and pistol belts. The third man, who appeared to be in charge, wore slacks that sagged below his belly and a red and white checked lumberjacket. He carried a rifle.

Garm spoke the word roughneck, and the man with the rifle nodded. "All vent well?"

Garm nodded. A Kraut. Well, no matter. In a deal like this you were bound to get all kinds. But he had a definite antipathy to Krauts. Over the years they had caused him a lot of grief.

The two men in coveralls said nothing, just stared and kept their hands near their guns. Apart from the pad lights there was no illumination except a single bulb on a long building some hundred yards off. A hangar, Garm thought, and it would do.

The man with the rifle said, "The Cessna is ready for you now. You can go to the house for refreshment, or zomezing maybe, but unless it is necessary I do not zink zo good, nein?"

Garm pointed at the light bulb. "What is that?"

"Hangar. Machine shop. Paint shop. A lot of zings. Ve—"

Garm pointed to the kid and spoke to the two men in coveralls. "Carry him over there."

He took the Kraut to one side as the men lugged de Ojeda away. "Tell the Cessna pilot the baggage will be ready in half an hour. I have something to do first. You got a first aid kit in that hangar?"

"Ve haf, yes. In the office. You vish it?"

Garm nodded curtly. "I vish it. I also vish privacy absolutemente. You got that?"

The Kraut nodded. "I haf it."

As he followed the man to the hangar Garm appreciated the fact that the Big Man had not lied to him in their London interview. His organization, the Big Man had promised, was efficient and would take orders as soon as the word was passed. Garm was head honcho and his word would be law. Only the Big Man himself could question or over-rule him. They had left it like that. So far Garm had no complaints.

The office was dark. The Kraut flicked on a light. It was just an office, except for an army cot with brown blankets stacked on it. Garm told them to put the boy on the cot.

The three men left. Garm took a large first aid kit from a rack on the wall. Carlos de Ojeda watched him, his eyes wide above the gagging tape. For the first time Garm got a good look at the kid's face.

Thin but good enough features, spoiled by a too small petulant mouth under a wispy mustache that looked as if it were penciled on. The eyes were wideset, the thin nose hooked a bit and the eyelashes were girlishly long. The clothing, now soiled and messed, was casual, mod and expensive. Garm thought the kid looked like a bum; Garm, at nearly sixty, wore his hair in a crew.

As Garm glanced through the kit he wondered how to go about it. There was little time and he wanted no trouble. He moved to the cot. The kid stared up at him, blinking his eyes rapidly. Garm smiled, as pleasantly as he could, and slammed the kid on the jaw with a big rocky fist. Once was all it took. Carlos de Ojeda slept.

Garm brought the first air kit to the side of the cot. He took a hunting knife from a sheath worn on his belt, in the small of his back, leaned over the cot, picked up the kid's left hand and examined the ring finger.

The ring was an old one, no doubt given to the boy when he was a child, and it was sunken into the flesh. Garm nodded in approval. It was just right. There was an heraldic device of some kind—the de Ojeda family was Castilian and went back for centuries—and a worn inscription that Garm could not read without his glasses. The old man, Simon de Ojeda, could have no doubts.

Garm had honed the knife for this job. It was razor sharp and it took the ring finger off cleanly, sawing through the small bone with a grating noise as Garm exerted pressure. He held the bleeding finger up, away from him, and poured half a bottle of mercurochrome on the stub. He twisted a rubber band around the stump as a tourniquet, wrapped and taped it with sanitized gauze. This took less than a minute; the boy scarcely stirred, crying out only softly. Garm looked at his fist and smiled. As good an anesthetic as any and a lot faster.

He placed the finger in a red Timex box, padded it around with cotton, snapped it shut and put it in his pocket. He bent to check the stump for undue bleeding. He must remember to tell them to remove the rubber band from time to time, to let the finger bleed a little.

Carlos de Ojeda moved and gave a little moan. Saliva trickled from his slack mouth. Garm watched him with an expressionless face. Punk!

He went to the door of the office and called out. "Okay. He's all yours."

CHAPTER 5

John Eagle took the small red box from the old man and carried it to a lamp on the heavy mahogany table. He opened the box and studied the severed finger and the ring it bore. After a moment he clicked the box shut and put it on the table by the lamp.

"You're sure? Absolutely sure. This is your son's finger and ring?"

Simon Carlos y Garcia de Ojeda was in his late sixties. He had married late in life, a patrician girl much younger than himself, and young Carlos was his only issue. He loved his son as only an old-fashioned

31

Spanish gentleman could, but he had never liked him and, were it not for his sainted wife, his lovely and long dead Catharine Rosa, he would have long since given the boy his patrimony and severed their relations. Carlos was a monster and stood for everything the elder de Ojeda opposed. Life in the big old mansion, standing on ten acres in the exclusive Humboldt district, had not been pleasant of recent years.

The old man came out of the shadows of the big library to stand beside Eagle at the table. He was, Eagle thought, in his somber black silk suit, a bit like a shadow himself. An emaciated shadow with a beaked nose and a tuft of white beard.

"It is the finger of Carlos," said the old man. "Beyond doubt. Or at least it is the ring of Carlos. To that I will swear on all the saints!"

He snapped open the red box and pointed. "You see how the ring is sunken into the flesh. So it must be my son's finger. I do not see how they could have—" He let the sentence trail off.

Eagle closed the box again. He thought the finger was genuine. He knew very little yet—it was why he had come, to find out—but what he had seen so far indicated that these people meant business. Eagle had come in great stealth and over a back garden wall, easy enough for a man with his Apache upbringing, but he had seen the watchers. Two in front, nonchalant and bold in a car, and two patrolling the back on foot. Eagle had let one of them pass within six feet of him just before he vaulted the wall. They were watching the back gate and an auxiliary postern.

Simon de Ojeda looked at Eagle intently with small eyes as hard and black as obsidian. Eagle was aware of the scrutiny and understood it. He had been a bare ten minutes in the room and they were not yet into the meat of the matter. What the matter was, other than kidnapping, Eagle was not sure. He smiled faintly; he was not sure of very much. Samson had called to relay Merlin's orders. Fly to Caracas, using a false passport, and talk to this old and important man. Go unarmed and do nothing but talk and listen. Report as fully and as rapidly as possible.

John Eagle, as number one Expeditor, was used to

32

situations like this. He had uttered a mild query. "What's it all about?"

Samson had laughed in his dry way and said, "I don't know much more than you do. Mr. Merlin did say that he might be able to repay an old favor. Something about helping out the friend of an old friend. You figure it. I couldn't, haven't, and of course I am not about to ask. So let me know soonest, eh?"

Eagle certainly would. As soon as he knew anything other than the fact that a young man, Carlos de Ojeda, had disappeared and lost a finger.

The older man led Eagle to a chair by the fireplace. There was no fire. Simon de Ojeda waved at a teacart laden with bottles and glasses. "Do you care for something, Mr. Eagle? Some sherry, perhaps. I believe there is some Tio Pepe—or something stronger?"

Eagle refused and held out his hand. "If I could see the letter, *Señor.*"

The old man took a letter from his inside breast pocket and handed it to Eagle. It was neatly typed, probably with a new ribbon, and was double-spaced. Eagle read:

TO SEÑOR SIMON de OJEDA—We have your son Carlos. He is well, but for the loss of a finger, see enclosed, and will remain in good health only so long as you cooperate absolutely with us.

First—you will not mention your son's disappearance, or this letter, to anyone. We are watching you and we will know. If you utter a single word, if you warn or alert anyone, be it relatives or the police or the military, *anyone at all,* your son will be killed. This we swear. We will kill him and send you his head. Believe this! Remain silent! In a day or two you will receive a letter by ordinary mail. I am, for freedom, The Wild Dog.

Eagle read the letter again before he handed it back. Nothing there for him. He was not a detective, a clue man. He was an Expeditor, he made things happen, and it usually involved killing.

"The letter was delivered by a message service," said de Ojeda. "A professional service. Shortly after it came

33

I was visited by the police. I did not call them in. My son's car had been found parked with three dead people in or near it—a girl, as I understood it, and two men. All three had police records. The police were most inquisitive about that, as to what Carlos was doing in the company of such people or, if he was not in their company, how they happened to be with his car. I could not tell them anything, though I was not as surprised as I pretended, and of course I did not tell them about the letter."

He took a slim cigar from a box on a desk and lit it. His teeth were small yellow bones under the white goatee. "The police visit worries me. They must have been seen. If this Wild Dog, these kidnappers, think I have disobeyed their orders . . ."

Eagle, who could not make up his mind about this old gentleman, sought to give comfort.

"I don't think you need to worry about that. The same people who grabbed your son probably killed those three. They may have been recognized and had to kill. But they would know the police would contact you about the car and they would discount it." He pointed to the letter which de Ojeda had placed on the desk. "Their prime concern is that you don't tell the police, or anyone, about *that*."

Simon de Ojeda nodded. "I haven't. I won't. That is why you are here, Mr. Eagle. And I thank you from the bottom of my heart for coming so speedily. I did not much hope that you would come, or that anyone could help me. It is all still very much of a mystery to me; why you got here so quickly, who you really are, who sent you, or if indeed anyone sent you."

Eagle smiled. "Someone sent me."

The old man sank into a chair across from Eagle. He puffed on his cigar, stared into the empty fireplace and at last said, "I did tell *one* person about the finger and the letter. A very old friend; he is now nearly a hundred years old, a former general and president of this country. I turned to him at once, as soon as I had seen the finger and read the letter. He is the one, the only person, to whom I could turn. I called him at once, within half an hour after receiving the packet. I thought the lines would be safe, and found him well

34

enough to speak with me. He listened and then told me to obey instructions and do nothing. He would do what he could. He thought it possible, just possible, that he knew someone who could help me. Someone who was in his debt from long ago. I did not understand all of what he said, for his breathing is not good and he does not speak well over the phone. But here you are, Mr. Eagle. Again I thank you. If you can save Carlos, I, and all I have, will be at your service forever."

Eagle listened to all this with half an ear. No doubt the old boy meant it. Save the kid and get half the kingdom. This did not much interest Eagle—not half so much as why Merlin was meddling in what was, so far at least, a purely criminal and police matter. A favor owed to an old, old friend of this old man? Passing the favor on, farming it out, as it were? Eagle shrugged and forgot it. Here he was. Merlin always had a reason.

"Who is this Wild Dog?" he asked the man. "That name mean anything to you?"

Simon de Ojeda nodded. "Yes. Perhaps more than it does to most people who see it in the newspapers from time to time." He tapped an ash from his cigar and looked at Eagle. A pretty calm and controlled old boy, the younger man thought; I'm beginning to wonder about the relationship he had with young Carlos. He's not exactly broken up.

De Ojeda leaned toward Eagle. "You are aware of my position in the Government, Mr. Eagle?"

"I am." Samson had mentioned that. The old boy was high in the cabinet, Minister of Geological Planning. Oil.

The other man waved a frail hand. "There may be some connection. I have had time to think and it may be that this kidnapping, this seizure of Carlos, is not for an ordinary ransom. I am a very wealthy man, true, but it may not be for money in the ordinary sense. This Wild Dog, as he signs himself, is a guerrilla leader named Emile Ortega. For five years now he has been fighting in the jungles, he and his pack of wild dogs, *canis azarae,* and our troops have never been able to bring him to bay. He is a fierce and ruthless fighter and a skilled political."

Eagle asked the necessary question.

"A communist?"

The old man shook his head. "I don't know. Perhaps. Perhaps not. Somehow I do not think so; I do not think of him as a *communista*. If anything I would say fascist —he boasts that he will someday take over Venezuela and run it for the benefit of the common people."

Simon de Ojeda laughed. "The usual lies. He wants to be a dictator."

Eagle was silent for a moment. This could turn out to be a real can of worms. Oil. Politics. God knows what else. Only Merlin knew, if even he did, and he wasn't telling the help.

He stood up, a big man, lean and hard with a craggy face and a way of moving, swiftly and effortlessly, that was the Apache heritage. Someone had once observed that John Eagle moved as though on his own personal set of ball bearings.

"I'll stay here tonight," he told de Ojeda. "I'll stay at least until we get that follow up letter. Better warn your servants not to mention my presence."

The older man nodded. "I already have done so. They can be trusted. Make yourself free of my house, Mr. Eagle."

Eagle grinned. "I'll make myself free of one of your beds, if I may."

He had left his ranch in Arizona on half an hour's notice and had been traveling ever since.

Simon de Ojeda said, "I will trust you absolutely, Mr. Eagle. I do this because I trust my friend and therefore I trust his friend also."

"I'll do what I can," Eagle told him. "But you must understand that it may take a little time. I was rushed into this thing absolutely cold. I have to get my bearings. And also I take orders. From the friend of your friend. I am directly responsible to my superior. In other words, sir, if he calls me off the case tomorrow, I will have to obey. This is all clear?"

The yellow teeth showed over the goatee. "Perfectly. But I hope you will not forsake me."

"By this time tomorrow," Eagle said, "I'll probably have a lot more questions and we may even have some answers. In the meantime I'll prowl a little and see what

I can find. When you have to explain me you can say that I'm security, a private bodyguard."

He remembered that Pinkerton had an office in Caracas. "Tell anyone who is interested that I'm a Pink."

De Ojeda looked askance. Eagle explained. "You'll have to come up with some excuse for hiring me. Anything will do, as long as we're together on it. Don't worry about it. This is just fallback stuff, in case."

The old man fingered his wisp of beard. "This Ortega, the Wild Dog, has threatened, indeed promised, to hang me as soon as he takes power. He does not agree with my oil policy."

Eagle did not want to get into that. It had nothing to do with him. He said, a bit curtly, "That will do. You're running scared and finally called for help."

Simon de Ojeda smiled and nodded. "I think I receive it. I have always had trouble with the American idiom."

Eagle laughed. "You received it. Okay—now I want a list of the servants and a little background on them. I suppose you trust them?"

"Implicitly. I have only five; two women and three men; they have all been with me over twenty years."

Eagle repressed a smile. Only five servants. The old boy was roughing it. Eagle had known, by the district and the look of the grounds, that he was in monied territory. Rich rich. Probably old money, at least some of it. Maybe some new money, too. Oil. Bribes and kickbacks, concessions. Who knew?"

They talked for another twenty minutes, clearing up odds and ends. As Eagle waited for a servant to conduct him to his suite, he said, "You had better lock your door tonight. Stay in your room unless you hear differently from me."

"Of course. If you think it best. Do you really think I am in any danger? I am, after all, something like the golden goose. Surely they would not—"

"I doubt it myself," said Eagle. "Just a precaution. Oh, take it easy on the phone, too. It's probably tapped by now."

De Ojeda shook his head in wonder. "You really think this Wild Dog has such facilities? He is daring and cunning, I know. Clever. That he is still alive proves that. But to come right into the city and—"

"Not the Wild Dog," said Eagle. "The police. I imagine they treated you with the greatest courtesy and asked as few questions as possible? And were a bit apologetic about those?"

The old man nodded and smiled. "You must have been there, Mr. Eagle. They were most considerate."

"That's because you're a potentate," Eagle said. He caught the expression on de Ojeda's face and added, "An important man. A high government official. Cops are like that."

The emaciated shoulders shrugged under the five-hundred-dollar suit. "I suppose you are right."

"Keep it in mind," Eagle said. "They'll have a tap on the phone. They'll do their best not to annoy you or get in the way but they'll also have someone watching the house. They won't just sweep this under the rug, you know. They can't. Three people murdered, and your son's car involved—they'll investigate as quietly as possible, but they will investigate. Exhaustively."

"A nuisance," said de Ojeda, "but I suppose it cannot be helped. I should be grateful for their discretion, I suppose. It may be possible to keep the story out of the newspapers."

"For now," Eagle agreed.

But not for long. He hoped to do his job, whatever the hell that turned out to be, and be long gone before the story broke. He was in Venezuela on false papers and among strangers. Merlin probably had connections here—where in the world didn't he have connections—but that wouldn't help now.

He had not mentioned the four watchers to de Ojeda. No point in it. He wondered how they were all getting along out there, or if the rats had left when the cat moved in. He hoped not, though doubting his luck. The watchers he had first seen, the Wild Dog's men, would probably cut out as soon as they spotted the police stakeout. Or maybe not. Maybe they would just retreat a little.

Eagle showered and put the same clothes on again. His one suitcase was at a hotel where he had registered under the name of Jerome Peabody. Mr. Peabody was in textiles.

He dozed for an hour or so, wondering just how much on the up and up the old boy was. You could say one thing for him—he had at least one powerful friend. Merlin was in on this. Which meant, as always, that Merlin had some angle, a particular axe to grind. Merlin never dabbled in run-of-the-mill crime.

One other thing. Simon de Ojeda was shedding no tears for his son.

Eagle stood by the window in the dark room and peered out. His suite, bedroom, sitting room and bath, overlooked the front of the estate. It had been raining off and on ever since his arrival in Caracas, but now had cleared. There was a sliver of hooked moon faintly visible through low clouds. Not a bad night for prowling.

He took off his jacket, tossed it on the bed, pulled off his tie and stuffed it in his trouser pocket. He had used a tie before as a garotte and might again. Eagle did not altogether agree with Merlin's edict about going unarmed into a preliminary situation. It had been his experience that preliminary situations had a way of turning nasty.

He searched the bathroom. It was massive, with white and gold paneling; the tub was the size of a small pool and the towels were heated. In the medicine cabinet he found both double and single edged razor blades. Eagle chose a single edge; the flange gave support for his big brown fingers, and he slashed at his image in the mirror. It was better than nothing.

How long would it be, he wondered, before the Caracas police began to apply pressure? So far they had been polite and discreet, in deference to Simon de Ojeda's high place in the government, but that would not last forever. The cops would be looking for Carlos de Ojeda, wanting an explanation of how his car had been involved with three dead people; if the old man was telling the truth, and the letter from the Wild Dog was not a hoax, they were not going to find Carlos. Certainly they had an APB out at the moment. When they got zilch they were going to come back, this time not so politely, and Eagle didn't want to be around. He was reminded again of his contract with Merlin. He was on his own. Merlin and the United States would disown him. Help, yes, if feasible, but there would be no acknowledgement. Eagle doubted that Venezuelan jails were very comfortable.

He waited another hour in the dark, then eased up the bathroom window. This side of the house was covered with a thick net of bougainvillea and ivy, the vines as thick as Eagle's wrist and mortared to the brick by time. Eagle hung like a bat on the wall and listened and looked.

Directly beneath him was a bed of hibiscus. A graveled walk bordered it and led into a clump of mango. There was a faint smell of orange and lemon trees in the air. The moon sailed out from behind a cloud, revealing tall palms in every direction. Fronds rustled with dry squeaks in a hint of breeze. It was humid and already his shirt was sticking to his back. Eagle regretted the white shirt, but there was nothing to do about that.

He leaped over the gravel and slid into the clump of mango. There is nothing as ghostlike, as silent, as an Apache when he wants to be, and now John Eagle reverted to his Indian skills. For an hour he prowled, a shadow among shadows, moving as freely as the breeze around the artificially wild estate. There *was* artifice here; money had been spent. Eagle skirted dark pools, crossed miniature bridges and stopped to rest in the shelter of a tile-roofed gazebo.

There were no watchers inside the grounds.

He had to go outside and this he regretted. He'd hoped to surprise at least one of the Wild Dog's men inside the walls. The gazebo would make an excellent spot for interrogation and a gagged man screamed silently.

From the gazebo a wide strip of closely barbered lawn led to the mansion. There were benches, and statuary given flesh color by the moon; where the vista ended there was a terrace. Above it, on the second floor, a light glowed. Must be the old man, unable or unwilling to sleep. The servants' quarters were on the third floor in the rear and the chauffeur slept over the garage.

40

One of the things that kept a man awake was a bad conscience.

Eagle ran with a long loping stride across a miniature llano, a grassy sweep bordered by chaparral. The grass ended in a brick fence, ten feet high, and Eagle saw the glint of moonlight on glass. A cheval-de-frise.

Broken bottles set in cement. Eagle backed off and studied the wall for a moment. He took off his shirt and wrapped it around his right hand. The leap was nothing in itself. His legs were of rubberized steel and he could run farther and longer than any of his cousins, the Navahoes. As a boy growing up on the reservation he often had done just that.

He breathed deeply, sucking the humid air into his big lungs, and for a moment memory came back—the last time he'd gone to see his foster mother, White Deer, she had mentioned that Joe Thunder Horse had been asking about him. Joe, now a computer programer, was one of the Apache kids Eagle grew up with and he had been the best runner in the tribe until John bested him by running sixty-five miles in a day. Joe had collapsed at fifty miles. Later they fought, with Eagle winning again, and afterward remained friends.

Eagle flexed his legs and got ready for the leap. Strange that he should think of Joe Thunder Horse just now. He hadn't seen the man in ten years.

He ran, timing it perfectly, leaped and hooked his protected right hand over the wall. He felt the sting as a glass shard penetrated the shirt. He dangled easily for a moment, feeling along the top of the wall with his left hand for a glass-free space. There. About a foot of smooth concrete. Eagle pulled himself up, taking the pressure off his punctured right hand, and maneuvered his knees into the glassless patch.

The man outside the wall, almost directly underneath the spot where Eagle balanced, flattened himself back against the wall and waited.

CHAPTER 6

Eagle's Apache nose saved him from being surprised.
He smelled the man below him. A waft of cheap hair
oil, a belch of strongly seasoned food, soap used to
cover up body odor; these all spoke to Eagle as he
balanced on the wall. Probably a cop. Just maybe one
of the Wild Dog's men, a city connection, but probably
a cop. A plainclothes stakeout. Jungle men had jungle
smells.

Don't kill him or injure him badly. Eagle, still on the
wall, feigned ignorance of the man's presence. He
whistled to himself, cursing and pretending to inspect
the cut on his hand. He wadded the shirt into a ball.
The man below played it cagily, silently backing against
the wall, gun in hand. Eagle saw the blue-gleam of the
barrel in moonlight.

He threw the ball of shirt as a distraction. At the
same time he leaped, aiming for the gun wrist. The man,
probably with orders not to shoot except as a last resort,
was caught off guard.

Eagle's aim in the dark was a little off. One of his
hard leather heels caught the wrist and the gun went
skating away without being discharged. His other heel
got the man in the head, just over the right temple.
Eagle lighted on his feet, in short running steps, and
whirled. The man was falling, his eyes glazed and staring. He slumped to the ground and did not so much as
twitch as Eagle bent over him. Eagle turned him face
up and went through his pockets.

Cop.

Eagle studied the police card for a moment. Emanuel
Perez. He wore a loud plaid sports jacket over an open
throated shirt. Middle-aged and pudgy and just doing
his job as best he knew how. Eagle patted the fat
cheek and put the police card back. He tossed the

42

revolver, a .38 Special, into a clump of prickly pear. Sorry, officer.

He recovered his shirt, crumpled and bloody, and put it on. He stood for a moment by the wall, hearing the man begin to snore, and glanced up and down the street. A far distant street lamp twinkled and a distant car passed. At this hour the exclusive enclave appeared deserted. But it wouldn't necessarily be so. He glanced down at the snoring cop and wondered how long it would be before a patrol showed, before the man was due to be relieved. He had until then, or until the man came to life.

Eagle was tempted to give it up for tonight. The Dog's watchers would certainly have withdrawn when the cops moved in. Eagle thought for a moment. Withdrawn, yes, but not given up. Not with a deal as big and as important as this. They would want to know what was going on. Eagle shrugged. He might as well give it a whirl. The chances were fifty-fifty and he was already out. He'd cold-cocked a Caracas cop, good for five years in a crummy jail, so he might as well go through with it. He hadn't much to lose.

He ran across the wide avenue and disappeared into a patch of thick-growing palms. For a few steps he was engulfed in semi-wild undergrowth, vines, burr and shrubbery, then he found a low stone fence. He vaulted it and was on a lawn. A lot of lawn; across it a few lights gleamed in a house, a big house to judge by the spacing of the lights. Night lights? Someone about at this hour? While he watched the lights for movement, Eagle sat down with his back against the wall and recast the layout in his mind.

The wide street behind him was the Avenida de Betancourt. Immediately on his arrival in Caracas, Eagle had driven about the district in a taxi, familiarizing himself with the terrain and waiting for darkness. He recalled it now. He had entered by the back way, but Simon de Ojeda's driveway, barred by a massive iron gate, opened on the Avenida. There were other gates, and driveways, up and down the street. On both sides, but well separated—it was unlikely that any of these people had less than four or five acres. Another driveway, then? A drive with a hedge cover from which a careful scout could observe the front of the de Ojeda place?

It was worth a shot.

Eagle had also been observing the lights in the house. Nothing had moved. What if the house was empty, deserted for the moment, and those were only safety lights. Precautionary? The Wild Dog's jungle people could prowl and discover that in five minutes.

Worth a look.

Eagle moved to his right, parallel with the street moving with no noise and little effort through the undergrowth. There was still the rear of de Ojeda's place to be considered, the way he'd come in, but he would worry about that later.

His guess was right. He came up to a driveway, on his belly and as soundlessly as a snake, and saw the little car. A Volkswagon. Eagle lay and watched for ten minutes; the man, smoking a cigarette, tossed it out the open window and immediately lit another. Eagle crawled closer and listened. No conversation. An occasional sigh or grunt, the throat cleared, the man blew his nose. One man alone.

How to take him? Eagle reached out and touched gravel. Hard to move silently on that. Hard to take a man in a car, for that matter. Probably he had the doors locked. Certainly he would be armed and certainly he would fire if alarmed. And time was becoming a factor. That cop back there would be yelling bloody murder any time now and the place would be swarming. Eagle pondered. All he had was the razor blade and his necktie. He should have brought the cop's gun, but it was too late for that now.

The man solved the problem for him. He opened the door of the Volks quietly, got out just as quietly and walked on the grass verge to the head of the driveway. Eagle nodded in approval. He should have known it. The man was supposed to be a watcher. Eagle could follow his thinking. A lonely job. Nothing was going to happen. The man was just going through the motions. Eagle moved silently on the grass. This time something was going to happen.

The man didn't even have time enough to reach for the gun in his shoulder clip. Eagle took him from behind, his left forearm like an iron bar across the man's Adam's apple. His right hand snaked into the man's jacket, found the pistol and flung it away into the bushes. Eagle held him so for a moment while he fished the razor blade from his pocket. He drew the edge of the blade ever so lightly across the man's throat. Eagle whispered. *"Se le termino, compañero. Muerte!"*

The man was no coward. He kicked back viciously at Eagle. Eagle, wide legged, expected the kick and took countermeasures. He increased the pressure, the muscles writhing and rippling in his great arms as he lifted the man off the ground and let him begin to strangle. He counted fifteen seconds and eased the pressure, whispering again, "You speak English, *compañero?"*

The man, eyes popping, all but dead, managed to nod against Eagle's arm. Eagle eased him down and knelt beside him, the razor blade at his throat. He gave the man a moment to catch his breath, then said, "If you sing for me sweetly, little yellow bird, maybe I will let you live."

CHAPTER 7

Merlin had one of his infrequent outings that day. He rarely left his stronghold on the island of Maui and when he did it was at the urging of Polly Perkins, his secretary and companion. This time, after much persuasion on her part, and much grumbling from Merlin, she prevailed—and he was loaded, wheelchair and all, into the Rolls-Royce van. Polly accompanied him. She wore her usual muumuu and her elegant feet were bare. Polly was one-eighth Hawaiian, of which she was vastly proud, and if she was graying at the temples, her ankles were exquisite.

Merlin continued to grumble as they drove. He was expecting, at any moment, a message from John Eagle in Venezuela. He smoothed his lion-like mane of white hair and glared at Polly.

"I promised a very old friend, an old man to whom I am much indebted, that I would give the matter my full attention. I really shouldn't be gallivanting around. I've seen everything on this damned island a million times. Suppose someone takes a shot at me? There are a lot of people who would love the opportunity, you know."

By now the Rolls was on a narrow crater road skirting the maw of Makaluha, ten thousand feet above the sea. The air was crystalline, velvety, laden with the scent of flowers. Polly smiled at him and opened a small louvered vent in one of the bulletproof windows. She patted his knee. "Relax. You're getting to be a terrible stick-in-the-mud; anyway, you know you're not in the least danger. There's a security car in front and one behind, and this thing is a fortress on wheels."

Merlin grunted, "Hah! Just like Ironside. Big deal."

"Ironside doesn't have a Rolls-Royce."

Polly was in high spirits that day. She giggled and said, "At the moment you look just like the war god, Ku. All you need is a club set with shark's teeth."

After a time Merlin stopped feigning and began to enjoy himself. It was true that as a very old man, and a cripple, he did not get out very often. His fortress, and the underground volcanic complex attached to it, was his home and his place of business. A billionaire many times over, he knew his business, the protection of the interests of the United States as he saw those interests. Merlin knew, none better, that he was crusty and opinionated, idiosyncratic—he often thought of himself as an aging spider in the middle of a massive and incredibly expensive web. With his money, power and skill, perhaps he made fewer mistakes than most. He liked to think so.

The van stopped at a crossing of the Lahaina-Kaanapali and Pacific. The warning sign read: *Akahele I Ke Ka'aahi*.

Polly laughed. "Look out for the fire cars."

Merlin nodded absently, hardly hearing her. At the moment he had no interest in trains. He wondered if there would be a message from Eagle when he got back.

Was there anything at all in this mishmash to warrant his interest and interference? Was there even a case? All he had so far was a vague communication, a plea that might have been garbled in transit, from a very old man whom he had thought long dead. An old man to whom Merlin owed one thing—his life.

It had been in 1916. Merlin was just out of Harvard and his father, that rough old tycoon, booted him straight from academe into reality. It was a time of political ferment—and great financial opportunity—in Latin America. Mexico burned while Villa and the other tinpot generals fought and looted; there were almost daily revolutions in Central America and farther south, in Venezuela and other mainland countries, the situation was little better.

Merlin chuckled, his thoughts a million miles from Polly, the van and the luxuriant Maui scenery. Polly, who carried knitting with her for times like these, let him be. She had done her best. At least she had gotten him out of his glass room, if not away from his memories.

There had been a well worn joke in those days, in the emerging banana and oil republics. You asked for a newspaper immediately on rising, or you inquired of a friend: "Who is El Presidente today?"

Such information was important. The oil rush was just beginning; leases and concessions were what it was all about. If your man won an election, either by votes or bullets, you rushed to get him to sign away everything in sight. You put up hard cash, as little as possible, to get future exploitation rights, and sometimes you had to produce more than money. In Merlin's case it had been guns.

Venezuela, 1916. Merlin, then using his proper family name, had been callow and inexperienced, green and sopping wet behind the ears. His father, who was already a multi-millionaire and was betting heavily on oil in the future, tossed him into the arena with the admonition that this was the way you learned. Sink or swim.

Merlin came close to sinking.

There was insurrection, fighting in Venezuela. Guerrillas in the Orinoco jungle. The two main contenders

47

for power were General Eleazar Medina and General Alonzo Lopez Venecia, whose guerrilla forces controlled most of the llano and jungle. Both were men of iron will and cunning.

Merlin bet on the wrong horse, in this case General Medina, but his grievous and near fatal error was in allowing himself to become politically identified with Medina. And, as this was not stupidity enough, he did a little wheeling and dealing on his own—without his father's knowledge, for he was twenty-two and flying high, feeling his oats—and ran a shipment of guns into Caracas. For this he was to receive vast oil concessions in the Maracaibo field.

It all fell apart, like a snowball in hell. General Medina, while drunk and suffering a collapse of nerve, shot himself in the head after cutting the throat of his current mistress. His army dispersed and two days later General Venecia was in the city; the executions began.

There was no help. Nothing that even his father, a powerful man on Wall Street and in Washington, could do. President Wilson was preoccupied with the war in Europe and the Mexican troubles, and he strongly disapproved of "oilbaggers," as he called them, meddling in South American affairs. He would not lift a finger to keep young Merlin from the firing squad.

His thoughts were interrupted as the Rolls van braked to a halt. He glanced at Polly, who was still knitting. "What is it?"

She peered out a window at the forward car. A security man left the car and walked toward the van. In his hand was a yellow slip of paper.

"A message," Polly said. The security car contained a powerful transceiver linking it with the communications complex under Makaluha. Merlin was never out of touch.

Polly went to the front of the armored van and slipped the bolt on a letter sized opening. While he waited, Merlin considered the landscape.

They had halted on a curve overlooking Kaanapali. Beyond lay the channel between West Maui and Molokai. On the mauka side, inland, there were stretches of sugar cane and the green crew cut of a golf course, fringed by red hibiscus and yellow plumeria. Beyond, just visible because the van had halted at the farthest outpoint of the curve, stretched the high slopes of Lanai. Beyond that extended the dark cutout of Kekaa. They were, at the moment, on the narrow waist of the island. Merlin's enclave, buried in the volcanic tubes of Makaluha, lay to the west. To the north was Kahului Bay and the airport. It was John Eagle's custom, when he flew in for a conference, to arrive at the airport under an assumed name. His papers would be impeccable as always—Merlin hired the best forgers in the world—and he would stay at the Sheraton-Maui until contacted.

Polly handed the slip of yellow paper to Merlin. He read it in a glance.

HEV COM R PRO BIRD

Heavy stuff in from Eagle in Caracas.

Merlin nodded at Polly. "Tell them to start back."

While she relayed the order through the speaking tube, Merlin got back into his thoughts. It was strange, most strange, how events worked out over the years. There had been trouble then in Venezuela and—he had only bits and pieces to go by so far—it looked like trouble now. It had been, essentially, oil trouble then and it seemed to be oil trouble now. But with a difference. Oil had been in its infancy then, a baby industry just starting to grow. Now oil was the very life blood of the planet. Without it the world, and his beloved United States, his country, would die of economic anemia. The United States, already in an oil shortage-engendered recession, needed vast transfusions of black crude blood.

They had told him he was to die in the morning. Against a wall in the old Capitolio prison. They had given him a good meal and a package of Camels and a bottle of good wine. Female companionship, a young *puta* would be provided if the *señor* so desired.

Merlin smiled to himself now as he remembered that. The young *señor* had not so desired. No woman. He would spend his last hours in contemplation and, though not a religious man, would seek to identify and examine his sins. The young *señor* had been a goddamned fool in those days.

49

Along about five, with dawn just below the horizon and his life running out, true realization set in. They *were* going to shoot him. With this realization came terror and, still, some disbelief. They knew who he was and what his connections were. He had made sure of that. He had bribed as many of his captors as possible, using IOUs since he was then penniless. They knew who he was and who his father was. He was not a peon, an illiterate ragged-assed Indian, or black, or of mixed-blood. He was who he was, scion to a great fortune and a United States citizen.

They were going to stand him against a wall and blow his guts out.

The old man, deep in reverie now as the van raced along the black topped road through the West Maui Mountains, stared out the window at The Needle without seeing it. It had all been a long time ago, but he remembered—how near he had been to whimpering, to falling on his knees and begging, as the cell door clanged open and they came in.

The General, Alonzo Lopez Venecia himself, had been mercifully brief. He could have toyed with the boy, tortured him with hope, but he came straight to the point.

"You are not to be shot," he told the young man. "You will be given a horse, a safe conduct pass, a little money, and one of my sergeants will escort you to the Colombian border."

Young Merlin managed to retain his dignity. He gravely thanked the general. But with life his brashness returned and he said, "Why not let me go by sea, General? There are American freighters in the harbor now."

General Venecia was a tall man with a long face and a nose like a hatchet. His reputation depended on who was doing the telling. He was from the high Andes, a *mestizo* with the usual mix of cunning and common sense. He regarded young Merlin with a faint smile as he answered.

"Because you would be seen and the story would be spread. I do not wish it known that I have pardoned you." He frowned. "This suffices your curiosity, young man?"

50

Not quite. Merlin had ventured, "Why are you pardoning me, sir?"

The general wore soiled khakis. His tunic bore no insignia of rank. He was in his early forties at the time and affected a drooping mustache that was beginning to show gray. He ran a finger along the mustache and considered Merlin. His eyes narrowed but the muscles around his mouth moved in what was possibly a contained smile.

"I do not envy your father," he said.

At that moment there was a disturbance in the corridor outside the cell. A man screamed and blows were struck. Someone was being dragged down the corridor. Guards cursed and the man was yelling over and over again, "No—No—No—No—"

The young man glanced at his prison window and saw the light, gray and thin leaking through the bars. The yelling and scuffling was cut off by the iron slam of a door.

The general watched Merlin. "That will be Corporal Dauria," he said. "You offered him a bribe, *sí?*"

Merlin could only nod. He was beginning to feel scared again.

The general nodded in return. "Yes. A bribe. The corporal did not report your offer."

There were sounds in the prison courtyard now. The high set window afforded no view, but the young man did not need that. The worst was the high screaming of the man as he was tied to a hook in the wall.

After the gunfire the general shrugged. "So much for bribe takers. There will be others. But you asked a question of me, young man, and I will answer it."

He twiddled his mustache a moment before speaking. "I too am a father. I hope he will not grow up to be as big a fool as you, but who knows these matters?" A shrug.

"I have looked well into your case and find that you are not guilty of much but being a fool. Considering your age and inexperience that is understandable. There is the matter of the guns, of course, a crime, but since *I* now have the guns, I will overlook that.

"There are other reasons also— I wish if possible

to have good relations with the United States. If sparing a foolish young scoundrel will help in this, it is a small price. The fact is, young man, that you are not dangerous enough, or important enough, to be shot. So you will do me a favor and depart immediately." He plucked at his mustache. "Before I change my mind."

As the young man headed for the cell door, flanked by two armed guards, the general called after him. "In the future, if you have one, you might remember this. I am not a priest lover, but they have a saying from their book—bread cast upon the waters, something like that. Keep it in mind."

"I will, sir," said young Merlin. He meant it with all the fervor of which he was capable. Just as he left Caracas with all the alacrity of which he, his mount and escort, were capable. He had never forgotten, not any of it, and he found it a bit strange, but not particularly mystifying or earth-shaking that the debt had finally come due fifty-eight years later. He would, of course, have to pay it.

Not to the general himself, oddly enough, but to a friend of the old man. The general had asked not for himself but for another. For one Simon de Ojeda, of whom Merlin knew very little at the moment. He was beginning to learn.

Back in his office, in the glass-walled room that revolved on its hydraulic swivel, he lit a cigar and got to work. Polly went to see about his midafternoon snack. Merlin powered his wheelchair to the big Venetian desk and read the decoded message from John Eagle. It had been sent in simple commercial code, by cable, and addressed to one of Merlin's business fronts in Honolulu. Decoded, it read:

FIRE WHERE SMOKE IS — RECENT MOVES OF SIR RODNEY HAMILTON RE OIL MAY BE RELEVANT—ALSO CHECK EMPLOYEE OF SIR NAME OF JOSH, JOSÉ, OR MAYBE JOSEPH GARMES? AM KEEPING NOSE FAIRLY CLEAN AND PROCEEDING PER INSTRUCTIONS—ADVISE SOONEST ANY INFO RE ABOVE—BIRD

Merlin pressed a button on his phone console and spoke briefly to a man by the name of Scalzo. Scalzo was a retired FBI man now working for Merlin and in charge of the D files. D for dangerous. Dangerous men.

Merlin powered his wheelchair to the glass window and watched Makaluha smoke. He rolled a long Havana in his mouth without lighting it and squinted at the volcano. He remained motionless, in deep thought, until Polly came in with his snack and his blood pressure pills. After she placed the tray on his desk, he motioned her to remain. There were times when it helped to discuss certain matters with Polly. She was an intelligent and sensitive woman and there were moments when he trusted her judgment over his own. On the not infrequent occasions when she disagreed with him, she spoke her opinions plainly.

When she had settled into a chair and tucked her bare feet in under her, he said, "Off the top of your head, what do we know about a Sir Rodney Hamilton?"

She smiled at the "we."

"There's a microfile on him. In the D files."

Merlin nodded. "I just sent for it. Is it up to date?"

She thought a moment. "Fairly, I think. I review those files every so often, you know. I remember seeing his file not too long ago. I don't remember too many details, but off the top of my head, as you say, he's something of a swinger and a wheeler dealer. Runs a private submarine instead of a yacht. Early fifties, I would guess, and some years ago he was considered the boy wonder of the international financial world. Had his picture on the cover of *Time*, that sort of thing. That's about all I remember, off hand."

Merlin lit his cigar and blew a cloud of smoke. "Why did I put him in the D file?"

As he spoke he watched her closely and saw her mouth tighten just a bit, as he had known it would. Polly did not altogether approve of the D file. On occasion, and with some asperity, she had pointed out that he was not God, no matter what his private opinion, and he had no business meddling in private lives. Or in private affairs that did not menace the United States.

Oil, he thought now. This could be of great concern to the United States. If this Sir Rodney was up to anything that would impede the flow of Venezuelan oil, even if it were only exorbitant profit taking, it brought the matter within Merlin's province. So he had maintained in the past, in various similar cases, and so he was going to maintain now.

Polly followed his thoughts and her mouth tightened a bit more. But all she said was, "You thought he would bear watching."

Merlin chuckled. "Looks as though I may have been right."

Polly shrugged. "I don't know. I don't know what this is all about."

Merlin gave her his sweetest, most charming smile. Though in the end he made the decisions, and always went with his hunches, he did not enjoy her disapproval. They had been lovers for a brief time, and friends for much longer; he respected her feelings and thoughts, but they would never see eye to eye about the D file.

"It doesn't," he had once pointed out, "make me a fascist brute or a communist subversive, or a voyeur, just because I keep tabs on some people I believe to be potentially dangerous to the world. Nothing much ever comes of it in any case."

On that occasion Polly had flared at him. "You're still meddling in private lives. You admit the D file only deals in potentialities, in what might be, not in crimes or antisocial acts per se. You pry into the lives of these people, you collect data on them, because you think that one day they *might* do something. You make yourself both judge and jury."

There had been no answer to that then, nor was there an answer now. Polly was right. He did play judge, and jury, and he meant to keep on doing it. An ounce of prevention—

Merlin had found that Polly got over her piques faster if she were kept busy. So he said, "Find out all you can about a man named Garmes. The first name may be Josh, or José, or Joseph. He somehow ties in with this Sir Rodney, though I haven't the faintest idea how. Does it ring any bell?"

Her memory was phenomenal; she scarcely needed to consult the files for everyday matters, but now she shook her head. "Garmes. No. It doesn't mean anything to me."

The old man, again with his beatific smile, ran his wheelchair over to her and patted her hand. "Go see what you can find out. And don't be too cross with me, Polly. You know how seriously I view this matter, and how much restraint and soul searching I go through. You think I'm wrong, I know, but I think I'm right and I'm the one who has to live with it."

She smiled suddenly and leaned to kiss his cheek. "If it were anyone but you I couldn't stand it. I still don't like it, the D file, but if it has to be I'm glad it *is* you. All right, I'll go see what we can find out about Mr. Garmes."

Merlin powered himself about the glass room, thinking that he did not like spats with Polly. It upset him. *And* he still thought he was right. He had started the D file many years before, long before he achieved his billions or had gone to ground in Hawaii. He had kept a list of men he knew, men with whom he did business, or, sometimes wined and dined, who might become tyrants, or war mongers, given power and money enough.

At first it had been only a list scribbled in a cheap notebook. As time passed it developed into the D file. And as the file grew so had Merlin's responsibility. He had spoken the truth to Polly—he exercised great discretion and caution, an elaborate system of checks and balances, before he plucked a file from D and declared it active. Only where there was a clear and present danger to democracy did he act.

It was true that he made the final decision.

Someone had to.

He had no illusions about Godhood; he knew he meddled and invaded privacy, if only as a last resort, but, again, someone had to.

A clear and present danger once established, Merlin saw little point in worrying about the niceties.

The microfilm came up from the library, along with a viewing machine. Scalzo, the ex-FBI man, came along with it. After he had positioned the machine for Merlin's comfort, he said, "I had a quick run through it, sir. A real slippery one. Slick as an eel. He's got a hole in his head, you know. Had the top of his head sheared off in a racing accident. Wears a silver plate. Sure hasn't interfered with his brain any."

Merlin nodded and dismissed him.

CHAPTER 8

John Eagle slept late, showered luxuriously, shaved and exchanged badinage with a bell bird that had somehow strayed far north from the Orinoco. Eagle was in good spirits this morning; he felt that he had earned his pay last night. He hadn't hurt the cop much and had left the Dog relatively unscratched. The Dog had talked readily enough, needing only an occasional small slash from the razor blade. Eagle thought that he had at least made a beginning. If all the Dogs, the pups of the Wild Dog, talked as readily—but they wouldn't, of course. He had been lucky to draw a weakling the first time out.

A servant tapped on the door to announce that Simon de Ojeda was waiting to breakfast with his guest. Just for the hell of it, Eagle tried his bad Spanish on the man.

"Que pasa? Have the police been here this morning?"

The servant had a face carved out of old mahogany, barely animate. He nodded, *"Sí*, Don. They came early. They were angry and insisted I awaken Don Simon."

"You did this?"

Without any change of facial expression the servant broke forth in a torrent of Spanish. Eagle grimaced and held up a hand. *"Hable usted mas despacio! Quiere repetirio."*

The man shrugged, but slowed his speech. "But yes. I had no choice. I told you, the police were very angry. One of their men, a *polizonte,* has been attacked. Badly injured."

Idle gossip, Eagle thought. These things always get

magnified. I left him a sore ear and a headache, nothing more.

The servant was slipping into high gear again and there was much that Eagle did not catch. He did not ask for a repeat. He tapped the man's arm and said, "Were you present when the *policia* spoke with Don Simon?"

The servant looked shocked. Of course not! They had gone into the library, very private. He was not a snoop. He did not listen at keyholes. He—

Eagle held up a hand. "Did you mention my presence in this house? To the *policia?*"

But no! He had his orders. *Señor* Peabody was a guest whose privacy was to be observed.

Noting that in the past few minutes he had been demoted from Don to *Señor,* Eagle gave the man a twenty bolivar note. He wasn't buying anything in particular, but it never hurt to stay on the good side of the help.

"Inform Don Simon that I will be there in a few minutes."

When the door closed Eagle went into the bathroom. The bell bird was still fluttering in vines near the window. Eagle burnished his shoes with a towel, a bad habit of his, and thought it over. It was natural enough for the cops to be mad. That was not important. What was important was that their patience must be running out fast, and sooner or later they would search the house. They had probably already doubled the watchers. It was not impossible that they might haul the Don, and any guests they might find, off to the *calabozo.* Eagle flinched and tossed the towel into the hamper.

He found Simon de Ojeda in the dining room, seated in solitary splendor at the head of an enormous table. The room was itself of institutional size, with a musicians' gallery at one end. As Eagle entered, the old man stopped picking at his food and rose to give his guest a courtly bow.

"Good morning, Mr. Eagle. I trust you slept well?" There was a twinkle, and a question, in the small dark eyes.

Eagle glanced back at the door. It was closed. The

Don said, "I ordered a buffet this morning. We will not be disturbed. It is useless, of course, to try to keep anything from them—servants always know everything—but I trust them absolutely."

Eagle smiled. "Your man called me Peabody this morning." He went to the buffet and began serving himself. He was hungry and the choice was extensive. Eagle had never been fussy about food, having been raised in Apache poverty, but he was not averse to the delicacies of life.

The Don sat down and smiled at his plate. He was not hungry. He very seldom was these days. Not since his beloved Catherine Rosa—he forced himself to put the thought away. He had done with praying for the time being. He had not slept at all, in fact had spent most of the night at his prie-dieu before Her image. There were times when he fancied that his Catherine Rosa and the Virgin looked much alike.

He watched the big man; what a *fisicio* he had, what a *constitucion,* heaping food on his plate. Enough for four men. He said, "I try to keep an international table. In my position it is necessary. I hope you find things to your enjoyment?"

Eagle nodded. The coffee was as black and hot as hell, the cream heavy and rich. In the spirit of internalionalism he put Spanish sauce on his *oeufs au buerre noir* and added kidney and crisp bacon. He always ate like a shark, and never gained a pound.

As he was leaving the buffet, Eagle noted an etagere in a corner. It was laden with murrhine cups set with what he would have bet were real rubies and emeralds. He paused for a closer look.

"My wife collected them," the old man said. "Those are Roman, mostly from the first century."

Eagle nodded and took a chair next to the Don. The old man let him begin before he said, "You left the house last night, Mr. Eagle? You encountered the policeman and injured him?"

Eagle nodded. "Sorry about that. It couldn't be helped. Bad luck on both sides. He was in the way. I didn't damage him much. His pride more than anything. That's what the *policia* are really screaming about, not a bump on a cop's head."

The Don watched him for a moment. He picked up a fork and stirred the small amount of food on his plate.

"You know, then, that the police have been here already this morning?"

"Your servant told me."

The Don's laugh was dry. "I do hope, Mr. Eagle, that you are not going to suborn my servants?"

Eagle was enjoying his breakfast. "I don't see how I can do that, sir. You say you trust them absolutely?"

"I do. I do indeed."

Eagle put down his knife and fork. "I believe that. What I don't believe is that you trust *me* absolutely."

The old man stared at his plate, moving the fork around and around. Eagle looked at the musicians' gallery and pictured the huge room filled with guests and laughter and wine and music. He wondered how long it had been.

Don Simon said, "I had a long night to think."

Eagle waited.

Don Simon spread his hands, pale claws, before him. "It has all been very sudden and very strange, Mr. Eagle. You will admit that? Just consider—I am suddenly in deep trouble. My son is taken, and three people are murdered. People he should not have known or associated with, if indeed he did. I am warned to keep silent. I am sent my son's finger, the flesh of my flesh. I am an important man, Mr. Eagle, forgetting all modesty —I am an important man and I hold a high position. In effect I control the mineral resources of my country. Billions of dollars. With my signature and with my influence in the committees, both in the Senate and the Chamber of Deputies, I can largely control the flow of those dollars. Not altogether, not totally, but to a very large extent I make oil policy in Venezuela."

Eagle nodded. "I also had a long night, and I accomplished a little. Not much, but a little. I also did a lot of thinking. Oil! I think that you are about to come to the point."

The Don tugged at the white swatch of beard on his chin and nodded vigorously. Eagle thought that he looked a bit like a desiccated billygoat.

"I was reticent last night," the old man said. "I did not withhold, you understand, so much as overlook.

Postpone—what you will. But consider my plight—I am tossed suddenly into this nightmare; I turn in desperation to the only source of hope I know, a very old and dying man. He tells me to wait, that he will try. I do not understand any of this, how or why or when, but suddenly you appear, like a genie from a lamp, and offer me help. I am not in a position to be, how do you say, choosy. I must accept help from any source. You will understand this, Mr. Eagle, and you will also understand why it is, how it is, that I have not until now been, again how do you *Norteamericanos* say it, exactly outgoing?"

Eagle grinned at him. "I sort of guessed that. That you weren't exactly opening the floodgates of information. That's not good. I am here to do a job for you, and I can't without all the relevant information."

Don Simon nodded vigorously, suddenly animated, a man who, after a period of long and agonizing thought, had come to a decision. "I agree. It is time all the cards were on the table. This is a most abnormal situation for me, you will understand. As Minister I normally can exercise a great deal of power, politically of course, and in certain other matters also, but in this thing I am like a babe in the woods. They have Carlos and I am helpless—what good to call in the Army, the Navy, the police and Air Force, only to have them kill my son? Catching the murderers, killing them in turn, would be of no solace to me."

Eagle refilled his coffee cup. "I understand all that. That is why I am here."

"Carlos was the apple of his mother's eye," said the old man. He looked past Eagle, far past, at something only he could see. Eagle waited patiently, hoping the old boy wasn't going to dodder again. He wondered if the Don was senile. Probably not. He could be sharp enough at times, when it suited him.

"Carlos was her gem, her jewel, her whole life," the old man continued. His gaze came back to Eagle. He smiled and raised a hand in deprecation. "You will forgive an old man if he seems to wander a bit. I feel that I must, in this instance, let it all hang out."

Eagle's jaw sagged a bit; the old man smiled again and clapped his hands lightly. "Carlos would put it that way. In this instance, one of the few since he was born, I would agree with him. It is a personal matter, Mr. Eagle, and I dislike inflicting it on you, but I have decided on absolute honesty between us and this is part of it."

Eagle nodded. "You and the boy don't hit it off too well?"

Simon de Ojeda pushed his plate away and clasped his hands on the snowy tablecloth. An attitude of prayer. Eagle cast a surreptitious glance at his watch. He had to get a cable off to Merlin.

The Don said: "I am most ambivalent about Carlos. I both love and hate him and at times I do not know which is the stronger. I married late in life, Mr. Eagle, a much younger woman, a girl, really, and perhaps I was too old to be a real father. I tried my best, or thought I did, but Carlos turned out to be a disaster." He waved a hand. "From my point of view, of course."

In Eagle's line of work he had to sort through a lot of dirty linen. He resigned himself.

"My son is a drunkard and a drug addict. A lecher. A despoiler of young women. Whether with whores or young ladies of his own class, it makes no difference to Carlos. He is profligate with money. My money and his mother's money. He is incapable of earning a bolivar for himself. He has been kicked out of four universities. He will not listen to me, nor to any older person, and it is impossible to have a calm discussion with him. Always we end by screaming at each other. Several occasions he has threatened to strike me."

Eagle decided to meet candor with candor. He could not see how any of this was going to help him in his task, but at least it would clear the air.

"Why didn't you kick him out?"

"Disown him?" The Don nodded. "I have often thought of it. Even mentioned it. Carlos laughed and threatened to raise a great smell in the courts. It would not be good for a man of my position, of my political prominence, to do such a thing. Aha, but I have been tempted."

Eagle decided how to play it. A bit brutally he said, "And now you have to pay to get him back."

"I must, of course. I love him as much as I hate

everything he stands for. I promised his mother, on her deathbed, that I would look after him. My Catherine Rosa knew that things were not well between Carlos and me, though she did not know the extent. While she lived Carlos made some effort to get along with me. He loved his mother deeply. I can at least say that for him. But when his mother died, before she had been in the earth a week, Carlos displayed the naked sword to me."

An elderly Don would naturally think in terms of swordsmanship. Eagle turned an illusion. "He took off the gloves?"

A nod. "As you say. His behavior became more and more intemperate and his demands for money unceasing. With women he became insane—there was scandal after scandal with everything and anything in skirts. There have been dirty talk and malicious hints in the poorer type of newspapers, the ones who lend themselves to such filth, and it has been suggested by a friend or two, by some of my peers in the Government, that I had best put my house in order or resign. I have no intention of doing any such thing."

Eagle could feel for the old boy. To men like this a promise, especially a promise to a dying wife, was sacred. But on the other hand—

Don Simon went on. "You see my position. I must struggle with it alone. I do not wish my son dead. I do wish him to go and leave me in peace, and to find peace for himself if that is possible. I would feel great guilt if I did not make every effort, pay any price, to have him returned safely. A severed finger will heal. In time that kind of loss can be lived with. It is the finger, you see, Mr. Eagle, that has me so upset, has thrown all my thinking out of joint. The finger, Carlos' finger, with his ring, changed everything. It frightened me badly that I had made such a miscalculation. It sent me to my old friend for help and as a result you sit here now."

Eagle held up a hand. "Hold it. You've lost me. I don't get the last bit. What miscalculation? What changed everything?"

"The finger, Mr. Eagle. I did not think Carlos would go that far. Would cut off his own finger to convince me to pay ransom."

CHAPTER 9

Eagle was a bit shaken. He went to the buffet to get more coffee. This was an angle he had not considered.

"You have reason to believe this is the case, Don Simon?"

"I do. Not proof, but some reason. I hope I am wrong. But you will see how I am in, as you people say, a bind. I could not go to the police even if I wanted to. The Wild Dog need have no worry about that. If Carlos is involved in this thing, of his own free will is staging a hoax to defraud me, his father, I cannot afford to let the truth come to light. The scandal would be the end of me politically."

Eagle returned to the table with his steaming coffee. "You're prepared to pay, then? To give your son a large amount of money for kidnapping himself? And what about this Wild Dog, the guerrilla fighter in the jungles? You're telling me that you think your son is in with this character? That they've done a deal together? I hope you see where all that leads, Don Simon. Carlos could end up in prison or even against a wall."

The white goatee trembled in agitation. The Don shrugged his fragile old shoulders and spread his hands. "All the more reason why the matter must be resolved quietly, privately, with absolutely no publicity. If I am linked, through Carlos, with this guerrilla—"

Eagle scalded his mouth with the coffee. The old guy was in a bind, all right. Torn between a promise to his dead wife and his career, his duty to his country and his position.

"You have no proof of this, Don Simon?"

"No. Only strong suspicions. Let me explain."

Eagle listened with a growing awareness that he was getting deeper and deeper into a cauldron. Matters were infinitely more complex than he had imagined. Or Merlin could have imagined. He wondered how much

Merlin really knew about this rat's nest—and wasn't telling him.

Simon de Ojeda, his hands clasped again in prayer, regarded Eagle down the long shiny table. "I must ask a pledge of secrecy, Mr. Eagle, about some of the things I am about to tell you. You will understand why when you hear."

Eagle nodded. "Okay. You've got it."

"A few months ago I began to receive various pressures. Letters, visitors, hints and rumors. All having to do with a new oil field in the provinces of Guarico and Bolivar. I should say fields, for they are extensive and extend on both sides of the Orinoco. They are not yet into production, but the oil is there. Enormous reserves."

Eagle's smile was sour. "I would have bet that oil would come into this sooner or later."

The old man nodded. "When does it not, these days! But I began to get these pressures. Subtle at first. Nothing overt, nothing to grasp at, but I have been in government a long time and I am sensitive to these things. Yet there was nothing I could place a finger on."

Eagle gnawed the last of his toast. "These new oil fields? This is generally known? I mean, they are not a secret?"

A shrug. "Who can keep an oil field secret? We did try to avoid publicity, to play it down. There is a certain amount of censorship in our press, Mr. Eagle. We simply omitted certain facts."

"I see. So who was responsible for the pressures?"

The old man was toying with a table knife, drawing designs on the cloth. "It took me time to find out. I employed a private agency, you will understand. I did not want questions raised in the Senate or the Chamber of Deputies. I have many political enemies. I found out, eventually, that the man behind the pressures is an Englishman. A financier of great power and wealth. Sir Rodney Hamilton. Do you know of him?"

On first impulse Eagle shook his head. He did not move much in financial circles. Then he felt a memory jolt. Hamilton. Sir Rodney Hamilton. Somehow familiar.

"He once appeared on *Time*'s cover, I believe. Man of the year. Does that help, Mr. Eagle?"

"Not much. I seem to remember, vaguely, but never mind. How does he fit into the act?"

The Don stabbed at the tablecloth. "I found that he was responsible for the pressures. Once I began to look I found out a great deal about Sir Rodney. He maintains a large ranch, a *hacienda,* in this country. He owns the island of El Blanco off our coast. He maintains a private submarine, I understand that it is painted gold! —and that will give you an idea of his type."

Eagle was skeptical. "This all came as a surprise to you? A man like that? You had not heard of him before?"

The Don's shrug was eloquent. "I asked myself that. The answer is that he is a secretive man. He keeps a low profile; always in the background, always shielded by other men and by dummy companies. I think, and this only after much racking of my brain, that I once met this man at a State ball. Three, perhaps four years ago. He managed to make no impression on me. Odd. Strange. Especially given the circumstances of his head."

Eagle looked puzzled. The old man laughed. "I know this only because of my investigation. Sir Rodney was once a racing driver and suffered a peculiarly horrible accident. The top of his skull was torn away. He now wears a silver plate that, as I understand, covers the entire top of his head. *Maravilloso, si?*"

Eagle nodded a bit absently. He was thinking that Merlin might just have a file on Sir Rodney Hamilton. He began to recompose the cable he meant to send.

He waited. Don Simon lit a thin tan cigarillo and blew out little clouds of blue smoke. He appeared not to see Eagle, to have slipped into another world in the way he had. Eagle cleared his throat.

The old man came back to the present. "In the course of my very confidential investigations, Mr. Eagle, I found that my son Carlos was well acquainted with Sir Rodney. He had not told me, never mentioned it, and I can see now that there was a great secrecy about their relationship. But Carlos always came and went of his own will; I cared little enough—my great wish being to avoid friction—so I suppose I should not have been so surprised. Yet I was when I learned that Carlos had been the frequent guest of Sir Rodney Hamilton. On the island of El Blanco, at the *hacienda* in the province of Guarico and on the golden submarine. It is, I believe, called the Nautilus Dos. My informants," the old man smiled thinly, "tell me that sexual and drinking orgies are commonplace aboard the golden submarine. This would explain, of course, my son's readiness to attend. Among other things."

Eagle lit one of his rare cigarettes and immediately squashed it out in his coffee cup. He felt more like a stiff shot of scotch. But he wasn't going to have it. The business was past being a mess and developing into a rat's maze. He looked at the Don.

"What you're telling me is that Carlos has been working with this Sir Rodney? To put these pressures on you. Meaning the new oil fields, concessions or whatever?"

The Don interrupted. "I think it is a possibility that Carlos was doing just that. I say *was,* you note. I did not yield to the pressures. I ignored them. No concessions were given, no deals made, nothing. The new fields, and the oil under them, belong entirely and absolutely to Venezuela."

Eagle would have bet that the old man had taken a bribe or two in his time, but he believed him now.

"The pressures stopped," the Don continued. "Suddenly—no more! Nothing."

Eagle was thinking hard. It figured. If the kid and Sir Rodney *had* been in cahoots, trying to shake down the old man for favored status, it hadn't worked. Maybe this Englishman had merely been looking for an in, trying to use a family relationship, seeking to get next to the father through the son. That sure as hell hadn't worked, matters being what they were between the de Ojedas. And maybe there was more to it, a lot more.

He watched the old man. "So the pressures stopped? When was this?"

"Three, four months ago. Two or three months after they began. Matters were as before."

Eagle got up and started to pace the big room. "All smooth and serene, eh? Just as before."

66

A nod. "As before, Mr. Eagle. Carlos went his way and I mine. We rarely spoke. When we did, we argued. Bitter words, I am afraid. And now—this! Carlos is kidnapped."

Eagle regarded the murrhine cups. "Or was he?"

A sound from the table brought Eagle around. Don Simon had stabbed the knife through the cloth into the wood. He left it there. His claw-like hand was trembling. For the first time Eagle noted how yellow the man's hands were. Yellow and shriveled.

"That is indeed," said Don Simon, "the question. Were it not for the finger I could readily believe it— that Carlos is working with this Sir Rodney to embarrass me, to bring new pressures, to make great sums of money from this new oil, by forcing concessions from me."

Eagle was curious. "Can he do that? Force concessions from you?"

"You mean my son, Carlos?"

Eagle nodded.

"Never!" Don Simon shook his head fiercely.

Eagle moved closer to him. "And if the kidnapping is genuine. If the finger is genuine and this Wild Dog really has your son—none of it anything to do with the Englishman—what then?"

Don Simon stood up. "Every cent I have. For the son of my dead Catherine Rosa. For my promise to her. But not a drop of oil. It is not mine to give."

Eagle sat down again. "What do you think of this Wild Dog angle? Of this Emile Ortega? Do you think there is any possibility that the *three* of them could be in on it, that Carlos, Sir Rodney and the Wild Dog are working together?"

The old man thought a long time before answering. "It is possible. Just possible. In my poor Venezuela, in this time of money and oil madness, anything is possible. Ortega, this Wild Dog, does have some support from certain elements in the Army and Air Force. Small; a few disaffected officers of no real importance, but it is there. I have no right to tell you this, of course. I—" He broke off.

Eagle gave an honest grin and raised a hand. "I gave you my word. Not a word leaves this room."

"Of course. Well, it is true. Ortega has to some small extent infiltrated our armed forces. But it is well in hand and our intelligence and security services will know when, and how, to act. Of the first and greatest importance, naturally, is that this Wild Dog be taken or killed. But none of this is of great moment in the present affair, Mr. Eagle. Not as I see it. I cannot see Carlos involved in any way with Ortega. My son is a coward. He has always been deathly afraid of pain. Even as a child he could not be cajoled to the dentist. I cannot see him submitting to such a thing as the amputation of his finger."

"There is another possibility."

"That he did not submit of his own will? That his finger was cut off by force and against his wishes?"

"It's a possibility."

Don Simon pulled the knife out of the table. "In which case the kidnapping is genuine, you think? Not a hoax?"

"Not necessarily. It could have started out as a hoax. Your son could have been in on it. Then once they had him, whoever, the plans could have been changed."

The old man threw up his hands with an expression of disgust. "It is all too much for me, Mr. Eagle. I thank God for your presence and I turn the burden over to you. I ask only discretion and, above all, secrecy. At least until we have the truth of the matter. Naturally, and whether or not you have success, you can name your own reward. I am a very rich man. Money as such does not concern me."

"Nor me. I work on a straight salary."

"Incredible!"

"A pretty *good* straight salary," Eagle added. "Now, we've got a lot of work to do. I have to send a cable, for one thing, as soon as possible, and I don't want to leave the house. Maybe one of your servants—"

The Don waved a hand. "Of course. It will be done immediately and to your exact wishes. You do not think the phone—?"

"Sure to be tapped by now."

"Yes, I suppose so."

Eagle said, "Do you want to tell me about the police visit this morning."

The old man smiled. "They are still polite. The courtesy wears a bit thin, perhaps, but it still exists. They are angry about the man you overcame."

"Did they explain why the man was hanging around?"

"Hanging around? Oh, I see. No. They did not explain. You were right, Mr. Eagle. They are suspicious and they are watching this house. They do not intend to let the matter drop."

"You could hardly expect that. No matter how important you are. Three murders. Have they found any connection yet between your son and the dead people? Or what his car was doing there?"

Simon de Ojeda shook his head. "They said nothing had been discovered for a certainty. Carlos is believed to have been seen with the dead woman at a bar, a place with a bad reputation. Nothing more than that. They were very vague. Very cool and correct, you understand, but not friendly. I am not in good odor with the *policia*, no matter what my high position in the government. They suspect me of something."

Eagle laughed. "They suspect you of not telling them the truth, the whole truth, and nothing but the truth."

Don Simon nodded sadly. "I know. They are right. In this situation—impossible."

"For the time being you will have to stick to your lies. You're pretty good at it."

Don Simon bowed in acknowledgement. "I am a politician, Mr. Eagle. I have been, in my time, a diplomat. It is natural for me."

"Do you think they suspect my presence?"

The old man shook his head. "I do not believe so. I watched for any hint of that, any suspicion. I do not think they know about you."

"Let's hope we can keep it that way."

Eagle had been waiting for the Don to ask and now he did.

"Your adventure last night, Mr. Eagle; other than damaging the policeman, had you any results?"

Eagle had seen no reason to volunteer the information. The less the old man knew about the more violent aspects the better—but a direct question must be answered. He did not entirely trust this old man, who

69

might be playing a devious game of his own, but to share the little he knew would not make or break him.

"I found one of the Wild Dog's men standing watch," he explained. "I had a little talk with him."

The Don's thin mouth twitched. He cocked one of his dark eyes. "A little talk? Of interest?"

Eagle nodded. "To a point. He didn't know too much. He was an underling, a private soldier. But whatever he did know, I got."

"I see. You persuaded him." The murky old eyes gleamed and for a moment Eagle thought of the Inquisition.

"It was easy to persuade him. Have you ever heard of a man called Garmes? The first name might be José or Josh. Or even Joseph. Joe? The man was a little incoherent by then."

"Garmes?" Don Simon repeated the name again. "Garmes. No, Mr. Eagle. It means nothing to me. I have never heard of such a man."

"It might be important," said Eagle. "Or may not be. I am not even positive I got the name right. His English was bad and my Spanish is not so hot, either. One thing I do know—he was telling the truth as he understood it. I had a razor at his throat."

Don Simon nodded in approval. "A razor, eh? You are a direct man, Mr. Eagle."

"The man had been in the jungle fighting with Ortega. He and some of his buddies slipped into Caracas three days ago to meet this Garmes, who seems to be in charge of this end of the deal. I got the impression that the man was mightily impressed with Garmes, impressed and afraid of him. Garmes is white, probably a Yankee, and not very young. A soldier of fortune, from what I gathered. Old, but mean."

Don Simon made a fragile yellow tower of his fingers and nodded slowly. "I am familiar with the type. Not so much in these modern times, but in the old days, in South and Central America, they were everywhere, such men. My guess would be that he is a mercenary hired by the Wild Dog."

"Or Sir Rodney Hamilton?"

"Or both, Mr. Eagle. Or both."

There was a tapping on the door and on the Don's

command one of the servants came in bearing a thick letter on a salver. "The post, Don Simon."

Even in crisis, thought Eagle, the wealthy and powerful stick to the amenities. A severed finger, a ransom note, must be delivered on a silver tray.

The Don handed the letter to Eagle, who said, "At least it got through. I was afraid the police might intercept it."

Don Simon shrugged. "They do not quite dare that yet."

The address was neatly typewritten with a fresh ribbon. So was the letter. It told them exactly what to do. And what not to do.

CHAPTER 10

Sir Rodney Hamilton spent the evening before his Caracas flight working alone in his home in St. John's Wood. He gave his man the evening out and locked himself in the study. Here, for hours, he pored over the contents of a safe and three filing cabinets, trying to make two plus two equal five. He failed. Three was nearer to it.

His major asset, the backbone of his multinational corporate structure, was ROYAL EURASIAN PETRO, LTD. The bellwether. Actually a holding company that held other holding companies. Ironically founded on oil, thus the name, it had wandered too far into diversification, and for the past two years the pressures had been inexorably down. On the Bourse, on the New York exchange, in the City. Down and down. He'd recoup a point or two one day, plunge ten the next.

If Sir Rodney had been a believer in retribution he might have glanced about for his nemesis. He believed in no such nonsense and he did not lose his nerve. It would all come right. All it needed was the guts to hang on and the brains to figure a way out.

He had gambled on gold and lost heavily when the United States entered the open market. He could not hold on long enough for the price to rise again; he needed the money from elsewhere to plug the holes in his corporate dyke. There were too many holes and he had too few fingers. The prognosis was one of disaster. Unless the Venezuelan ploy worked.

Until last week, just before his trip to Tokyo, he had hoped that the British Government might pull him out. REP was the fourth largest oil concern in the country and on the surface it looked like saving. Sir Rodney had seen to that by an elaborate and sophisticated technique of cooking the books. This was thieves' argot and Sir Rodney did not mind using it. It was all a matter of accounting systems. They differed enormously.

The worst had happened to him last week, at the worst possible moment, when the Labor government was trying to make up its mind. Had the Tories been in, Sir Rodney could have swung it.

The stock market hit a twenty year low.

The pound weakened badly on foreign exchange markets.

The OPEC cartel was making new and threatening noises about embargo. Venezuela, one of the OPEC gangsters, as Sir Rodney thought of them, had recently nationalized its iron ore industry, and the concessions of U.S. Steel and Bethlehem Steel were to be terminated the first of the year. It was not a favorable time to go seeking concessions. And yet concessions he must have. Sir Rodney gazed at the stack of paper on his desk and rubbed his silver skull with nicotine stained fingers. If he could get control of sixty-five to seventy percent of the production of the new fields along the Orinoco he would be home free. He would play with the gangsters and not against them.

But it all had to be done before Venezuela got around to nationalizing oil. He had to get in and make his profits before that happened. He could stall nationalization, by spending enough money in the Venezuelan Senate and Chamber of Deputies, but he could not fend it off forever.

There was still time, barely, but not a moment to waste. The iron ore concessions had been supposed to run until 2000; the oil concessions ran until 1983. The new government, under Perez, was slightly left of center. This bothered Sir Rodney not at all. You did not deal with governments in a body, en masse; you dealt with individuals, men who could be bought, men who sought to line their own pockets. It usually worked for him. It had not worked with Simon de Ojeda.

It was just as well that the phone rang at that moment. Sir Rodney got a spleenful when he thought of that righteous old cock. Not that the son, Carlos, was any bargain. Well, they would see. He picked up the phone, at the same time glancing at a clock. A few minutes after midnight. Who?

"Father?"

He nodded at the phone and ensconced himself with one buttock on the desk. "Hello, Jennifer. You're the last person I expected to hear from. I thought you were in New York."

"I was. I flew in just a few hours ago. Mother sent for me. She's gotten very ill, Father."

The last thing he wanted at the moment was to be confronted with Berenice and her problems. Even thinking about REP's losses in tankerage—the Worldscale breakeven rate was 80 and last month REP had done 35—was preferable to getting involved with this woman whom he had not seen in twenty-two years.

"I'm sorry to hear that," he said. "What can I do?"

"It's cancer," Jennifer said. "Cancer of the cervix; they don't know yet if it's operable. I'm sending her to a nursing home near Salisbury and calling in specialists."

"Fine," said Sir Rodney. "Yes. I suppose that is best." He reached for a sheet of paper and studied it. It was a digest of some of REP's current difficulties. One horrendous figure struck Sir Rodney at a glance.

EARNINGS PER SHARE—$0.17

"Father?"

"I'm here, Jennifer."

"I'm frightened. I think Mother's going to die."

"I'm sorry. But we'll all die, Jennifer. You, me, your Mother. What can I do?"

He wondered—he could no more suppress the thought than he could have ascended to Heaven—if Jennifer was wearing a bra. She frequently did not. He had considered remonstrating with her about it, but had kept his silence. He thought a father was not supposed to notice his daughter's breasts even when they were swinging ripe and full a few inches away.

Her tone did not change. It was as cold and crisp as before as she said, "I don't expect you to do anything. I never have. But there will be great expenses and I intend the bills should come to you."

"Of course, Jennifer."

The silence was long and he guessed that, whatever it was, she was having trouble getting it out. At last she said, "Mother asked me to call and tell you."

Unusual. He could not remember the last time Berenice had instigated any communication between them. She had her house near Old Sarum, in Wilts, and her daughter and her own life and for all he knew had been content.

"She wants to see you," said Jennifer.

"I find that hard to believe, Jennifer."

"She has gotten very old, Father. And she's sick. She cries so easily."

Sir Rodney had no intention of going down to Wilts. He abhorred nursing homes and hospitals. His one experience, when they had put the silver plate in his head, had been quite enough.

"What exactly did she say, Jennifer?"

"That she wanted to see you."

"Her exact words?"

"She—she—" Jennifer's voice broke, her cold mien broken by emotion. He nodded to himself. As a child Jennifer had been very emotional. Only in her late teens had she adopted an armor of reserve, learned to take a distant stance. This he attributed to her growing suspicion, or more likely full realization, that her father regarded her as he did. He had sought desperately to prevent this, had used every guise to cloak what most civilized people considered a perversion, but he knew he had failed. He wondered how long Jennifer had known.

Jennifer was in control again. "She's been under

74

heavy sedation, Father. Vague, you know, and she slurs her words. But I understood her. She said, 'Tell your father that I have always loved him and that I would like to see him once more before I die.' "

Sir Rodney doodled on the REP report on his desk. He drew a heavy line through the heading—ASSETS (JUNE 30, 1974) $1,866,134,000.

A lie. Only he—and perhaps a few canny auditors who guessed and kept quiet—knew how much the figure was overblown.

"Will you come down, Father?"

"It's not possible," he told her. "I have to fly out to Venezuela tomorrow. It's absolutely most urgent. I'm sorry, Jennifer."

He was an imaginative man, in many ways a sensitive man, but he did not need these faculties to read the silence that followed. Disbelief and dislike. Cold indifference. Hatred?

"I thought your answer would be something like that. Goodbye, Father." The connection snapped.

Sir Rodney stared at the phone. After a moment he realized that the receiver was still in his hand. He replaced it, lit a cigar and began to pace the room. Why now? Why now of all times, when he was fighting for his financial life?

Why him, for that matter? He had never loved Berenice. Of course he'd lied about that, to get her to bed, but everyone did that. Women *knew* that. They expected lies and pretended to believe them. It was all part of the game, a game women loved and enjoyed as much as men. Berenice, once he had introduced her to sex, couldn't get enough, was always willing and eager and ready to learn new tricks. Until she got pregnant and demanded marriage.

He poured himself a spot of brandy and drank it. He was surprised to find that he was sweating heavily; his stomach and head felt odd. Damn! This was no time to come down with some bug, not with what he had facing him.

He had been twenty-nine then and at the peak of his racing skill and fame. He'd won some big races that year. Had come in fourth at Indianapolis. Won the Grand Prix at Monaco.

Two years before he'd hit the oil spot at Brands Hatch and lost control of the BRM at 180 mph. The car had gone somersaulting wildly, a roll bar collapsed, and the gritty top of a concrete retaining wall had scrubbed away the top of his skull.

Sir Rodney poured another tot of brandy and, forgetting Berenice for the moment, recalled the miracle. As if the wall had not been a wall at all, but a surgeon's saw—the cut could not have been more exact, the tolerance more infinitesimal. Bone gone, skull ground into pulp, the amazed doctors found the dura untouched, the delicate arachnoid and pia mater inviolate. It *had* been a medical miracle, and he had spent nearly a year in the hospital.

He was getting one of his headaches. Sir Rodney found a bottle of pills in his desk and shook one out. He caressed the silver skull with his blunt fingers, wishing they were drills so he could dig down through the metal and root out the pain. He took the pill with more brandy and wondered if his doctor was a liar. Probably. The Harley Street quack swore the pills contained no opiates, nothing illegal or habit forming, but they worked, worked swiftly and well, so they must contain at least one narcotic.

He sat at his desk again and tried to recapture his train of thought, to reimmerse himself in the papers. No good. He put them away, locked up and went upstairs to his bedroom suite.

As he polished his skull he thought again of Berenice. And was for a moment tempted to relent. He really couldn't spare the time; on the other hand, if the poor stupid bitch was dying, and still loved him after all these years, it would be a kindly effort on his part to make the trip down to wilts. He could not see that it mattered in the slightest—he could offer her no more comfort now than when he had sent her packing—but maybe he should make the effort.

Weakness. He steeled himself against it. Cast your die and abide by it. He abhorred, detested and feared weakness in himself as in others. If you were going to be a success, a bastard, the only way to make it work was to go all the way, one hundred percent, without hedging or relenting. He had crossed that barrier a long time ago, when he knew his nerve was gone and he could not race again, when he decided to spend the rest of his life in the pursuit of power and money. You couldn't change once bitten, once a real bastard, and there was no use trying. Especially not now. His only chance for survival now was to go on being what he was—to become even more so—and this did not allow for sentiment, pity or compassion, even for himself. That was weakness and weakness, in his position, was sure to bring disaster.

The pain had gone, vanquished by the pills, but he could not sleep. More and more, recently, he had difficulty sleeping. Conscience? That made him laugh.

Still no sleep. In the end he did what he did not want to do. He allowed himself a fantasy, a sexual scene with Jennifer. Feeling unsafe, exposed, even though the images were locked in his brain and shielded by a silver door. No one could ever know.

Wrong. Jennifer knew, if not in detail, she knew the general thrust of his thoughts and feelings toward her. Her problem, he considered as he began to masturbate, was to know, to react and guard herself, without appearing to know. Without ever bringing it out into the open. His problem, too. Never make an overt advance.

His penis was half flaccid and he stroked harder, at the same time wondering if he were getting old in that respect, approaching an age when sex would cease to interest him. He knew it happened, but could not imagine it for himself. He never had any real trouble with Cynthia Vorhees. Her mouth was magic. He disliked having to pay her for it, but in the end it did not matter. You always paid, one way or the other, and if he'd married Berenice he would still be paying. And not just in money. He would have had to put up with her, *live* with her, submit to her meddling and her supervision of his life. He would have had to pretend to love her until death. No way, for him. He had done the right thing all those years ago. And had not begrudged her money since, though some might have thought him less than generous. Perhaps with the mother he had been, still was. On the daughter, on his child, he had lavished money. And love. Love that over the

77

years, since Jennifer had become nubile, had somehow, without his quite knowing how, changed its name and form.

His head twinged again. He left off masturbating and rubbed the silver plate nestling so snugly just a micron from the dura mater. A silver curtain fronting the gray and white stage, the two pound blob of tissue and convoluted muscle that contained a cosmos, in itself entire and private. An X-rated and taboo mental movie. He again began to play with himself, remembering Jennifer as he had last seen her months before, when, in London for shopping, she had stopped by his main offices in the Hamilton Building. Something to do with her taxes, he could not remember exactly, and she had stayed only for a quarter of an hour. Lounging on a corner of his desk, long-legged in a Maximilian pants suit of gabardine. No bra, as usual, beneath the soft yellow cream silk of her blouse. Her breasts flopped about like two silky doves with every movement. He had stared that day, he remembered now, and Jennifer had known and reddened and gone quickly.

Now, as he stiffened and approached spurting, he felt a twinge of anger and resentment. Who had a better right to her? She was *his!* He alone had produced her, nurtured her, loved her and lavished a fortune on her. Had taken her from her mother as soon as possible— that poor excuse for a woman—and kept her in the most expensive schools in the world. True that he had never been able to break the cord between daughter and mother, but he had attenuated it. Had he been a less busy man, when she was younger and more malleable, he might have taken her to live with him, but that had proved impossible. He had then been working sixteen hours a day and been constantly on the go, building the fortune which was now on the verge of slipping away from him.

Sir Rodney Hamilton slowed his stroking to prolong the sensation. In the fantasy, as Jennifer sat on his desk, he found the courage to move near her, between the carelessly flung Maximilian legs, and to watch her eyes and her expression as he opened her blouse. He knew the texture and conformation of her breasts and nipples, having studied her once when she lay naked and sleeping in his villa on the Cote D' Azur.

She widened her eyes and breathed softly, "Oh, Father," but made no move to stop him. Her breasts trembled in his hand, which were themselves trembling. Jennifer had eyes of the darkest brown, her mother's eyes, with glints of silver in them, like pale mica, and the clear corneas of innocence.

"Oh, Father." She leaned to press her moist lips against his cheek.

Sir Rodney spasmed onto his hirsute chest. He writhed and groaned aloud. The fantasy exploded like a pricked balloon.

Incest. It was only a word, he told himself as he went into the bathroom to wash. A semantic trap. The world, his world, rated it the highest and most horrible of sins, yet he had read of cultures in which it was deemed proper and natural. There were few such, he admitted, as he wiped down with a wet towel, but they existed.

No good, of course, trying to tell that to society. Hypocrites and liars all. Incest was a scare word, a terror word, and yet there was more of it, much more, than the world cared to admit. The practical thing was, the whole trick—don't get caught. As with most other significant acts in the world.

Sir Rodney looked at himself in the bathroom mirror and rubbed a big hand over his polished skull. He wondered, as he often did, if he were a bit deranged. Wasn't everybody, to some extent? It was not a sane world.

He went back to bed, thinking that fantasies never hurt anyone as long as you did not attempt to act them out. He found relief in them and knew that he would never, in actuality, lay a hand on his daughter. Even so he could not understand, and did not like, the shame and nag of guilt he felt at moments such as these. He had murdered men in his day, or had them murdered, which was the same thing, and had felt less guilty. Such nonsense. He was an existential man; there were no sins other than man-made ones. And he only thought them, spun little sexual plays in the cavern of his mind. Yet the guilt feeling was there. He did not understand it. He was a man alone, he would live alone and die alone, and he brooked no master, no code, in the world. He gave nothing but lip service to fools, remained determined behind his façade.

Another spasm of rage shook him. Why in hell's fire should he care about some long dead and rotted Jewish prophets? They had all been a bit mad. And he had never pretended that the tenets of Judeo-Christianity were his own. Fuck them all. He must go, as ever, his own lonely and dangerous way.

As he drifted into sleep, the gonadal pressure relieved, and the forbidden images drifting, forming and reforming behind his eyelids, his thoughts returned to the coup he intended.

He was betting on another war in the Mideast. If it came and the United States supported Israel—anti-Semitic feeling was growing in the States, true, but not yet enough to effect a reversal of American policy—then another oil embargo was certain. This time it would be total. The United States would be a beggar, cup in hand. And he, Sir Rodney Hamilton, could fill that cup with oil if he could achieve the concessions he needed in the new field along the Orinoco. At his own price.

With the millions thus gained—he was thinking in terms of twenty dollars a barrel—he could invade the American stock market while it was still in the doldrums and buy and buy and buy. Selectively, of course. There were bargains galore, bargains crying to be snapped up, if a man had the money and the guts to buy and hold on.

He had the guts. He had the plan and the boldness to carry it through. All he had ever needed was a lever to exert pressure on Simon Carlos y Garcia de Ojeda. Now he had the lever. Or thought he did. Sending the finger had been a good touch, Garm's idea, and surely the old man loved his son enough to save him. One would think so, certainly; these old gentlemen of Castilian descent were given to strong emotions.

A good thing, he thought, that I'm not the bloody little bastard's father. I wouldn't fool with the worthless little so and so for a minute. I'd let the Wild Dog cut off his head and put it in the mail.

Sleep invaded him. Just before he succumbed he

smiled. The irony—the kidnapping had been young Carlos' idea in the first place. Not the finger part of course, but the kidnapping itself. It had come up one day, during idle talk, when Carlos was visiting Sir Rodney on the island.

Sir Rodney had laughed and downgraded the idea as too melodramatic. And filed it away in case old Simon proved obdurate. As he had.

CHAPTER 11

As soon as it was dark, John Eagle leaped over the wall again, and made his way across estates and over back lots until he found a cruising taxi. He went to his hotel where he took a shower, changed shirts and made a reservation for Quito. The capital of Ecuador was roughly a thousand miles from Caracas and as he booked a return flight, less than an hour after his arrival, Eagle acknowledged that the sleepless time had arrived. He had been through it before.

It was a drag, having to fly to Quito to make a phone call, but Merlin did not have a scrambler connection in Caracas. The nearest one was in Quito, where Merlin was heavily into oil and maintained a bank both for profit and as a front.

He flew a subsidiary of Lufthansa, Condor Flugdienst, a non-stop jet and was in Quito in less than three hours. He made a phone call; the president of the bank met him half an hour later and admitted him to the bank by a side entrance. The bank president, a dapper little man who appeared to have Indian blood, selected a key and opened a cabinet to reveal the phone. He nodded politely and said, "I will wait in the outer office, *Señor.*"

Eagle waited until the door closed, then dialed through. After a few rings, Polly Perkins answered.

"I'm in Quito," he told her. "My flight back to Caracas leaves in less than an hour. Is he available?"

"Just a moment, John."

Merlin came on the line, his voice steady and mellifluous. A good sign, which Eagle had noted before. When Merlin was pleased, on top of things, his voice was that of a younger man.

"How is it going, my boy?" He was purring.

"Will you please scramble, sir."

Eagle pressed his own button. Merlin said, "Done. Now?"

Eagle filled him in to date. The old man listened without once interrupting.

When Eagle had finished Merlin said, "We've come up lucky here on Sir Rodney Hamilton. I have him in my D file and, from what I've seen so far, that is where he belongs."

Eagle had no idea what the D file was. He kept silent. Merlin never told him more than he needed to do a job.

"A monstrous ego," Merlin went on. "Overweening. The-world-is-made-for-me kind. Dangerous. Keep that always in mind. He just may be one of the great white collar criminals of all time."

"Do you think he's behind the kidnapping of Carlos de Ojeda?"

"Everything so far indicates that he is. We're accumulating more data by the hour and putting it through the computers. I've got London working on it and making hourly reports. This Garmes you asked about may be Garm—a Joseph Garm. An older man, a soldier of fortune. Very rough, from what we know to date. I'll have more on him later."

"That's one of the problems," said Eagle. "Later. I may be out of touch for some time. It's hard to say how long. I'm returning to Caracas as soon as I hang up, but I don't want to go back to the de Ojeda house. It's a trap. I've been lucky up to now, getting in and out, but that won't last forever. And the police are running out of patience with the old Don. I can't risk going back in. I can't do any good in a Venezuelan slammer."

Merlin chuckled. "Agreed. I have other plans for

you in any case. Dependent on how much time you can wangle. You say the first meeting is set for tomorrow night?"

"Yes, sir. It was all very specific in the letter. Don Simon is to meet someone. I explained it. Comic book stuff. His chauffeur is to drive him around until someone makes contact."

"I think you had better be in on that, John. Can you arrange it?"

"Looks like I'll have to. The police will probably have a man on him. Maybe not. Shouldn't be anything I can't handle. And if I do—what then?"

Merlin told him.

When he had finished Eagle said, "Stalling tactics might be a little risky. I saw the finger; this is a rough outfit we're playing with. If they get unhappy they just might send the boy's head along parcel post."

"I don't think so," Merlin said. "I'm guessing, playing a hunch, but I think that if you and Don Simon handle it right they'll go along with a little stalling. Sir Rodney has to have time to arrive on the scene and set the stage, as it were. This thing is more complex than it appears on the surface, John—this man is after something that can't be accomplished overnight. I won't go into all of it now, no reason to trouble you, but it involves politics and, I am beginning to believe, revolution. But your job is to save the boy. If at all possible. Stick to that."

"Of course, sir. But there is still the matter of communication. I'm not too familiar with the NSA area."

"I know." Merlin coughed; Eagle could see cigar smoke exploding. "The fact is, John, that we're a bit delinquent in that area. It's being remedied now. Within twelve hours a Double-Blue net will be functioning. You had better make a note of this address."

Eagle wrote down the street and number. At the moment it meant nothing to him, but if Merlin said so there would be a safe house there within twelve hours. And the means of communication.

It all made Eagle feel a little better, a little more secure. If there was such a thing in his job.

They spoke for another five minutes during which Eagle kept glancing at his watch. If he missed his flight back to Caracas he would have to wait six hours for the next.

Merlin summed up and asked Eagle to repeat after him. His hunch had been right. He wouldn't be getting a lot of sleep for a time.

"That is Plan A," Merlin said, "and for the time being it will be the prime one. You will go to Plan B only if something goes wrong, at your end or mine. You will, as always, use your own judgment once you are in the field."

He did not have to ask, but he did just to get it on the record. "I have permission to kill?"

"As always, my boy. If justified."

Just before he hung up Merlin said, "There are times when we could all hark back to the Old Testament. I believe this is one of them. An eye for an eye, John, and a tooth for a tooth. In this case, a finger for a finger."

"Yes, sir. Goodbye." Eagle went to catch his flight back to Caracas. He hoped it worked. If they were given time it just might.

CHAPTER 12

"You're sure he's gone to Caracas?"

"Positive, Ian. I told you. I booked him through myself."

Ian Thomas parted the curtain a trifle and stared down into the street. He was in Cynthia Vorhees' flat on the Bayswater Road near Notting Hill Gate. He had just finished making love to Cynthia and, his lust satiated, had gone back to worrying. He thought he was being followed. It made no sense. Unless—

Cynthia lay on the sofa, her dress still pulled up to her waist. She nursed a drink and wondered why she continued the affair with Ian Thomas. The thing had been on going for almost two years now. Poor drunken seedy little Ian. Getting on, he was, and not such a great lover. Just now she'd had to get him to erection with her mouth.

She supposed it was because Ian treated her like a woman, a person. Sir Rod, as she had come to think of him, treated her like a hired cocksucker, though the job was worth it.

Ian let the drape fall back into place and turned away from the window. "You're absolutely positive? You saw him get on the plane?"

"Of course not. He doesn't take me to the airports with him. I suppose his chauffeur drove him. How should I know? Anyway, why shouldn't he have gone to Caracas! He does a lot of business there. He's got a ranch, or a *hacienda* or whatever and an island there. His submarine is there. You're not making sense, Ian. Why should he bother to have you followed is what I'd like to know."

He came to the sofa and leaned to kiss her lightly on the mouth. Why do I put up with him, she thought. He gives me at least a pretense of affection. A woman needs that. Even if half the time he doesn't get me off.

Ian Thomas made himself a stiff drink, half a glass of scotch, and came back to the sofa. He toyed with Cynthia's chestnut furze, tracing his fingers lightly over her labia, still moist from him. She tightened her legs.

"Stop it, Ian. You'll have me all stirred up again."

He caught a tendril of curly pubic hair and twirled it on his finger.

"I guess I'm a little uptight, as the Yanks put it, but I would have sworn I was followed here. And if I was —who else but bloody bastard Sir Rod?"

Cynthia pushed his hand away and tugged down her skirt. "He wouldn't bother."

Ian shook his head. "Maybe he would. Oh, not in person. I don't expect him to come breaking the door down. But he could bloody well hire private detectives."

Cynthia sipped at her drink. Eyed him over it. So far his lovemaking had only served to arouse her. He did that sometimes—aroused her and then went off and left her hanging high and dry. Not this time, she determined. This time he's going to finish what he started.

Her thoughts were not really on the matter at hand,

Ian's suspicion that he was being followed, and she was startled at his vehemence.

"He could bloody damned well hire private detectives to spy on us, Cyn. And he bloody well would if he suspected anything. I know the old bugger better than you do. He goes into a fury if anyone tampers with what he considers he owns."

"He doesn't own me, Ian. Or you."

He did not look at her. He went back to the window and lifted a corner of the drape. He felt uneasy. Her statement was not exactly true. In a sense Sir Rod *did* own him. Owned his silence—for what Ian did not precisely know, except that it concerned Joe Garm— and owned his future. He was in his late forties and, but for the cushy job on the *Graphic* he would be washed up. On the street. Everyone in the world knew he was an alcoholic. Sir Rod certainly knew it. And yet he'd all but promised him the managing editor's job as soon as old Carruthers retired. Which would be when Sir Rod said so.

He thought of the two thousand pounds hidden in a closet in his flat. Which he did not intend to declare or pay tax on. The hell Sir Rod *didn't* own him!

He saw nothing suspicious in the street. There had been a man, Ian had been sure, but now the man was gone. Probably had never been there, except in Ian's head. Booze and tension would do it.

But Cyn was wrong. Dead wrong. Sir Rod was capable of anything. Hubris, arrogance, that was the bloody bastard's trouble. Arrogance, too much money and a conviction that he was above the law. That he could do any bloody thing in the world that pleased him. Silver-bald old sod!

In spite he turned on Cynthia. "The hell he doesn't own you. Maybe you more than me. I don't spread my legs at his beck and call. Or suck his cock whenever his bloody majesty is pleased to drop his pants."

It had been a mistake to ever tell him what went on with Sir Rod. Not that he wouldn't have guessed— drunk he might be, scruffy and seedy, in final judgment a failure, but he was sharp enough. He had been a top flight newsman before the alcohol got to him so completely and, at times, he still flashed signs of what he must have been. Cynthia decided not to become angry. She meant to be satisfied this time, either by his point or tongue, and she did not want an angry scene. It would take a little coaxing as it was—Ian did not like to go down on her.

She gave him a half smile. "I do it for an extra fifty pounds a week, love. Not because I like it. Look at it this way—we both work for the bastard, you in your way and I in mine, but he doesn't own us."

Ian Thomas resisted a temptation to peer into the street again. She was probably right. He was seeing things. Imagining. Nerves. Nerves and booze.

He filled his glass this time, drank, wiped his mouth, gasped, and went over to sit beside her again. He pulled up her skirt and she did not object.

"You're missing the point," he told her. "One of them, anyway. Bloody Sir Rod *think*s he owns us and it amounts to the same thing. And what a man with all that money and power *thinks* is what counts. Money and power get their way in this world."

"Not always."

It was in part an idle statement. He had his finger in her, working slowly. Cynthia lay back on the sofa and unbuttoned her blouse. She began to caress her nipples with her fingertips. The sensation she craved was just beginning, it would be a long time before she achieved orgasm and she sought a way to keep him at it and to bring her home in the way she liked best. She closed her eyes.

"Not always," she repeated. "He doesn't own his daughter. Jennifer Hamilton. She hates him. She goes her own way."

She caught his interest. He stopped fingering her and looked up. "What do you mean?"

Cynthia took his hand and put it back where it had been. "Don't stop doing that. I mean what I said— Jennifer hates him. Not that I blame her. I think he's after her. Or would be if he dared."

"What in the bloody hell are you talking about?"

Cynthia moved against his finger. "Do you know Jennifer Hamilton? Have you met her?"

"Maybe once or twice. I've seen her picture often enough. In the magazines—and the scandal rags."

Cynthia kept her eyes closed. The sensation was growing, feeling better and better with each passing moment.

"She gets into those messes to spite him," she said. "I don't believe all those wild things you read about her, but some of them must be true and she does it to get back at him. I'm sure of it."

Ian Thomas laughed. "Great Bloody Christ on the mountain! Now you're an amateur psychologist. Really, Cyn—"

She shook her head. A flood was rising in her pelvic region. "Not a psychologist. A woman. And I notice things. A lot of things. I said he would like to have her, didn't I? It's true. I've seen him look at her when he's off guard. He undresses her with his eyes. His own daughter. I know you think I'm just a stupid totsy, Ian, but I know that look. Any woman does. I think our Sir Rod wants to fuck his daughter more than anything else in the world. Even money and power."

Ian considered. He stared at her pudendum without really seeing it. His finger, an automaton, stroked her clitoris. It was a fiery red, swollen, penile. Her inner thigh muscles were in light spasm.

Without looking up he said, "You actually think the bastard is having it off with her, with the daughter?"

A light was glimmering in the back of his brain. Self interest, gain, a possibility to be explored. Not that there was anything certain to it. Cyn was a raving lunatic. And yet—

It was nearly time. Cynthia said, "I told you she hates him. She would never let him touch her that way. Or any way, if what I've noticed and heard means anything."

"Heard?"

She groaned softly. "Don't stop. Yes, heard. I listen in sometimes. She is very hard with him. Cold and harsh."

"I would think that it would be the other way around."

"No. Sometimes, not always but sometimes, he tries very hard to make her like him, to get on the good side of her. It's pitiful. There are times when I feel sorry for him."

"You feel sorry for him!"

"Please, Ian, let's not talk any more right now." She pressed his head between her two palms, exerting a gentle downward pressure.

"Please, Ian. Do me that way."

For once he did, if not with gusto at least with competence; it left her drowsy and filled with gratitude. Once in the street, walking toward Pembridge Gardens, he began to think about what Cyn had told him. Incest! Was it possible?

He tugged his Burberry about his throat against the raw day and acknowledged that of course it was possible. He was a newspaperman. He knew that anything was possible in this worst of all possible worlds. But was it even probable? If so, how could he find out, prove it, remain safe and make a profit?

Ian Thomas had barely begun to toy with the idea, running it through his head for size, weighing the pros and cons, when he heard the taxi pull up beside him. He did not really hear it; he was so lost in his thoughts as barely to acknowledge it on the periphery of his consciousness. By the time his mind cleared, and he was acutely aware of the taxi and the two burly men, it was too late.

Merlin's men took him south for a time and changed to a private car near North Cheam. Ian was paralyzed with fright and gave them no trouble. He believed them when they said he'd receive no bodily harm if he cooperated, but he was still shaking with terror.

The Humber sedan took the A217 Bypass to Cheam Road, where it cut over west to the London Road. They drove for a long time, allowing Ian to smoke but not to talk, and it was well after dark when they left the main road and, after a quarter of an hour on winding lanes, stopped at an isolated cottage.

Inside they gave him a badly needed glass of scotch and allowed him a few minutes to compose himself. When the questions began, Ian Thomas answered as fully and truthfully as he could.

CHAPTER 13

Eagle got back to his Caracas hotel in time to catch a few hours sleep, an unexpected bonus. He ordered breakfast sent up, along with the morning papers, and dawdled in his robe.

The hour of truth, as the Spanish liked to say, was approaching. He was running things now and it was a question of how much he told, or did not tell, Don Simon. As little as possible, concomitant with the old boy's safety and reputation and that of his son. Eagle's job, at Merlin's behest, was to get the old man and Carlos out of a mess, not deeper into one. The trouble was that there were a lot of factors to be considered—and things that could easily go wrong.

Eagle did not intend to re-enter the trap, the Don's mansion, and he'd made provision for that. He leafed through the papers—he read Spanish better than he spoke it—and waited for the phone to ring. The *policia,* or so he hoped, were not interested in or even aware of a Mr. Peabody and Eagle wanted to keep it that way.

He could find no mention of the kidnapping in any of the papers. There was a paragraph or two, buried in the want ads, to the effect that the police were still searching for the killer, or killers, of the girl and the two men. There was not even a mention of Carlos de Ojeda's car. Eagle smiled at that. The Don had a bit more pull than he pretended. Censorship, pressure, whatever, had all but killed the story. That could change in a hurry, of course, if they ever tied young Carlos in with the guerrillas. Or if they sent his head by registered mail. The cops were keeping a low profile, bowing to pressure and avoiding stepping on toes. Important toes. So far. But those cops were there. Waiting. Venezuela was not exactly a police state, but neither was it the USA.

The phone did not ring. Eagle finished the papers,

90

saving the comics in *La Verdad* for the last. He smiled at Blondie and laughed outright at Beetle. No phone.

He stretched on the bed and ran it all through his head, over and over again. Merlin had filled him in and now it pretty much made sense.

Merlin was probably right. Sir Rodney Hamilton, the man with a hole in his head, was probably behind the thing.

Eagle could almost summon a twinge of pity for the knight. Chances were that Sir Rodney did not dream of Merlin's existence, was unaware of Nemesis dogging him. Eagle shook his head. Here the old scoundrel was getting ready to rip off the world, with no idea that someone was walking behind him. Sir Rodney was in for a nasty surprise.

Eagle glared at the phone. Don Simon was to go about business as usual today, and call Eagle from a safe phone. There were public booths in the Senate Building.

Eagle went to the bathroom and had hardly begun shaving when the phone rang. He cursed. Every time. He sprinted for the instrument.

"Peabody here."

Don Simon's voice was conspiratorial. "I am calling from a kiosk near the Pantheon. Is it wise to speak freely?"

Eagle could see little reason why not. The Don had picked a booth at random and the police were unaware that Peabody was Eagle. Even if the cops were tagging the old gentleman, which was unlikely, all the tail could do was report a phone call. Eagle took a chance and ruled out any ultra-sophisticated listening devices.

"Okay. Anything new?"

"Yes. Another policeman came this morning. A Lieutenant Garcia. He is of what they call the Special Police."

"Secret and political?" Eagle had been afraid of this.

"Yes. He was, this Garcia, most courteous and considerate of my position. There has been no advancement in the case. Carlos has not been found nor have the killers been apprehended. He admitted, this Garcia, that they are watching my home and Carlos' apartment. I did not think it wise to inquire about phone taps."

Eagle nodded. "Just as well. Other than that there is nothing new?"

"Nothing. You are prepared to go through with our plan this night?"

"I am. And I must insist that you do your part. Exactly as we agreed."

A sigh came over the wire. "To remain in my lonely house and do nothing. I do not like it, *señor,* but I have given my word."

Eagle hoped he would keep it. Aloud he said, "You have plenty to do. You've got to build the smokescreen. Remember to act normally in every respect but one— you're to drop subtle hints, start rumors, that a big oil concession deal may be in the making. Nothing concrete, and nothing that definitely ties you in personally, but hints and whispers. Sir Rodney will pick them up soon enough."

"You have definite information, then? Sir Rodney Hamilton is behind this? He is working with the Wild Dog and the disloyal elements in the Army and Air Force?"

Eagle thought for a moment, wondering how exactly to phrase it, then said, "We're *pretty* sure of it. We're still collecting information. I'll know more after I see his people tonight, but I think we're on the right track."

The old man sighed over the wire. "Filthy. A powerful and gifted man, but filthy. To steal a man's son. I have done many things in my life, as a man must to survive, but never would I—"

Eagle cut him off rather abruptly. "I'll report as soon as I can. Remember to stick to the plan. Exactly."

The Don promised that he would. "Go with God," he said. "And be careful."

Eagle had every intention of being careful. He was unarmed and messing about with dangerous people. He was walking on eggs.

With the oncoming of darkness a light rain began to wash the streets. Eagle took a taxi to the suburb of Las Mercedes. He left it near the great supermarket, the Auto Mercado, and killed time by walking through the store. Prices, he noted, were higher than a giraffe's ear. He left the store by another entrance.

Juan Castenada, the Don's chauffeur, was waiting in

a nearby parking lot with the black limousine. He greeted Eagle with a questioning stare. Eagle said, "Did you bring the things?"

"In the back seat, *señor.*"

Eagle got into the limousine. On the seat were a black Homburg hat, which the old man wore, and a dark rain cloak with shawled shoulders. The Don was elegant but old-fashioned.

Eagle put the Homburg squarely on his head, tugging it down as far as he could, and tossed the cloak over his big shoulders. "Walk around the car," he told Castenada. "At ten feet or so and tell me what you think."

The man complied and said, "At just the first glimpse, *señor,* and in profile, perhaps. For a few seconds. No longer. You are too big, *señor.*"

Eagle smiled. "Maybe. But I'll have to do. And it should only take a few seconds. Okay, Juan, let's get going."

He gave the chauffeur the instructions as he and the Don had interpreted them from the Wild Dog's last letter. The letter had been explicit, had contained a list of do's and don'ts and Eagle was at the moment contravening some of the instructions. He figured his chances at about fifty-fifty and was counting on the enemy being somewhat rational. Flexible. Willing to compromise to a degree to attain a much desired objective.

They skirted the university and worked their way to the west into the Las Flores district. Eagle slouched in the seat, making himself as small as possible. To his right the Railroad Station and the Capitolio were bathed in white floodlights. They were headed for the Pan-American Highway.

Eagle said, "Are you nervous about this, Juan?"

The man nodded. "*Sí.* I have never dealt with gangsters before."

Eagle smiled to himself. Gangsters was as good a name as any, he supposed. Juan must have seen a lot of Yankee movies.

"You know what to do?"

Again a nod "I have my instructions from Don Simon. I will obey."

"Good. See that you do nothing else. You are a driver of this limousine and nothing else. You will see nothing and you will hear even less. In other words, Juan, you are a man who is not here. *Sí?*"

"*Sí.*"

Juan Castenada had been born and raised in Caracas and knew the city better than he knew his own backside. He skirted La Vega, hit the Pan-American and stayed on it for five miles. After passing a line of neongarish motels he slowed and began to watch for a side road. They were now running parallel with double railroad tracks. The tracks hooked suddenly to the left and over the highway. After the level crossing Castenada slowed even more, braking nearly to a stop, and found a narrow graveled lane diving to the right. The declivity was steep and there was barely room for the limousine. In a moment they had left the highway behind and were crawling through rainy desolation. The headlights tunneled ahead through the soft rain.

Eagle rolled a window down and caught the smell. Gypsum. Right so far.

"An old cement plant, Juan?"

"*Sí, señor.* I remember it. They have not worked here for many years now, but the smell never leaves."

The lane widened into a large open area. There was a bend and, as the lights scythed around, Eagle caught a glimpse of ruined silos like upended monster cannons alongside rusty trackage. A gantry frame, with no crane or car, straddled the tracks like a wicket.

The limousine approached a siding with a rotting loading platform. "Stop here, Juan."

The car halted. Castenada turned off the lights on Eagle's order. They sat in silence, the rain ticking on the roof, virtually each discrete drop audible. Eagle listened and his Apache ears picked up a sound near the silos. He could see nothing and all he could smell was the gypsum. They had chosen well. The deserted cement plant sat alone in its campo, the approaches easily guarded. There would have been watchers back at the turn-off, probably with walkie-talkies, who had called ahead. Eagle slouched a bit more in the seat. Cautious bastards. What in hell were they—

The limousine was bathed in a sudden explosion of

94

light. Three or four powerful flashlights probed them from near the silos. Eagle sat stiffly, in profile, the shawl collar of the cloak pulled up around his neck and cheeks. He couldn't fool them for more than a few seconds. He *was* too big.

Someone called from the dark behind the blaze of lights. "Don't move. Both of you keep your hands in plain sight."

Eagle raised his hands. Juan Castenada did the same. "Don't get nervous," Eagle told the chauffeur. "Just keep cool and steady. Nothing is going to happen to you."

Castenada muttered something about the Virgin.

A light bobbed toward them, an enormous bright eye peering in the window of the limousine. A voice behind the light said, "You're not Simon de Ojeda! What the hell goes on? What are you trying to pull?"

Here was the crux of this assignment. Eagle could see the reflected sheen of blued metal in the speaker's hand. A lot of hand gun. Probably a .45 Colt, U.S. Army gun.

Eagle spoke with aplomb. He had been rehearsing all day and now he achieved just the right tone—a mix of seriousness and flippancy.

"Take it easy," he said. "This is no double-cross. Everything is going to be okay. I think we can do a deal. My name is Peabody and I'm working for the old man. He was afraid to come himself. You've already grabbed Carlos. He thought you might grab him as well. That should make sense to you."

"I'll decide what makes sense," the man said. He was wearing a ski mask and his voice was a roughened baritone, as though from an old throat injury.

Eagle waited. The window was down six inches. The man put the light squarely on Eagle, blinding him, and studied him for fifteen seconds. His chuckle was not one of amusement. "Why the getup? The old man's hat and cloak?"

"I figured you would have watchers all the way. I wanted you to keep the appointment. I told you. The Don wants to talk business. If the deal is right he's willing to go along."

"Hold it," said the masked man. He waved the light

at the chauffeur. "You. Get out. Walk over there and stand by that silo. Keep your mouth shut and watch yourself."

"He's all right," Eagle said. "Just a driver. He takes orders from the Don."

For the first time the man brought the .45 into full view. He waved it at Castenada. "Get going."

Juan Castenada walked to the indicated spot. Two beams of light criss-crossed on him. The chauffeur fumbled for a smoke. Eagle laughed. "He's scared shitless."

"You're not scared?"

"Come on," said Eagle. "Let's not over-do the melodrama. I've been trying to tell you—I'm not here as an adversary. The old man wants to be friends. He *wants* to be agreeable and work things out so everybody makes a nice fat profit. But his name has to be kept out of it—he won't become involved in anything public —and a lot of details have to be worked out between him and your principal. That's why I'm here. To set it up. So, any time you're ready we can get down to business."

"Get out of the car," said the man. "Keep your hands in sight. Lean against the car."

The frisk was fast and professional. Eagle leaned against the car, legs wide spread, as the man went through his wallet. So far it was going pretty much as he'd expected it would.

"You expect me to believe you're a Pink?"

"That's what the ID card says," Eagle said mildly. The card was not in fact a forgery. Merlin was a major stockholder in the giant detective agency, though he did not often abuse the privilege. Only the name was a phony. Jerome Peabody.

The wallet was thrust back into his pocket. "Turn around," said the masked man. "Take off that stupid hat and coat."

Eagle cast them away. The light played up and down his rangy frame. "For two cents," the man said, "I'd give you a lead belly button. You're fucking things up and I don't like that. Why didn't you dumb bastards just do as you were told!"

Eagle read the tone as genuine anger and weary

resignation. He knew then that he had a chance to bring it off. Barring slips. He made his own tone more harsh. "You ready to listen now?"

The masked man nodded. "Get back in the car. Keep your hands where I can see them at all times."

Eagle did so, wondering how far to push it. This was Joe Garm, he was sure of it, and he weighed the advantages of secret knowledge against those of shock value. For the moment he was indecisive. He'd wait and see.

"So talk."

"It all makes sense," Eagle explained, "if you understand the Don's attitude and his problems. He's an old man and he's scared. He was afraid to come tonight because he thought you might torture him."

The masked man laughed. "Who's being melodramatic now?"

Eagle shrugged and waved a hand. "You've got to admit—all this cloak and dagger business . . . . Anyway —the Don is a very rich old guy, as you know, and he's got a lot of powerful friends and connections. None of which he could use in *this* connection because he doesn't want the cops in any more than you do. Let me tell you again—he wants to do business if he can without getting his own ass in a sling. Keep that in mind and you'll understand this.

"He came to us because he didn't have anywhere else to go. We've got an office in Caracas, you can check it in the yellow pages, and we do a lot of highly confidential work. We come high, but we know how to keep our mouths shut."

"A fucking private eye," the man said. "I still don't believe it."

"Believe it," said Eagle. "We don't work against the law, but we don't always sleep with it, either. We can be pretty neutral—for money. And some of us have been known to moonlight."

Hard eyes watched him through the eyeholes of the mask. "So that's it? You're working for yourself? The agency isn't involved?"

Eagle's big shoulders moved. "Could be. What does it matter? What matters is that we set up a deal. I've got a message for your boss from mine. The message is that there is no problem if the details can be worked out."

"What details?"

Eagle decided to fire another barrel. "Listen. So you can take all this back and your boss will know we're leveling. Your man is Sir Rodney Hamilton, the one they call Silverskull, and he's after oil concessions in the new fields along the Orinoco. He tried to make a deal before, but the Don couldn't play because there were too many people watching. Too much pressure. A man in his position has to be very careful."

"And now things are different?"

Eagle nodded. "Yeah. Different. Political situations change all the time. Right now, if everything dovetails just right, it might be possible to pull off a deal. If the price is right and if the old man can be protected. A big if. The thing has got to be absolutely foolproof. The Don is too old to be a fugitive and nobody likes a firing squad. Which brings up a point—the old man must in no way, in absolutely no way, be tied in with that tinpot guerrilla and his people. This Wild Dog. The Don is willing to deal, if he does deal at all, only with Sir Rodney."

The masked man chuckled. Eagle decided he would reveal his knowledge of Joe Garm's identity. A hard case, even from the little that Merlin's people had come up with so far, and probably responsible for the kidnapping of Carlos de Ojeda—and the killing of the woman and two men in the overlook where Carlos' car had been found. An old man, or nearly so, and a killer. A dying breed. An anachronism. Such a man, Eagle reasoned, would be vunerable personally, have his own peculiar code of honor. The problem was in finding a litmus that would bring it out.

The masked man chuckled and waved the Colt in the direction of the silos. Juan Castenada, still transfixed by the lights, was lighting another cigarette. He was visibly shaking and sweating.

"Keep your voice down," the man said. "I've got some of Ortega's punks with me. They're a pretty wild-assed bunch and they're trigger happy. Sometimes they scare me."

Eagle would play his hunch and go with his knowledge, such as it was, of men of Joe Garm's type. To make the whole business work, to gain time, he needed to establish a rapport with this man.

"I imagine," he said quietly, "that it takes quite a lot to scare you, Mr. Garm."

It could have gone either way. Eagle was naked before the gun. The next three seconds were the longest of his life.

Garm did not move the Colt. He said, "You've been doing some pretty good homework. So you know who I am. Big deal."

"All right," said Eagle. "We'll do this thing, go our own ways and never see each other again. I've got a lousy memory and I hope you have."

Garm nodded. "Bad enough."

Eagle had been listening for something in the man's tone and he thought he heard it. A hint of tolerance and acceptance. For the time being Garm was accepting Eagle as one of his own kind—a scuffler out for the fast buck and not caring much how he made it. It was the illusion Eagle sought to establish, the roles he wanted played—he and Garm were paid hands, mercenaries, hired intermediaries dealing in other people's troubles and money. If they both walked a chalk line there was no reason for a falling out. Do the deal, take the money and run.

Garm did seem friendlier. The iceberg melted a drop or two. "For a laugh," he said, "I'll let you in on something. The snatch was young Carlos' idea at first. He wanted us to pretend to grab him and put the arm on the old man for a few million. Sort of chills your shit, don't it? No good little prick."

Eagle shook his head. "Why didn't it happen that way?"

"Sir Rod wasn't ready for that yet." Garm laughed. "Tell you the truth I think it sort of fazed him. He's like me, kind of old-fashioned, and in our time you don't do things like that to your old man. I shit you not, Peabody, I just don't get these kids today."

Sir Rod. They were getting it more and more out into the open. Eagle felt pleased with himself.

"Speaking of Carlos," he said, "and before we get into the details of the next meeting, I think we had better settle about the kid."

"Settle what? What's to settle? We keep him until Sir Rod and the Don get together and come to an understanding. If that doesn't happen we kill him. Case closed."

"Not quite closed," Eagle said. "The Don doesn't want him back."

Garm still wore the ski mask. The eyes that studied Eagle were hard and bright and not particularly surprised.

"Like that, eh?"

"Like that. As I get it, Carlos is a no goodnik from way back. Been a thorn in the old boy's ass for many years. This is the chance of a lifetime."

"I'll be a sonofabitch."

Eagle kept silent. Garm said, "The Don actually told you that?"

"Scout's honor. But it has to be done right. By that he means quietly. Don't let the Wild Dog have him and no public demand for ransom. We don't want to make a martyr out of the kid. That's a big jungle out there, with a lot of rivers. Nothing to it."

Garm laughed harshly. "The poorass little punk sure don't have many friends, does he?"

"Do it right, don't fuck it up, and the Don will be grateful. It could help grease things between him and Sir Rod."

Garm laughed again. "Not much surprises Sir Rod, but I think this will. He'll get a kick out of it, too. Christ, what a switcheroo. If the old man is on the level, of course. But if this is a gimmick, if you guys are farting around, playing cute—"

"The Don means it. He wants Carlos out of his hair. Of course he'll have to play the grieving father bit."

Eagle thought that Garm was going to buy it. Not swallowing yet, perhaps, but certainly nibbling. So far the ploy was serving its purpose—getting them off balance and stalling for time. Eagle needed at least a couple of days.

"Do it any way you want," he told Garm, "but do it right. In the meantime the Don needs two or three days to make some arrangements. There's an oil bill coming up for a vote next week. He's chairing the committee that decides who gets what and he needs time to buy some people, or put the squeeze on, whatever. I don't know a goddamned thing about Venezuelan politics. But the word is, like I told you, that the Don can do it, if there's no static and no fuckup. That means quiet and deep, way down under the surface."

Garm shook his head. "Sir Rod wants an eyeball to eyeball with the old man. How do we work that?"

"We don't; not for the time being. Maybe never. Why take the chance when it isn't necessary? I can deal for the old man. I am dealing for him. That's why I'm here."

Garm still shook his head. "I don't know. I don't think Sir Rod will go for it. He's flying out from London for a head to head talk with the Don."

Eagle pushed it a little. "He can't force it now. You don't have a lever any more."

"The hell we don't. I can give the kid to the Dog. Ortega is slobbering to get his hands on him anyway. He wants to execute him publicly, then chop him up and send the pieces all over the country. With notices in all the papers. You're not gaining a damned thing, Peabody, by having us kill the kid unless we do it quietly. He's just as much a hostage as before."

"Shit!" Eagle had expected this but he threw in the reaction as part of the mutual con game.

"We'll work it out," said Garm generously.

"It will be dangerous. The cops are all over the place. They haven't put any real pressure on the Don yet, but they will. They won't just let it drop."

"That's the old man's worry. And yours. You should be able to handle a few cops."

"There are all these rumors about a revolution brewing," said Eagle. "Disaffection in the armed forces and all that shit. This would be a piss poor time for anything to break about an oil ripoff. The whole sky could fall on us."

"I don't know anything about that," Garm said, and Eagle knew he lied. And knew that Garm knew he knew, and did not care.

They talked for another few minutes and Garm said, "I'll pass all this along to Sir Rod. He won't like it, but he's a pretty patient type. You'll come probably to the island in two, three days at the latest, and we'll tell you how it's going to be."

Eagle did not pretend ignorance. He was supposed to have done his homework. "La Blanca?"

"Yeah. Sir Rod owns it. There's a phone. All you have to do is call and we'll send a boat in for you. No big deal. People come and go all the time. Just be sure you don't have any cops on your ass."

"The cops don't know about me." Eagle hoped.

"Keep it that way. Well, I'll see you then. You and your driver can leave now."

As they drove back into Caracas Eagle said to Juan Castenada, "That wasn't so bad, was it?"

"I am still praying, *Señor*. I heard them talking about me. I could not see them, but I could hear. They were admiring my throat—to cut."

Eagle knew it was unnecessary but he said it anyway. "You will forget all this, Juan. This night did not happen."

"*Sí, Señor*. I told you. I have my orders from the Don."

Eagle supposed that there was such a thing as old-fashioned servant loyalty. He seemed to be seeing an example.

He relaxed and began to consider his schedule. Tight. He glanced at his watch. A little over an hour to get to the airport and catch a plane to London.

An eye for an eye, Merlin had said, and a tooth for a tooth.

Eagle hoped—faintly—that it wouldn't come to that.

CHAPTER 14

When Eagle deplaned in London he made a phone call from the airport. He talked, but mostly he listened, for half an hour. Then he rented a car and drove down to Salisbury. He was still Jerome Peabody, still traveling in textiles. As far as he knew the Peabody persona was not blown, not wanted and was as good as any. Joe Garm, and Sir Rod, would undoubtedly be checking it out in Caracas. A discreet inquiry would reveal no Peabody attached to the Caracas Pinkerton office. Not even a moonlighter indulging in skullduggery on his own time. Eagle had not expected the Pink impersonation to hold up for long; they were a legitimate and reputable company and Garm should have been suspicious from the first. But he had played along, apparently accepted the lie and that was all that mattered. Eagle figured that he had two days.

During the drive to Salisbury he replayed the thing in his mind, back and forth, inside and out, searching for weak spots. There were plenty of them.

One thing he had was information. Ian Thomas, whoever the hell he was, had been talking steadily. Singing loud and clear. A lush, Merlin's man had said on the phone, and all they'd had to do was ration the booze. Discount half the man had blabbed, Eagle thought, and they still knew a hell of a lot more than they had before. Some of it was pretty sick.

He came into Salisbury from the west, skirting the water meadows of the Avon. The Cathedral spire—he remembered reading somewhere that it was four inches out of plumb—poked a gothic finger at the leaden, late October sky. It was a dank day, with a fine mist smoking up the windshield, and he'd encountered some light snow on the way down.

When he spotted the cheerful lights of a pub he pulled into the parking lot. After ordering a sandwich and a pint of bitter he called the Nine Yews Nursing Home. A woman answered. Eagle asked about the visiting hours

"Three to five, sir. Every day."

He glanced at a clock over the bar. A quarter after five. He put regret into his voice.

"Too bad. I've probably just missed her, then. Miss Hamilton? Miss Jennifer Hamilton?"

"You have that, sir. I'm sorry. She's just left. I saw her leave myself. Not five minutes ago."

Eagle sighed audibly. "Well, thank you. I can probably catch her at home. How is her mother, by the way?"

"Who is it that's calling, sir?" A faint note of caution now.

"A friend of the family," Eagle said. "Known them for years. I grew up with Jennifer."

It didn't come off. The voice said, "I am not permitted to give that information over the phone, sir."

Eagle said thanks and hung up. He went back to his sandwich and beer, thinking that the lady's prognosis was probably not good. Berenice Boggs. Probably terminal cancer. Merlin's London people had been working like fiends. Eagle munched his sandwich.

It was a minor moral dilemma. The cancer would rivet the daughter to the spot. She would not likely go gadding while her mother was dying. It made her easy to get at, but taking her away from her mother at this time was a nasty trick. After a moment he shrugged his big shoulders. It had to be done.

He drove into the center of Salisbury and found a parking lot near the Poultry Cross. On Bridge Street he found the map he wanted at a stationer's shop. He had a backup man in Salisbury, and a phone number, but he did not want to use them unless absolutely necessary. He was accustomed to working in wilderness, in desolate places, and working alone, and he did not like to change his habits.

Berenice Boggs, Jennifer Hamilton's mother, had a house in a village called Old Sarum. The map showed it to be about ten miles to the northeast, between Salisbury and Amesbury. Eagle walked back to the High Street and over to the Close, pondering whether or not to go in and have a look at the Cathedral. It was one of the great ones and he had plenty of time. He decided against it; after a second of internal debate he went back to the parking lot for his rented car. Dusk was thickening now; it would soon be dark.

Nor did he linger in the village of Old Sarum. He drove through it once, found Cottontree Lane on the far side and marked the small detached villa sitting in a well-wooded plot. At least there was some cover. He drove past until the lane dead-ended, then he turned and drove back. As he approached the house again a car was coming toward him. Eagle slowed and allowed the car to make a left turn ahead of him. It was a sporty little MG with the top up and a girl was driving it. Jennifer Hamilton. Must be. The target for tonight, Eagle thought and found himself approving of the target.

For a millisecond she was caught in the flash of his lights. A pile of hair—it could have been any color in that illumination—on a proudly tilted head. The profile was sharp, clean cut and gone in a moment. Leaving an impression of beauty and youth. A fur jacket precluded any glimpse of her figure.

Eagle drove on. The London man had said that Jennifer Hamilton was a dish. Eagle had the feeling that he should have seen her picture somewhere or other but he couldn't quite place it.

Eagle drove out A36 until he found a motel. He set his mind for midnight. And he woke up at ten of the hour. The motel was quiet, with only four cars in the parking spaces and a night light burning in the office. Eagle left as surreptitiously as possible. An hour later he parked a quarter of a mile from Berenice Boggs' villa —a plebian name to be associated with so much money —and began hiking.

The weather had worsened into a cold fine rain. Before he left the car, in a turnout he had noted earlier, Eagle gathered his kidnapping equipment from the glove compartment. Two pairs of handcuffs. A roll of wide adhesive tape. A dozen clean men's handkerchiefs. He stuffed them into the pockets of his light topcoat and set off again.

He met no one on the road; only a few lights were visible. A village like Old Sarum went to bed early. About Jennifer Hamilton he was doubtful—she was a sophisticate and a swinger—and the thought had been plaguing Eagle that she would be throwing a party tonight. Or perhaps having a man in to sleep with. Either would fuck up his plans but good, and he would have to try again. He still had thirty-six hours, and in dire necessity he could probably stall Joe Garm for another twelve, but the sooner the better.

He went over a stone wall and approached the house from an oblique angle. The going was easy and he used his flashlight only occasionally when he got into trees, then shielding it with his hand. He did not really expect trouble, this being England. In the States there would have been fences and dogs and maybe even security guards. Or perhaps not. This was the mother's home, not the daughter's; the poop was that Sir Rod had not seen the woman in over twenty years and certainly did not lavish money on her. Not prime kidnapping bait.

Nonetheless Eagle was counting heavily on shock and surprise. Things like this just did not happen in quiet rural England. Tonight they would.

A light burned in an upstairs bedroom. The villa, though substantial, was of modest size. A light burned downstairs, in what had to be the living room, and another in the kitchen. Night lights. Eagle stood in a copse and watched for half an hour. Nothing moved downstairs. Once a silhouette, of a woman, flitted across the bedroom window. Eagle moved stealthily to the driveway, making no sound on the blacktop. The MG was parked at a side door. He felt the radiator. Cold. She hadn't been out recently. Probably reading in bed. Reading and thinking about her mother dying in a nursing home.

Eagle had an unfamiliar twinge of conscience. As a rule such things did not bother him. Usually he dealt with rough people and had no qualms. It was a job and he was well paid for it.

This was a little different. For the first time in a long while he found himself questioning Merlin's judgment, near to resenting the burden Merlin had put on him. Jennifer Hamilton was an innocent, caught up in a mess she doubtless could not understand and knew nothing about.

Eagle could always abort the mission. That was his privilege. And then provide Samson, and Merlin, with good and sufficient cause for so doing. But this case had worldwide ramifications. . . .

Eagle took a miniature burglar's kit from his pocket and went to work on the side door, thinking furiously how he'd handle it. How to take her without frightening her half to death? Charm, he supposed, might work if she gave him a chance. A suave burglar ploy. Explanations and reassurance. Reason.

The lock was pitiful, child's play, and opened to the

third probe he used. He lifted the door so the hinges would not squeak and stepped into a warm foyer. He closed the door noiselessly behind him, feeling the knob indentations through the very thin dark gloves he wore.

A drugget of yellow light fell into the foyer from the living room. The stairway lay straight ahead. That could be a problem, getting up stairs without creaking. You could stay to the inside, close to the wall where the risers were strongest, but that didn't always work.

Eagle moved to the foot of the stairs and stood listening. There was faint light in the upstairs hall. An open door. He heard the girl sigh and there was a flutter of magazine pages. He put a tentative foot on the first step. The bed creaked as she got out of it and padded barefooted into the hall. Eagle flattened himself into shadows along the wall.

Jennifer Hamilton went to the bathroom and, probably out of long habit, closed the door. The moment Eagle heard the click of the latch he was up the stairs, loping silently on the thick carpeting.

The closed bathroom door was to his right, the open bedroom door to his left. He ran on tip toe to the bedroom and stepped behind the half open door. It was a large comfortable-looking room with a messy, lived-in look. He guessed it was the mother's room. The bed was big and rumpled, with a brass headboard. A reading light was clipped to the rail and books and magazines were scattered on the bed. On the night stand stood a bottle of whiskey and two glasses, one containing water and the other half an inch of whiskey.

The toilet flushed. Eagle stepped away from the crack in the door. So far it had been almost too easy; the girl suspected nothing, but he didn't want to louse it up by carelessness. The nearest neighbor lived a hundred yards down the road and he doubted that her scream would carry that far, but he had no desire to find out.

She came into the room, past him, and he took her from behind. At first caught in shock and surprise, she did not struggle. He got his hand over her mouth and his arm about her waist, lifted her and carried her to the bed. She was naked, her bare belly firm yet soft under his touch.

Eagle held her off her feet, dangling, and spoke softly into her right ear.

"I'm not going to hurt you. Don't scream and don't fight and everything will be all right. Understand me?"

She writhed and kicked back at him. He tightened his grasp on her waist and she gasped into his smothering hand. Eagle wasted no more words. He cut off her air with his forearm and pushed one of the handkerchiefs into her gaping mouth, thrusting the cloth well back with his fingers. He twisted her arms behind her and handcuffed her in a swift one-two-three motion. He tossed her on the bed, wrong side around, snapped a cuff on her ankle and one around the brass rail of the headboard. She lay gasping up at him. Her eyes were wide and fearful and at the same time furious. She had dark brown eyes with silver flecks; over and above the shock he could see outrage in them. No one had ever dared, in all her pampered life, to treat Jennifer Hamilton like this.

For a moment Eagle stood looking down at her. He smiled and hoped it was reassuring. "I tried to tell you," he said. "Now I'm afraid we'll have to do it the hard way."

She chewed furiously on the handkerchief, trying to push it out with her tongue. She made baby sounds like naaaaa and gaaaaa. Eagle smiled and patted her head. She jerked away as though he were an adder.

For a few seconds he studied her nakedness. Her eyes blazed but he would take his time. It was not simple voyeurism; he had motive and method in mind. If he could tame her it would make matters easier all around, and she must understand that he was not a rapist.

He was, he acknowledged, looking at one of the most attractive females in the world. Jennifer was a fairly tall girl, slim and supple, with long tapering legs and, insofar as he could see, not a blemish on her flawless close-textured skin. She had been tanned, not too recently; the bikini marks were fading. Her breasts were of medium size, pink buttoned, firm and well separated without any flow of fatty tissue. Her navel seemed larger than that of most young girls. She had an abundant brush of luxuriant red-gold pubic hair

Eagle pulled a sheet over her. "You can see that I'm not a rapist," he told her. "I would have acted by now."

She continued to glare at him. Eagle put a big hand on the back of her neck and exerted a light pressure. "I'll take the gag out in a minute. If you try to scream I'll just squeeze a little, like so, and you'll black out. I know exactly where the nerve is.

"I have to talk to you," he went on. "About your father. It is very urgent and important, to a lot of people, and I want you to listen."

Her eyes widened and she pushed with her tongue at the handkerchief. Eagle reached for her mouth but did not yet pull out the gag. He gave her a genuinely regretful smile.

"You want to promise me not to scream or kick up a fuss? It won't gain you anything and if other people become involved they might get hurt. You want to be sensible?"

She nodded.

"You mean it?"

Another nod.

Eagle pulled out the handkerchief. He kept his fingers on the back of her neck.

Jennifer gasped and took a deep breath. "What about my father? Who are you? Why are you doing this to me? If you mean to rape me, it's all right. I mean I won't fight you. Just don't kill me." She had, he thought, a lot of guts. Took after her father, no doubt.

He sat on the bed beside her, still keeping his hand on her neck. "I said no rape. No harm at all. I want you to listen and cooperate with me. It will make it easier on both of us."

She was breathing easier. "Cooperate? Cooperate in what? What are you talking about?"

His smile was benign. "In your own kidnapping. Only for a little while."

"My own kidnapping? You're insane!"

"No ransom. Nothing like that. You won't be harmed and it won't cost you anything. You want to listen now?"

"No! I want you to go away and leave me alone. I—"

He squeezed her neck ever so slightly. She jerked away. "Don't. You said you wouldn't hurt me."

"It doesn't hurt," Eagle said gently. "You just go to sleep. Come on, Jennifer. Do listen. You might be able to help your father, save him a lot of grief."

"I don't give a damn about my father. I hope he rots in hell."

Having been filled in by the London people, given a near verbatim report of Ian Thomas' babbling, Eagle was not too surprised. Nor too believing. Ian Thomas was a drunk who thought his life was in danger. Any gossip he repeated must be taken with a large grain of salt.

He thought it best to feign surprise. "You don't want to help your own father out of a mess?"

She tossed her head, the mass of her red gold hair sparkling. Her eyes were narrow. She had a thin straight nose and a just slightly too large mouth which at the moment, without lipstick, looked dry and cracked. The lower lip was sensuous.

Suddenly her manner changed. She nodded. "I might help him. I don't love him, I hate him, but I might help him. What do I have to do? What kind of trouble is he in?"

Eagle had been wondering how much to tell her if she proved amenable. Not that it really mattered how much she knew, because she would be out of circulation for a time, but a contented associate was preferable. He decided to spill the whole thing.

He put it in synoptic form, cutting corners here and there and of course leaving out any mention of Merlin. Jennifer listened, nodding now and then, no longer fearful of him, and once she said, "That's my pop all right. That's the knight. When chivalry was in flower old Dad missed the boat. Anything for a dirty buck."

When he finished, she said, "So what do you want from me?"

"Just to stay kidnapped for a time. So that when he checks it out he'll be convinced. You have to disappear for a time without trace. Then he'll play ball with us. You may not love him, or even hate him, but our information is that he loves you. That's our lever."

Her mouth curled in contempt. "He loves me all

right. He loves me too much. Only not the way a father is supposed to love a daughter."

Eagle nodded. "We've heard rumors."

She stared at him. "My God! How could you possibly —I mean I never mentioned that to a soul before. I'm too ashamed. It's squalid and dirty. I get the creeps when I think about it. My own father and I'm afraid to be alone in a room with him. But how could you know anything about it? I mean—this is disgusting. I don't want to talk about it."

"Then we won't. How about it, Jennifer? Will you help us out? If you hate him all that much it should be a pleasure to do him a bit. Or if you have any love for him at all you can help him, keep him out of deeper trouble. If we can stop him now, and get the de Ojeda boy back alive, we just might be able to square things around."

Jennifer Hamilton began to cry. Quietly, her lovely face contorted in a grimace of inner pain, the tears sliding down her cheeks. Eagle, who had an empathy strange in a man of his rough profession, felt her torment. The hurt, the revulsion and the love—for part of her loved her father—that she had carried all these years. Sir Rodney Hamilton, KCBE, must be a sonofabitch to end all sonsofbitches.

It might have been mental telepathy. Jennifer looked at him and said, "Isn't it a bitch? In a lot of ways, you know, the old bastard is a lot of man. He was a hell of a race driver and he made his money, all that money, on his own. His own will and guts. And he won't even come to see my mother when she's dying." Fresh tears flowed.

Eagle glanced at his watch and remained silent. Plenty of time. And he had it nearly under control now. She would play along he was almost certain.

She was trying to smile and not doing too well. "He's a knight, you know. A sir. KCBE. Knight Commander of the British Empire."

"I know."

The smile disappeared in a vicious twist of the sensual mouth. "You know what I call him?"

"What?"

"KCBE—Knave, crud, bastard and asshole."

"Asshole? That doesn't——"

"I know that. I couldn't think of a nasty word starting with E."

Eagle cradled her tear-streaked face in his hand. She did not flinch from him. According to his briefing she was promiscuous and well known around the world, among the so-called beautiful people, as an easy lay. He wasn't going to push it, he told himself, but if offered he did not think he would turn it down.

"How about it, Jennifer?"

"All right. I'll do what you want. You can take these damned things off me now. I won't make you any trouble."

He removed the cuffs. She stretched and chafed her wrists and ankles for a moment, then pulled the sheet taut over her breasts, the nipples plainly visible through the cloth, and gave him a strange smile.

"On one condition."

Eagle scowled. "What condition?"

"That you take me along. To Venezuela. Let me talk to the old fool. I've always been able to wrap him around my little finger."

Eagle explained again and said that it was better to stick to the original plan.

She did not argue the point, but said, "All right, then. Just take me to Venezuela and I'll stay out of the way until it's all over. I promise I won't be any trouble. I don't want to be kidnapped; it's sure to be a bore and a lot of trouble, and anyway my way is better. He'll think I've been kidnapped and that's just as good."

Jennifer twisted a magnificent diamond off her left ring finger and handed it to Eagle. "There. He's sure to recognize it. He gave it to me for my birthday last year. Ninety thousand dollars."

Eagle slipped the ring into his pocket. "I'll see that you get it back when this is over."

She puffed her mouth at him and he sensed that she was viewing him in a new light. Her glance wandered up and down his body now and then. Maybe the reports were right.

"What about your mother? Isn't she in a pretty bad way?"

"She's dying. Cancer of the cervix. Oh, the doctors

give you a lot of shit, try to smarm you, but she's going to die."

"And you still want to fly off to Venezuela?"

She put a hand on his. Her nails were ragged, much chewed and unpolished. "Yes, damn it. For only a few days. There's nothing I can do here and I get so depressed I could kill myself. Mother might not die for weeks yet, or months, and anyway she's so heavily doped for pain that she hardly knows me. Please. I told you I won't be any trouble. I—"

She broke off with a nervous laugh. "I don't even know your name."

"John will do."

"All right, John. Take me with you. I can leave this minute. I have my passport with me and money and everything I need. I'll buy the tickets to Caracas. First class. Okay, John?"

Eagle considered. Her motives were ambivalent, he doubted she clearly understood them herself, and when he was in the field he had authority to change any plan. Originally they had planned to hold the girl in the same isolated cottage where Ian Thomas had been questioned. Thomas had been released now, with dire threats of what would happen if he talked and the cottage was as safe as any place in England.

England. That was the catch. The English police were as efficient as any in the world and if Ian Thomas did find the guts to talk—

Jennifer thought he was weakening. She put a hand on him, her eyes widening as she felt his erection. Eagle had not been fully aware of how much her nakedness had stimulated him.

"Well," she said. "Well!" She was no longer a frightened woman. Her mouth went a bit slack and she licked her lips.

"I think," she said, "that you had better take me with you. I think we can solve all our problems." She gave him a look. "You seem to think so in spite of yourself."

Why not? He could play along and have her picked up in Caracas. The backup team, what Merlin called the Double-Blue net, would be in operation by now and there would be a safe house, and communication with

Merlin. Too, the Venezuelan police were not as efficient as the English, not so alert and eager. She would be close at hand just in case the finger trick did not work.

She would have to be closely watched, but that was true in any case and it would be easier in Caracas. A bolivar bought more protection than a pound.

Jennifer leaned to kiss him. She kept her eyes tightly closed. Her breasts had hardened and the nipples were standing out. For the moment she had forgotten everything else, and Eagle supposed it was as good a surcease as any.

Jennifer flicked him once with her tongue and then lay back on the bed. She narrowed her eyes at him. "What are you waiting for? Get out of those clothes."

Her eyes admired his body as Eagle stripped. She kept licking her lips and her mouth was wet. "You're one hell of a magnificent brute," she told him. "But I suppose you know that."

Eagle kicked off his shorts. Back on the Apache reservation, growing up with his friends, and at an age when such things were compared, he had been known as *kaki somn gunt*—the well hung one. There had been the usual juvenile jackoff club with the chiefdom going to the one who could spurt farthest. Joe Thunder Horse had come in second there, too.

Jennifer raised her knees. Her face was slack, some of the prettiness gone, and for the moment she looked older than twenty-two.

"I'm sexual," she told him. "I'll wear you out. I can't get enough. There isn't enough in the world for me."

"Let's see about that."

Eagle kissed her, fondled her, then mounted and thrust deep. She was more than ready, her vagina wet but tight, her juices leaking down her inner thighs. She seized him about the neck and pulled him down on her as her buttocks went into a frenzied, circular, driving motion. She moaned loudly as she climaxed after a short time. Eagle drove steadily at his task.

She cradled his head to her breasts and whispered, "That was just the first. I'll have many more. Let's keep going forever."

Later, as she slept soundly, Eagle found the phone. The man who answered listened for a time and then said, "So I am to understand that it's all off here? You won't be needing us or the cottage?"

"That's it. We abort here. Call Caracas and alert them. Repeat exactly as I gave it to you. I don't know what flight we'll be on so they'll have to watch every incoming flight. Now, you got all that?"

"I've got it, sir. I'll pass it on to Caracas at once. Good luck."

"Thanks," said Eagle.

CHAPTER 15

Jennifer Hamilton's moods changed like the colors of a chameleon. During the first half of the flight she hardly spoke at all. Eagle let her be. He had planned to pump her a bit, to tidy up some odds and ends, but in her present sullen and uncommunicative mood, it was no go. Instead he sought to keep her amused, speaking lightly of his Apache upbringing. Later he would try to get a few drinks into her in the piano lounge. She was having twinges of conscience now, he thought and she had had time to think matters out and had discovered her self interest. Hate Sir Rod she might, or half love and half hate him, but he was the man with the money. Her lavish style of life depended on him. Thief and fraud he might be, buccaneer and financial pirate, would-be incestuous father, but he was also, as Don Simon had put it, the golden goose. From whom all blessings flowed. When Jennifer was finished considering the implications of that, what would her decision be?

Finally, after a couple of martinis in the lounge, he caught her interest. She was skeptical.

"You really were raised among the Apache? Red Indians? I don't believe it."

Eagle shrugged. She still knew him only as John. "It's true," he assured her. "I swear it on my tomahawk. I was born on the reservation. My father was a Scot and

115

my mother an Englishwoman. She died giving birth to me and my father drank himself to death."

That was not quite true. His foster mother, White Deer, had told him that his father had been killed by a bulldozer toppling on him. He *had* been drunk. At the time he'd been a civil engineer building roads near the Apache reservation.

Jennifer was still doubtful. She was on her third drink. "What's your Indian name, then?"

Eagle smiled. "Charley Two Bellies. John for short."

"Fool."

"All of that," acknowledged Eagle. "I just do the best I can."

With the fourth drink she began to talk about herself. By this time she was babbling a bit and her tone became a little shrill, but she was not really drunk. Eagle listened attentively, culling for bits that might prove useful. Strangely enough she did not once mention her father.

She was, he discovered, more athletic than he would have supposed. She belonged to country and athletic clubs all over the world and had won trophies in tennis and swimming and golf. She belonged to a parachute club.

"You could have fooled me," he said. "You don't strike me as the athletic type. Where are your muscles?"

She smirked. "They're there. You just can't see them. I don't get all my exercise in bed. And a girl has to stay in shape even for that."

When they went back to their seats she arranged a magazine so that she could use her hand beneath it. She whispered, "I've never done it on a plane. I've read about it and heard about it, but I've never done it. Could we try, do you think?"

Eagle glanced around. The aisle was busy with stewardesses and passengers coming and going. He shook his head. "No way. You'll just have to be content with fantasy."

Jennifer smiled and kissed his cheek. She unzipped him and slid her hand into his shorts. "I'd like to kiss it," she said, "but I suppose I daren't?"

"Better not. The vice squad might be aboard."

"Fuck the vice squad."

Eagle remained limp. After a time she fell asleep; he

removed her hand and zipped up. Jennifer began to snore lightly. He arranged her pillow and his own and dozed lightly, still thinking, until they arrived in Caracas. It was raining as they left the plane and went through Customs. Jennifer was groggy from sleep and gin and he took her arm. They were both traveling light, with nothing to declare, and they were through customs in less than half an hour. No official blinked an eye at the Jerome Peabody ID or at Jennifer's well stamped passport.

All quiet on the Caracas front.

She took his hand as they walked to a taxi stand. "What do we do now? Can I call my father on the island? I might be able to talk some sense into him."

"No. I've got people meeting us."

They stood under an awning out of the soft rain. A thermometer in a *farmacía* window said 83. Eagle opened his collar and mopped his face. He took her wrist, just in case she had some nutty idea of making a break, and looked around for his people. They were supposed to meet every flight. Where in hell—

A blue Ford, a battered Falcon, pulled in to the curb. There were two men in the front seat. The man beside the driver leaned out. "Mr. Peabody?"

"Yes." Eagle pressured the girl toward the car. For a moment she resisted. "Who are those men? Where are we going?"

"Eventually to see your father. Come on now. You made a bargain."

Jennifer had become tense. She sat straight-backed in the seat as they drove away from the airport. Eagle patted her hand. "Relax."

To the men in front he said, "Where's the house?"

The driver answered. "Miranda. Casa Villadiego."

"Communications in?"

"Yes, sir."

They were on a thruway and driving fast. It was beginning to get dark. Eagle said, "Have you got the object?"

The man handed back a small jeweler's box. "Yes, sir."

Eagle settled back. Jennifer stared at the box. "Is that it? The—what you told me about?"

117

He handed her the box. "Yes. Take a peek."

She made a face. "I don't know if I want to. I—I might throw up."

"Do it out the window, then." He reached to take back the box.

"No. I'll look."

He watched her face. She removed the lid and looked into the box as though peering into the coffin of a dear friend. Curiosity and revulsion played on her face.

"It won't hurt you," Eagle said.

The dead finger was a match for her living one, her left ring finger. It was clean and the nail was polished. Eagle wondered only briefly where they had gotten it. Probably they paid off a morgue attendant or a funeral home employee.

Jennifer wrinkled her nose and said, "Ugh. It smells funny."

"Formaldehyde."

He took the ring she had given him from his pocket and slipped it on the finger, held it up for her to see. "A perfect fit. An eye for an eye, a tooth for a tooth and a finger for a finger."

"Put it away. I feel a little sick."

He tucked the finger, with the ring on it, back into its box and put it in his pocket. They were getting close now, driving rapidly along dark roads, and he tried to lighten the moment by grinning and saying, "You're chicken. I'm surprised. A girl who makes parachute jumps. Free fall, at that."

She ignored him and peered out a window. "This isn't the city. Where are we? Where are you taking me?"

Eagle gestured toward dim lights glowing over a tall, wide iron gate. It stood open.

"Betancourt Park. This is where we part company for a time. Not for long and I'll be in touch. Don't be afraid."

She looked at the two men in the front seat. "You're going to leave me alone with them?"

"For a little while. They won't hurt you. They work for me and they're responsible to me." He spoke loudly enough for the men to hear.

Jennifer's chin firmed and she narrowed her eyes.

118

"No! I won't go with them. I came with you and I'm going to stay with you. You promised to take me to my father."

Eagle had not promised this and he said so.

She tossed her head in aggravation. "Well, I assumed you really would. It makes sense: I'm the only one he'll listen to, and then only sometimes. But I could try. Maybe—"

She was working herself into a lather. Eagle said, "I thought you hated your old man. What do you care what happens to him?"

Jennifer screwed up her face and spat words at him. "I know what I *said*. And it's true, sometimes. I do hate him. Everything I said about him is true. But I love him, too. He *is* my father. I don't want to see him hurt, or maybe killed, or get into terrible trouble. I do owe him something."

"He's already in terrible trouble."

"I know. Maybe I can get him out of it. I know a lot of influential people."

"And there's the money," Eagle said softly.

She glared at him and did not answer.

"You wouldn't want that to stop," he went on, "and you wouldn't want him to go broke. Or what you would consider broke."

Headlights blinked ahead of them. Three times. They had been following a blacktopped lane through heavily wooded terrain.

The driver blinked the Ford's lights in answer. The other car turned on its lights.

They stopped opposite the waiting car, a nondescript Chevy with one man behind the wheel. Eagle opened the door. "All out. Transfer point."

Jennifer hung back. "I told you I don't want to go with them. I won't."

"The hell you won't." Eagle yanked her out of the car. She fought and swung at him with her fist. "You bastard! You crummy sonofabitch! You lied to me."

She was amazingly strong and agile and she nearly writhed away from him. As he caught her, her dress ripped and one breast fell out. She kicked at him, trying for his balls. Eagle ran out of patience. He snapped commands and in a minute they had her gagged and

119

cuffed, in the rear seat of the Chevy. The two men who had picked Eagle up at the airport got into the car with her.

"Easy does it," he told them. "I don't want her bruised any more than she is now. VIP treatment, but keep her secure."

He took the driver of the Chevy aside and they talked for a quarter of an hour. The man, a fairly young man with a badly broken nose, was in command of the Double-Blue net in Caracas. He listened, nodded and made a few notes. When Eagle was satisfied, he got into the Ford and drove away.

CHAPTER 16

The night was humid, drizzling and moonless, and Eagle sweated heavily. After leaving the park he consulted an ordinance map, memorized the bearings and drove out of the city to the northwest, staying in the Federal District and beyond La Guaira. He passed the overlook where the two men and the girl had been killed, and Carlos taken, but he did not stop. There was nothing there for him now.

Isla La Blanca lay thirty miles out between the islets of Cayo and Orchila, in shark-infested waters, and Eagle hoped he would not have to swim tonight. The confrontation with Joe Garm could go either way. Eagle had done his homework, had done all he could, and now the coin would be tossed.

He passed through a fishing village. A filling station and a few stores were still open. Singing and the sound of guitars came from a *cantina*. Beyond the village the highway widened, skirting the sea, and he could see lights in the shore villas as he continued eastward. Joe Garm had been explicit in giving directions. This was a part of the Gold Coast where the rich had summer homes.

He reached a crossroad and turned left, down toward the ocean. No houses could be seen now and the track ended in sand at the foot of a sturdy concrete quay. A phone kiosk stood on it. Eagle walked to the end of the quay and gazed out to sea, the soft drizzle laving his face. The faintest of oil smells came through the dank air. Small waves laced around the quay; the sea was flat, a sheet of black. For a minute or two Eagle peered into the salty murk. Some thirty miles out lay the fiefdom of Sir Rodney Hamilton, complete with retainers, minions and his own yellow submarine. How did a man get that way?

He walked back to the phone kiosk. The light came on as he opened the door: A house phone with a blank dial. He twisted it all the way around and waited, counting. Ten—eleven—twelve rings.

"La Blanca."

"Garm?"

"Yeah. This Peabody?"

"Right. I'm ready to come out and talk now."

"About time, I'd say. No trouble? Nobody with you? You're not trying anything funny?"

"Would I do that to you, Garm?"

The man chuckled. "You'd better not if you want young Carlos back. Okay, I'll send the boat in. Be half an hour or so. Okay?"

"Okay." Eagle hung up.

He went back to the Ford for the keys. He buried them in the sand behind the kiosk, marking the spot with a black pebble. As he paced up and down the quay, waiting, he wished he had disobeyed orders and brought a gun. His equipment, arms and jungle gear, had been flown into Caracas and taken to the safe house. Joe Garm was a killer and Eagle had a gut feeling about this upcoming confrontation. He shrugged. Too late now. He was in the soup, and had to sink or swim on his own. He grinned at the mixed image. It had been a risk either way, still was: the cops could get him first. Their finding a weapon on him meant the slammer for a long time and he was no good to Merlin in the slammer. He was no good to Merlin dead, for that matter, but he had taken the gamble— Garm would doubtless search him—and he'd better not

121

moan about it. When things turned against him he would just have to come up with something.

He heard the boat before he saw it. A sound of power in the dark. A minute later he saw her lights curving in toward the quay. There were light stanchions on the quay; he found a box on one of them and flipped the toggle. The quay stood bathed in light, gray-yellow in the mist and fine rain. Eagle buttoned his sodden topcoat to the chin and waited.

She was a Chris-Craft yacht, about a sixty-eight footer, with a flying bridge and a pulpit. A white ghost, her bright work dulled by moisture as she slipped out of the murk, she burbled as she was reversed expertly to nuzzle at the truck tire fenders. The man at the wheel leaned to call, "You Mr. Peabody?"

"That's me."

Another man was holding her in with a boathook. He snapped at Eagle. "Jump aboard, sir. We're not tying up."

Eagle leaped. The man hauled the boathook inboard and turned to him. "My orders are to search you, sir."

"Be my guest." Eagle stood, arms raised, as the man gave him a fast and expert frisk.

"Do all guests get this treatment?"

That was ignored. The man pointed to a companion-way. "You're to wait in the cabin, sir. You'll find it very comfortable. There's a bar if you want anything. The run to Blanca takes about half an hour when there's no sea. Okay, sir?"

It had to be okay. Eagle descended the luxurious cabin, found a deep leather chair and relaxed. No drink. He had to keep a clear head and perfect muscular reaction. He felt in his pocket for the finger box and, after reassuring himself that it was there, lay back and closed his eyes. Not meaning to nap.

He did nap. A hand on his shoulder brought him awake as the man said, "We're into Blanca, sir. You must have dropped off."

Eagle made no attempt to smother his yawn. "Yeah. I've had a rough couple of days."

The man was not interested. He accompanied Eagle topside. The yacht was tied up at a long dock. On the dock, at the head of a ladder under a solitary arc light, a man waited for him. Eagle climbed. The man extended a helping hand as Eagle reached the top. Eagle ignored the hand and swung onto the dock. The man backed away a few steps as though regretting his gesture of help. It had been a mistake. Both men knew it. The welcomer was carrying a rifle and he had gotten too close to Eagle. Eagle noted it and hoped for more mistakes when he really needed them.

"I haf a jeep," the man said. He gestured down the dock. "You vill go and vait for me, blease. I haf business here a moment."

Eagle nodded and turned away. As he walked he heard the man ask the sailors if Eagle had been properly searched.

Eagle climbed into the jeep and waited. Rubbernecked. Red lights blinked on top of tall radio masts. A quadrangle of dim light must be a helicopter pad. No landing strip was outlined but he figured one to be there. He peered out to sea. The rain had stopped and the weather seemed to be clearing suddenly, as it often did in the sub-tropics. He thought he saw a light across the water but could not be positive. There was no wash of tide or current around the dock, not even a hint of surf, and he thought he must be on the landward side. The house was probably across the island overlooking the sea.

The heavyset man came lumbering up to the jeep. He was not carrying the rifle. A gunbelt was strapped around his paunch and he stopped six foot from the jeep to pull the belt around so that the holster would be on the far side from Eagle as they drove. The handgun looked like a Python .357.

The man put his hands on fat hips and stared at Eagle. He wore slacks that sagged about his ankles, and a red and white jacket. A green Army fatigue cap was pushed back from a high balding forehead. He said, "I am Hans Volkral. You are Mr. Jerome Peabody, I sink, and I hope ve are going to get along. No trouble?"

Eagle shrugged. "Not from me. But let's get going. I came here to see Joe Garm."

"Ia, Mr. Garm. He is vaiting for you at der castle. Ve vill go now, immediate."

Eagle nodded again. "Fine with me. Immediate."

Volkral told him to push over as far as he could. As he squirmed his belly under the wheel Volkral pushed the holster still farther around to his left. Eagle, who had no intention of trying anything at this stage, grinned. "Quite an installation you've got here."

"Ja. It iss. Sir Rodney iss very rich man. On the vay I show you somesing."

A friendly Kraut. To a point. Eagle would have bet that Volkral was an old Legionnaire and that he would kill you at the drop of a hat. Or his employer's command, whichever came first.

Volkral wheeled the jeep expertly up a narrow black-topped lane, the lights revealing a hillside littered with scree and boulders. When they reached the top of the hill Volkral braked the jeep and pointed. "Sir Rodney's submarine. Not many even rich mens haf der own submarine, I think nein?"

"Nein."

Eagle had been boning up on the Nautilus Two. The Caracas papers had featured it, and Merlin had reported on it. Now, as he looked down on the concrete submarine pen, he thought that Merlin was right about Sir Rodney. An ego swollen to bursting. The bastard thought he was a country!

Her gold paint flamed in a reticule of working lights. Men in dungarees and sweaters swarmed over her upper hull. Her sail, or conning tower, jutted like a saffron flag. Eagle's Apache eyes read her markings easily.

NAUTILUS II
HAMILTON

A flag was stenciled on her sail which he took to be that of Royal Eurasian Petro, Ltd., Sir Rodney's prime company. It was plum purple: Gold and purple; the colors of royalty.

He said, "She isn't as big as I thought."

"She is old British," said Volkral. "P class. She vas sunk vunce and raised, then they sell her for scrap. Sir Rodney buys her but does not scrap. Instead he fixes her up. Der Englanders vere fit to be tied. Iss against

124

international law for private individual to haf submarine. Hah. Sir Rod tell them to fix themselves. Gets a registry from Central American banana country. And here, der island, is just outside Venezuelan waters. They can do nothing."

Eagle grinned.

Volkral appeared fascinated by the submarine. He kept talking about her. "Iss diesel und electric. They take out her guns and seal her tubes, ja, make party rooms and bar, plenty of state rooms. Iss hard on the girlies, nein? Vunce you got them in a submarine they cannot run far, I sink."

Eagle agreed. "Nein." He doubted that Volkral had ever been invited to the parties. "Let's go, huh? I came to see Joe Garm, remember."

"Ja." Volkral drove on. They climbed the lane, peaked at a ridge and began to descend. A sea breeze had set in, sweeping the mist away, and below them Eagle saw the lights of the castle. As they approached he saw that it was indeed a small castle, turreted and massive-walled.

"Vas builded by Guzman Blanco," said Volkral. "He vas a dictator. They kick him out in 1889, I sink."

"You're a mine of information, Volkral."

"Ja. I am Cherman. I like facts."

"Good. Is it a fact that Sir Rodney Hamilton is here now?"

Volkral thought a moment. He had had his orders. After a few seconds he decided that answering the question would not contravene them.

"Nein. Sir Rodney is not here. He iss inland, at his ranch, since yesterday."

So much for that. Joe Garm, as Eagle had suspected all along, was going to be the front man all through the operation. Eagle was not meant to see Sir Rod. The old man, Don Simon, yes—but not Eagle.

He saw no harm in pushing it. "Is there a kid here, a boy, by name of Carlos de Ojeda? Garm kidnapped him. He killled three people doing it."

Volkral gave him a wall-eyed look. "I know nothing of such things. You haf maybe der sick imagination, I sink. And I sink maybe I vill answer no more ques-

125

tions. Ve be at castle soon and Mr. Garm vill maybe gif you some answers, Ja?"

Eagle shrugged. They might not shoot you for trying.

They crossed a dry moat spanned by working a drawbridge. No portcullis. Eagle felt a little cheated. As the jeep crossed a cobbled courtyard he noticed a basement, or was it a dungeon?—lights. A steady dynamo sound took over as Volkral killed the jeep's engine.

Volkral waved a hand. "Gum. Mr Garm is vaiting for you."

CHAPTER 17

Joe Garm's every instinct told him to kill Peabody. Or whatever his name was. That in itself was maddening— Garm had been working his balls off, spending money and casting a wide net, and had come up empty. Peabody was not Peabody, Garm damned well knew that, but who in hell was he? Nobody knew. All of Garm's connections, and he had many, had come up with zilch. Peabody was a shadow that came and went and shouldn't be there at all. Pinkerton had never heard of him, not surprising since the Pinks were a legitimate outfit and did not employ gunmen.

Peabody was a gunman, a professional, and yet more, much more, than that. Garm knew it in his bones. As a man who'd lived by guns, and his wits, for over forty years he recognized the kind.

Joe Garm was a simple man. He hated complications. He did not like to lie if he could help it, because he forgot details and got tangled in the lies. He liked things to be what they seemed, open and shut, and now he had the feeling that this job was slipping out of control. His half million, his quiet retirement was at stake, and he intended to do something about it. As soon as possible.

A man put his head in the library door. "That guy's here, Mr. Garm."

Garm nodded. "Send him in. I won't need you. But you better hang around in the corridor just in case."

The man lingered. "I like specific orders, Mr. Garm."

Garm chuckled. "Okay. If he tries to leave without my permission, meaning that if I am not with him at the time and tell you it is all right, you kill him. Specific enough?"

"Yes, sir."

While he waited Garm slid the .45 Colt from its holster, inspected it and snapped off the safety. Not that he anticipated trouble. Eagle wasn't armed. Garm felt no compunction about shooting an unarmed man if the man was a threat to him. And he had come to feel more and more, to know in his gut, that this Jerome Peabody *was* a threat to him. Not only to this whole unique operation, but to him personally.

Garm went to stand by a fireplace in which a small log fire drowzed. There was bric-a-brac on the mantel and over it hung two crossed halberds, long hardwood spears with combination axes and point heads. Clumsy and heavy weapons; Christ only knew their origin. Maybe old Guzman Blanco had brought them over from Spain.

He went back to the desk and carefully arranged the chair in which Peabody would sit, squaring it around so that Peabody would be full chest to Garm behind the desk. He took his own chair behind the desk, flipped out the Colt and swept it across the desk. He nodded in satisfaction, then frowned and moved some wire baskets, books and the pen set. Peabody must not have a chance to throw anything.

When Eagle came in Joe Garm was seated behind the desk with his feet on it. He wore slacks and a bush jacket and had an open holstered Colt .45 web-belted around his waist. Eagle sensed immediately that Garm meant to kill him.

Garm nodded and motioned at the chair. "Mr. Peabody. The elusive Mr. Peabody. Sit down."

Eagle cased the room as he sat. His mind registered everything of importance. As he sank into the chair he deftly slid it forward a few inches so his feet could

127

reach the desk. He studied Joe Garm's steak-colored bulldog face, wattled at the throat and white at the temples. The pug nose had been broken a lot. The wide-set eyes were like the steelie marbles he and his Apache peers had swapped on the reservation.

Garm began. "I'll say one thing for you. You've got plenty of guts."

Eagle nodded modestly.

"Before we get into this," Garm went on, "I don't suppose you would like to tell me your real name and who you're working for? It might make things easier."

"I don't suppose I would."

Garm chuckled. "You're going to stay Peabody if it kills you?"

"Will it?"

"Could be," said Garm. "You're a disturbing element. A loose end. I don't like loose ends."

"I'm mad for you," Eagle said, "but that's not the point. We're here to do business. Let's get to it."

Garm leaned back in his chair. He interlaced his fingers and crossed them on his chest. "Okay. Let's. First off, things have changed a lot since we met."

"How changed?"

Garm held up one finger. "One—we don't buy the shit about Don Simon wanting the kid killed. Two— we're withholding judgment about the Don being ready to deal for oil concessions if the climate is right. Maybe and maybe not. That has to be worked out between the Don and Sir Rod. Face to face. We think you're bluffing and stalling for time. What we don't know is why. You can't change anything. We hold all the cards. If the old man wants his kid back he has to deal for him. Our way."

"I'm going to put my hand in my pocket," Eagle said. "Don't get excited."

Garm nodded. "Go on. I know you're not armed."

Eagle took the little box from his pocket and tossed it on the desk. "You might forward this to Sir Rod in his jungle home. It might change his thinking even further."

Garm examined the finger. He slid off the diamond ring, held it up to the light, then slipped it into his pocket. Then he began to laugh. Eagle kept his face impassive. He knew he had lost the trick.

When Garm stopped laughing, he said, "Good try." He reached into a desk drawer and flipped a 4x5 glossy photo at Eagle. It was a picture of Jennifer Hamilton in a bikini. One of the string jobs. Only her pubic hair and nipples were concealed. She had a drink in her hand and was laughing out of the photo. Laughing at him, Eagle thought. Maybe he deserved it.

Garm was leering again. "Tit for tat, eh? Tit for tit might have been more interesting except that Carlos don't have tits. Anyway it won't work. I've had men watching the airport ever since you disappeared, Peabody. Around the clock. Some of the Wild Dogs; Ortega calls them his urban squads, and they're good."

He pointed at the phone on his desk. "I knew five minutes after you were back in Caracas. And she had all her fingers then."

Eagle was silent, waiting to hear of further disasters. Garm said, "I don't think you people spotted us?"

Eagle shook his head.

Garm grinned and shrugged. "I thought not. We didn't press it. The last thing in the world I want to do is to frighten or hurt the little lady. She's Sir Rod's daughter, for Christ sake. But we know where you've got her and my people are watching. We can take her any time we want."

Eagle shook his head. "I wouldn't try that. She could get hurt. Sir Rod wouldn't like that."

Garm waved an impatient hand. "I know that. It's a delicate situation, damn it. And I'm not going to monkey with it. Keep the girl for now. It's stalemate. Your people have got the girl; I'll tell you the address just so you'll know I'm not bullshitting you—the Casa Villadiego in Miranda—and my people have got your boy. We don't want any trouble there, no cops, so we'll cool it. Unless you try to take her out of Venezuela. Then all hell will pop. Okay with you?"

Eagle nodded curtly. Jennifer might still be a lever, but with a bastard like Sir Rod it was hard to be sure. He'd believed Jennifer when she said her old man wanted to fuck her and only lacked the courage to make an overt pass.

"So we go back to square one," said Joe Garm. "All this shitting around has just wasted time. Don Simon has to meet Sir Rod and talk it out. That means the old boy has to come here, to the island, and we'll fly him to the ranch. It can be done at night and who the hell is going to know? The whole thing won't take more than ten, twelve hours. The Don can be back before the cops know he's gone."

Eagle disagreed. "I doubt that. They're pretty hot about those killings, the three you killed, Garm, and they're watching the old man pretty closely. I'm not even sure they're buying his story, but they're still being polite and pretending to. If he wasn't a Cabinet member, he'd be in the slammer now. I don't see how he can meet Sir Rod. Too dangerous and too compromising."

Garm had not blinked when Eagle mentioned the murders. Now he said, "What makes you think I killed those people?"

"Because it figures, Garm. I know you now."

Eagle slid the chair another two inches toward the desk. Garm did not appear to notice. Somewhere in the castle a generator hummed.

Garm wondered how much of the truth to tell Peabody. Not that it mattered, but Garm was enjoying the conversation. Enjoying the power of life and death. He still didn't know who Peabody was, or how he had gotten into the act, and this puzzled and worried him. He did know that Peabody was a menace, a trouble-maker and a meddler, and had to go. But not just quite yet. There was always the chance that Peabody would give something away, would reveal his background and his employers. Garm had never doubted that Peabody was working for someone. The frustrating, the tantalizing question was, exactly who? Sir Rod must have a lot of enemies. It was important that the Big Man know who was trying to fuck him up. There might be a bonus in it for Garm.

He stayed the movement of his hand toward the Colt.

Garm was bluffing. His position had suddenly deteriorated from a position of strength to one of weakness. Peabody could not know this—Garm had known it only for the few hours since he'd talked by radio with

Sir Rod at the *hacienda*—and Don Simon would be a hell of a lot easier to bluff than Peabody. . . . Sir Rod had not wanted to keep Carlos de Ojeda at the *hacienda*. He had given the kid to Ortega, the Wild Dog, for safe keeping. Garm had advised against this, fearing a double-cross, but the big man hadn't listened. Ortega hadn't double-crossed them. He, and his men, had mistreated and antagonized the neighboring Indians, the Motilones, until the Indians turned on them. The big man didn't have the whole picture, he was keeping his billionaire ass safe in the *hacienda,* but it looked bad. The guerrillas and the Motilones were still fighting. And the Motilones had Carlos. They had surprised the Dogs, ambushed them and taken the kid prisoner.

Garm knew that he had to fly in there and straighten matters out. He was working on the details now. The one thing he hadn't counted on, the last damned thing in the world he'd expected, was Indian trouble. The Motilones were normally peaceful and friendly. But they were cousins to the Jivaro, who were head hunters, and rumor had it that some of the Jivaro had recently drifted north from Brazil. They were troublemakers.

Like Peabody, this bastard across the desk. Let Peabody know, or guess, that Garm didn't have the kid any more, that he had nothing to bargain with, and all bets were off. Peabody had known Garm wouldn't kill the boy early on. Garm saw his half million and his easy retirement going down the drain. But with Peabody out of the way there was still a chance they could bluff the Don. Peabody was the obstacle. He was as good as Garm himself, as tough and experienced and unscrupulous, and he had to go. Soon. No matter what he'd thought earlier.

Apaches, basically savages, possess an instinct for survival far surpassing that of the ordinary white man. John Eagle was no ordinary white man. He had been raised from infancy by Apaches, was one of them in all but blood, and now he sensed Garm's thoughts.

Eagle doubled his legs and kicked hard at the desk. It was heavy but he moved it enough to wedge Garm temporarily into the knee space and to hinder his draw. Eagle leaped for the fireplace.

As he wrenched one of the halberds from the wall

131

Garm fired. The bullet nicked Eagle above the right elbow, scoring the flesh, battering against the fieldstone and ricocheting crazily around the room. The roar of the Colt filled the library.

Eagle spun about, the halberd high over his head and drawn back as he felt for balance. He stood sideways, presenting as small a target as possible.

Joe Garm was on his feet, grinning, leveling the Colt at arm's length, pointing the dark blue finger at Eagle.

Garm said, "You sonofabitch. I should have done this the other night."

Eagle had grown up knowing how to hurl a lance. He and his friends had defied the law a thousand times by hunting buffalo from horseback.

Garm squeezed the trigger.

Eagle hurled the halberd. It was heavier than any lance he had ever used, but he had found the balance point and he felt it going true as it left his hand. He put everything he had into the throw.

The heavy .45 slug ticked through the quarter inch of loose flesh about Eagle's middle. Just above his left buttock. In and out, bringing a spurt of capillary blood and doing no real harm.

The point and axe of the halberd penetrated Garm's stomach. He stared at Eagle, clutching at the hardwood pole, both hands greased with blood. He hadn't fallen; he kept moving his hands along the pole in an obscene masturbation and trying to speak. Blood choked off his words. When he fell, the end of the pole jarred into the floor and shoved the blades deeper into him.

Eagle yanked down the other halberd and raced for the door. He reached it just as it opened inward. Garm's man, gun in hand, stepped in. Eagle slashed at the hand with the axe part of the halberd. The dull old halberd didn't sever the wrist, but the gun went spinning away. Eagle shoved the point into the man's throat, tearing out the jugular. The man went down, gasping and screaming and apparently trying to stop the blood with his hands.

Eagle scooped up the dying man's gun, a P-08 Parabellum, and thrust it into his belt. He was bleeding like a stuck pig himself, feeling it hot down his pants leg and inside his shirt. Nothing serious but he had better stanch it as soon as possible.

He had used his eyes and memory on the way in; now he turned right in the corridor, instead of left toward the front, as they would expect, and ran toward the generator sound.

He plunged through the first door he found. Down winding stone stairs to another dimly lit corridor. The generator sound was louder. Still no sounds of pursuit and he saw no one. With Garm dead it would take them a little time to get organized. Who was second in command? Probably the Kraut, Volkral.

There was a red light over the generator room and a sign said DANGER. Eagle propped the door back so as not to get trapped, and entered. He worked frantically, trailing blood, throwing every switch to OFF except the main. This should bring them straight to him.

The room was dark but for a central light over the whirring generator. Eagle snatched a heavy crowbar and a sledgehammer from a tool bench, and studied the generator and main switchboard for a moment, imprinting them on his mind, then he yanked the switch. The room went dark and the generator began winding down.

Eagle worked in the dark, from memory, smashing with the hammer and wedging and prying with the crowbar. In two minutes he had given the repairmen a week's work. Still no one came.

He put the tools down quietly and edged out the door. The corridor was black; no sounds and no moving lights. Garm's people, including the Kraut, did not seem all that anxious to move in and catch lead in their asses.

A waft of sea breeze moved down the corridor. Eagle moved against it, understanding why they did not come to him. Volkral, it must be Volkral, was playing it cagey. They were on an island thirty miles from the mainland, and they would be watching the yacht. The Chris-Craft was the only way off the island. He had heard nothing to indicate that a plane or a helicopter were on the island. Both might be at the *hacienda* or they might be in Caracas being serviced.

He used a handkerchief to plug the hole in his side,

securing it as best he could with his belt. The bullet burn on his arm had stopped bleeding. He kept going, feeling his way in the dark, following the breeze until he came to its source. A window was open on the wall somewhere over his head.

Eagle used his cigarette lighter to locate the window. Six feet over his head, a narrow window stood propped open with a stick. He closed the door and searched the room with his flaring lighter. He was in some kind of store room. No sweat. He tugged a couple of empty crates below the window and mounted them. He left a little skin on the narrow window frame but in a minute he was through and lying against the cold stone of the castle's foundation.

He heard voices and saw flashlights moving about. None close to him. They were waiting. Surely they had an auxiliary generator. Or they could tie into the yacht or the submarine.

That would take time. Eagle crawled toward the dry moat, slid down the slope and bellied across it to the far bank. It was hard to believe his luck so far. Only one thing explained it—the Kraut's certainty that Eagle must come to the yacht. That probably meant no extra boats and no plane or 'copter. Eagle had noticed a tiny dinghy on the yacht but it might as well be in Caracas.

Apparently there was only one way off the island. The yacht.

And yet—as Eagle wormed his way up the moat bank he made a decision. He would try the submarine pen. It was a long shot but it might come off. His life was forfeit with the dawn. They would hunt him down at leisure.

His sense of direction worked. After ten minutes of running and crawling and dodging he was on top of the hill where Volkral had stopped to brag about the submarine. Still no power. Men were working in the pen, by flashlight; they were shouting and gesticulating with the lights. Eagle started down the hills on his belly. The workmen were calling out in English and Spanish and Eagle heard enough to understand that they were waiting for the central lighting system to be hooked into the yacht.

134

There was no moon, but the weather had cleared enough for starsheen and as Eagle crawled toward the pen he saw dark piles of something, roughly pyramid-shaped, near one corner of the pen. Ruts led past them to the gate in the submarine pen. Eagle, using elbows and knees, had been making a slug's progress parallel to the track. He left it now and moved toward the pyramid. This would afford some cover.

Five piles of supplies on wooden platforms. Securely tarped and roped. Eagle lay prone and studied them. Supplies for a submarine.

It was just possible.

He sweated, working against time. Even inept workmen, working in the dark or by flashlight, would not take much longer to hook up the yacht to the castle and pen. A knot baffled him momentarily and it took enormous strength to rip out the grommet. He crawled under the tarp, snugged it down and risked using the lighter for a count of five.

Bingo!

Eagle grinned. It was beautiful. A rubber dinghy all neatly packed, compressed and awaiting only the popping of the gas cartridges to inflate. Strapped to it were a short paddle and various emergency kits. Shark repellant.

Eagle listened. Not far away, just beyond the submarine pen wall, two men were discussing women. Another man interrupted.

"What the hell goes on? Was that shooting up at the castle?"

Someone answered in a liquid Spanish accent. "What shooting, *compadre?* I heard nothing. Nor will I. I advise you to do the same."

A third man chimed in. "Listen to him, Ralph. You don't see or hear a goddamned thing. Just do your job and draw that fat paycheck."

"I dunno—I swear them was gun shots."

"I said forget it. What the hell's holding up the lights?"

"The Krauthead and the dumb fucking sailors can't find the right wire."

Someone took a leak. Over the tinkle of piss on stone someone said, "No skin off our ass. We get paid."

Eagle heard the drone of a plane.

A man said, "There's the Cessna coming back. Is he shit out of luck! How he's gonna land without lights?"

"He ain't."

The plane came in low over the island. The engines blipped and a man said, "He better watch it or he'll ram them towers."

"He's madder than hell. Can't figure what's going on."

A man laughed. "Maybe they can get him down by flashlight."

"Come on, you guys. There's Captain Vitale nosing around. We better go look like we're anxious to work."

They left and Eagle did the same. He slid under the tarp, tugging the rubber dinghy after him. It was bulky and hard to handle. He turned onto his back and, holding the dinghy on his stomach, like a rat carrying an egg, Eagle scuffed his heels and made slow progress toward the far wall of the pen. Sweat poured from him. If the lights went on now—

Beyond the submarine pen he got into boulders and scree that cascaded in a steep fallaway to the water. Eagle slid the dinghy down the scree like a sled and followed it; to hell with the noise. It would be louder in his imagination than in reality, and in the pen they were pounding on the hull with loud boom-boom-booms like gongs. He picked up the package of yellow rubber and waded into the sea.

He swam out a hundred yards, towing the package. On the island flashlights moved and darted like glow-worms. Eagle popped the gas cartridge; the dinghy hissed and began to expand, a writhing mass of yellow dough. He trod water and watched the dinghy being born. When it was delivered he climbed aboard and began to paddle as hard as he could for the mainland. The night was excessively humid and sweat flung from him with every stroke. Occasionally he stopped to fling water on himself. The sea was like tepid bathwater. He had achieved a terrible thirst and began to think of ice cold beer.

He was well out of view when the island exploded in light. Eagle stopped paddling for a moment to watch. The plane, which had been circling all this time, blipping its engines and blinking its lights, began to slant in for a landing; the tower and runway lights had come on. From his concealed vantage, looking out of darkness into light, Eagle could make out the yacht, the castle lights and the skein or work lights over the submarine pen.

He thought of the torn grommet and picked up the paddle. He wasn't out of it yet. Volkral was no dummy and if the damaged tarp was noticed and the dinghy missed, they would come after him. Get him, too. Either from the yacht or the plane. They'd machine gun the hell out of him.

Eagle took a deep breath of salt air and put his back into it. The tide was with him. But he knew that his only real chance was if the dinghy was not missed, if Volkral, convinced that he must still be on the island, waited until dawn to root him out and kill him.

CHAPTER 18

"You can scratch Joe Garm," Eagle told Merlin. He was on the scrambler from the safe house in Caracas. "I had to kill him."

The Casa Valladiego, the safe house in Caracas, was so far just that—safe. Eagle had dumped the Ford, taken a taxi and walked in the front door as bold as brass. With Joe Garm dead the snake was temporarily headless. Eagle figured he had a few hours grace.

Merlin said, "What of the boy?"

Eagle's guess was that the kid was still alive and being held at Sir Rod's *hacienda*.

"Carlos is still their ace in the hole. Without him they've got nothing to bargain with."

Merlin and Polly were in the revolving glass room. Before him on the desk Merlin had a thick sheaf of Xeroxed sheets, a compendium of computer printouts and raw intelligence from all over the world. When

Merlin stamped a MOST URGENT imprimateur on a matter, the results were speedy and costly. He had gone all the way on this one.

Eagle continued with the sitrep. "The situation here is stable for the moment, sir. They're watching us. They've got the house surrounded, but they're making no moves. My guess is that they don't want cop trouble any more than we do."

"God forbid," said Merlin. "How does it go with the girl, and with the old gentleman, Don Simon?"

Eagle explained. "Jennifer is in her room. Locked in and mad as hell. She threw a wash basin at me. Don Simon is keeping a low profile."

Merlin chuckled. "That bit of business with the girl certainly fell flat. The finger ploy was only a ploy. Polly warned me against it but I wouldn't listen. Garm will have radioed Sir Rod that she is in good health; after all I've learned of the man, I don't think we can bluff him."

Eagle was not so sure. "I lost the ring. I had to leave in a hurry. But we have got the girl and I think we had better hold onto her until we see how things go."

"Right."

Merlin riffled through the mass of Xeroxed material on his desk. Amazing, simply amazing what a man like Sir Rodney Hamilton could get away with. Very nasty, some of it. A thought struck him. He had a bad habit of taking Eagle's successes for granted.

"I was remiss in not asking before," he said. "How is *your* health, John?"

"A couple of punctures, but nothing much. I lost a little blood, but I've been patched up and now I'm okay."

"Well enough to go into the interior?"

"Yes, sir." Eagle had known all along that this was coming.

"I'm afraid you'll have to have a face to face chat with Sir Rodney, my boy, and point out the error of his ways. And the consequences. I see no other way."

"Yes, sir." Eagle knew it was already set up, in the works.

"We haven't the facilities in Caracas," said Merlin. "I intend to remedy that, but it can't be done in time

138

for this operation. You'll have to fly to Quito. You'll find everything ready and waiting."

Eagle would have bet on it.

He heard Polly say something to the old man. Merlin said, "I know, my dear. I'm just getting to that."

Merlin said into the phone: "This situation is a bit more delicate than some you've handled, John; it must be handled with kid gloves. We're going to have to cut a few corners, shave a few edges. In short, make some kind of deal. One that gets the boy back and keeps the police and military out of it."

The hole in Eagle's side itched like hell. They'd shot him full of penicillin, sprinkled some magic powder on his wounds and now his head ached, too.

"I understand about the police, but the military?" What had Don Simon told him about disaffection in the Army and Air Force? It hadn't seemed to worry the old boy much.

"OK," said Merlin. "Garm killed three people, or so I am assuming, and is now dead himself. We might be willing to let the affair cancel itself out, but the Caracas police won't be. On the other hand we can't very well give them Sir Rodney because you killed Garm."

"Probably another one, too," Eagle admitted. "At least he was bleeding a lot from the throat when I left."

Silence while Merlin thought it over. He said something to Polly Perkins. The air between Venezuela and Hawaii hummed with recondite space noises.

"Ordinarily it wouldn't matter," Merlin said, "but in this instance your cover is broken. The girl. Sir Rod won't talk and Don Simon won't talk and we won't talk. But the girl, Jennifer, given sufficient pressure, might. Perhaps out of sheer spite, to get back at her father. And even the little she knows, if the police get it, might be enough for them to ask for an Interpol warrant. Do you see where I am leading, my boy?"

"I do. Kid gloves. Sir Rod gets out of the bind if he plays ball and promises to be a good boy."

"And returns Carlos without further damage. And pays a heavy, an enormously heavy, indemnity."

"Frankly, I don't think he'll go for it. He must be in desperate financial trouble or he wouldn't have started all this."

"He is. Indeed he is. I've proof of that on my desk. Along with other data, a mass of it, including more pertinent matters. The military I mentioned.

"Some of this is educated guesswork, extrapolation, and some of it is fact. I have certain sources in the Venezuelan government. There *are,* as the old man told you, some areas of disaffection in the Venezuelan Army and Air Force. Malcontents. Young hot headed officers. There has been some liaison between them and this Ortega. My opinion, and that of my sources, is that they hope to use this Wild Dog to spark a revolution and then dump him when it is successful. Their grievance, it appears, is the present government's policy on oil prices and concessions. The rebels want to nationalize immediately and drive the price sky high. They want the billions right now."

Eagle wanted desperately to scratch. He said, "I'm surprised they haven't killed Don Simon. He *is* more or less the oil policy."

"I'm sure it has occurred to them. But enter Sir Rodney. He is using both of them, the Wild Dog and the rebels, and he sells them this wild idea of putting pressure on the Don by taking his son."

Eagle noted again that the kidnapping had originally been Carlos' idea. Merlin chuckled. "Irony there. Hoist by his own petard. He'd probably forgotten he ever planted the seed."

Polly said something which Eagle did not catch. Merlin spoke aside, his voice muffled, and then came back on.

"Since you're going up against Sir Rodney you'll need a little background. You might find a weapon in it somewhere and it won't hurt you to be *au courant* now. It just might shock him into having second thoughts if he finds out how much you know.

"His purpose in all this is to make a killing in Venezuelan oil and dig out of his own financial hole. My extrapolation, and the computer model, indicate that he hopes to gain concessions, and a controlling interest, in the new Orinoco fields. He'll try to get Don Simon, and the Venezuelan government, to accept stock in Royal Eurasian Petro. To this end he has been trying to prop up the stock artificially. My sources tell me that Royal Eurasian is in a bad way.

"Thus the kidnapping. Sir Rodney is a good amateur psychologist. He knows these elderly aristocratic Castilian types. Knows Don Simon's devotion to his wife's memory. He also knows the whole thing is a long shot, but he took the gamble. If he wins, judging by his past record and his recent activities, he probably plans to plunge heavily into the American market. A coup to delight the hearts of the old robber barons."

Polly Perkins was speaking again in the background. Eagle heard Merlin sigh and said, "Yes, I suppose you're right. But I loathe using such material—even against a man like Sir Rodney."

Merlin came back. "You know how I feel about blackmail, my boy, but in this instance we may have to consider it. There is very nasty talk out of London, and it may be just that, talk, that Sir Rodney is inclined to incest. Whether literally true or not you may be able to fashion some sort of lever from it."

"I think it's true," Eagle said. "I have Jennifer's word for it. She says nothing has ever actually happened and I believe her. She didn't seem particularly shocked or angry about it—it's just another reason for hating her father."

Merlin sighed again. "Shocking. Well, use it if you can and must. We've got to stop him one way or another. If he ever gets control of the new oil, he'll invoke the force majeur clause—there's one in every contract—and jack the price out of sight, and the United States will be forced to deal with him on his terms. He's a real menace to the world—and must be brought under control."

Eagle asked the question.

"In the event, that I cannot bring him under control? That I cannot reason with him?"

A long pause. Then, "Once the mission begins, John, you have full powers. As always. Your mission is to find Carlos de Ojeda and bring him out alive. If Sir Rodney or his men interfere, you may have to take measures, of course."

Eagle was still a little puzzled. It was not like Merlin

to be indirect. Eagle decided to try bluntness. "You mean kill Sir Rodney if I think it necessary?"

"Only as a last resort. If there is no other way. The main idea is to get young Carlos out. Once we have him safe, Don Simon will be able to handle Sir Rodney. In the courts, by police action, there are a great many ways once the boy is safe. I cannot, will not, give you a direct order on this, John. You will have to use your own judgment. Mine is not to kill Sir Rod if it can be avoided. Rogue and scoundrel that he is, he is still an important man and his death will make waves. Get the boy! Then we can release the girl and let Don Simon and the Venezuelan government take over. Have I made myself clear?"

"Yes, sir." Eagle hung up and made ready to fly to Quito.

CHAPTER 19

Eagle flew directly from Quito to a forward base a hundred miles south of Calabozo. Merlin's people, as always, performed a miracle of logistics. In two days they had set up camp in a pleasant zone of cow trees. On all horizons the llanos swept away, a sea of knee-to-waist high grass, broken only occasionally by clumps of thorny acacia and chaparral. The camp was on high ground, and dry, but the rainy season had barely ended and the llanos were in large part inundated. A series of talus mesas, innumerable stipples of gravel, were connected by a web of ditches and shallow lagoons. Farther to the south, beyond San Fernando de Apure, the riverine jungles began.

The crew were licensed as oil prospectors, with the necessary vehicles and technical equipment. Heeding a last minute flash from Merlin, they armored the vehicles with planking and fine steel mesh. For Indian trouble.

Jim Darby, the man in charge of the backup team, briefed Eagle on the eve of his departure.

"That's Motilone country. Normally they're peaceful enough. Little people, damn near pigmies; they keep to themselves and harm nobody. Leave them alone and they'll leave you alone."

It was the first Eagle had heard of Indian troubles.

"That's all I need," he told Darby. "What's got them riled up?"

Darby shook his head. Merlin's last communique had been sparse.

"As I get it the Wild Dog and his guerrillas have been pushing them around. Making slaves of them, killing them for the sport of it, nice things like that. The trouble is that it isn't just the Motilones—they're not such a tough people and might have taken it, or just moved away. But some of the Jivaro have moved in, and worse than that—"

Eagle knew something of the Jivaro. "What could be worse than that? The Jivaro are head hunters."

Darby nodded. "Cannibals. The Waimiri-Atraori. The meanest Indians in Brazil and they've been moving north into Venezuela recently. They're pushing a lot of new roads into the Roraima Territory and pushing the Indians out. You've got mad Indians. Last year alone they killed fifteen government people and road builders. And they *are* occasional cannibals. Or so I get it. It's hard to be sure."

Eagle was growing more pissed off by the moment. "Rumors?"

"Rumors usually have something behind them."

Eagle shrugged. Nothing to be done about it at this late date. He would have to avoid the Indians if he could and cope with them if he must. He set about triangulating his drop, working on the large scale map with compass, protractor, ruler and a plastic triangle. Darby checked him out.

Eagle set the pin of the compass to a rough estimate of the position of the Hacienda de Hamilton, as he called it. If it had another name he didn't know it. He drew a circle with a radius of fifty miles. Darby said, "You're doing it back asswards."

143

"Drop me anywhere on the circumference," he told Darby, "and I'll be within easy walking distance."

Darby snorted. "For you, maybe. Not for this old man. That's rough country. And we've got the data for an absolute fix, so make it."

Eagle smiled. Darby was not all that old, but neither had he been raised by Apaches. On the other hand he was a cartographer and navigator.

On arriving in Quito, Eagle had again spoken with Merlin. For a time, earlier, there had been consideration of a frontal approach—Eagle was to fly inland, land on the *hacienda* strip, stroll to the gate, and state his case. All open and aboveboard.

Eagle put the kibosh on that in a hurry. "Won't work. By this time Sir Rod knows Garm is dead. The Kraut, Volkral, will have flown inland with his gunmen. If they don't shoot us out of the air they would nail me as soon as I landed. Volkral would look for disguises. I've got to do it the hard way. Appear like a ghost from the wrong direction, the Orinoco side. Get into the *hacienda* and corner Sir Rod before he knows I'm in the neighborhood."

Merlin knew it was best that way, too.

Eagle drew lines with the ruler from Calabozo, Manapire and Caicara. Where the lines intersected he made a large dot. The *hacienda*. With a pencil he tapped the circle he'd drawn. "We'll skirt this to the west and drop me on the southern segment." He made a dot on the circle. "Right about here."

Darby nodded approval, but he looked sour. "That's liable to be mangrove country. Mangrove and swamp jungle. Lousy with snakes."

Eagle grinned. "I get along very well with snakes. Okay, is that it?"

Darby took out a notebook and consulted a long penciled list. "I guess that's it."

Eagle stretched and yawned. "Right. I want to go in just before dawn. When will the chopper have to leave here?"

"About two."

"Wake me at one-thirty," Eagle said. "I'm going to catch a fast forty." He went to his own tent and took

144

five minutes falling into sound slumber that was long for him.

When woke up he began to dress from the skin out. First the plastic body suit with the temperature regulators and the chameleon factor. Like the lizard after which it was named, the suit would change colors to match the background.

The body suit had twenty pockets, all cleverly concealed. Eagle loaded them with gear, most of it built especially, laboriously and by hand in Merlin's labs, for missions such as this.

When he finished loading the pockets, he slipped on a lightweight belt and holster containing the gas pistol. This looked like an oversized Luger with an enlarged snout—and it fired steel fletchettes vaned for accuracy. Eagle was deadly with it at fifty yards and it was all but silent. Very few of his victims ever heard the slight swooshing noise the pistol made.

Before he holstered the pistol he slipped a fresh gas cartridge into place and checked the fletchette chamber. Three of the lethal steel needles were in place. He carried two spare clips.

He donned his outer garments. Jungle boots, high-laced and waterproof. Lightweight pants, a bush jacket and an Aussie hat. His cover story, in case he ran into a jungle patrol, was that he was a freelance prospector looking for oil as well as gold. He had forged papers to prove it.

Having dressed, and slipped a hunting knife into each boot sheath, he made a final check of his back pack. This was a conventional pack, crammed with mostly conventional articles, the sorts of things a freelance prospector would normally carry in rough country.

"Conventional also were the weapons he carried openly—a .30 M-1B carbine with a dozen spare clips in an ammo belt. The little carbine was small enough to be handy in brush and jungle, and it was spiteful for its size. His hand gun, holstered to the ammo belt, was a Colt Trooper six shot chambered for .357 magnum.

Eagle was whetstoning the blade of his machete when Darby came into the tent. "Ready?"

Eagle nodded. "As I'll ever be. You people?"

145

"All set. Let's get going, then. I want that copter well out of the drop zone before the sun comes up."

They let Eagle down into a mangrove swamp. While the Huey chopper hung stationary, flailing at the humid air, they winched Eagle down in the basket. He waded up to his hips in black water as they sent down his pack and the rubber boat.

Darby leaned out to shout. "Try to work the base every twelve hours."

Eagle cupped his hands and yelled over the blatting of the Huey. "I'll try. Don't get nervous if I don't make it right on schedule."

Darby nodded and waved as the helicopter rose and swirled away, swallowed by the lowering dark sky. When its sound died, Eagle forgot it. He had work to do.

He inflated the boat, the size of a child's backyard pool, and tossed his pack and the carbine in. There was barely room for him. He took a compass reading with his flashlight and began to paddle. Mangrove lay all about him and clutched at the boat with arthritic witch-like roots. Eagle used the light continually to seek channels. He was not concerned with human enemies in the mangroves. Once the boat was bumped by a twelve foot log that was no log—his light picked up the baleful gleam of crocodile eyes.

Eagle muttered. "I'm not breakfast, you sonofabitch."

As pearly light began to seep into the east, he worked out of the mangroves to a spit of gravelly mesa beyond which he saw what looked like dry llano. He pulled the boat up on the spit, deflated it and buried it. He took another compass reading, double-checking, then slipped into the pack, picked up the carbine and started north at a jog trot.

The first day was without incident. He jogged tirelessly, paying no mind to the eighty-pound pack except occasionally to ease the straps where they chafed him. He saw no human being. He lunched on food pills and tepid water from his canteen, then assembled the tiny transmitter and called the base. He could send but not receive.

He sent his position as he reckoned it by compass and the sun—concealed half the time by dank gray cloud—and took up the journey again. The going was so far easy enough for him. At times he waded in water to his knees, slowing him up, but mostly he encountered dry mesa and soggy llano with now and then a salient of jungle. As it grew dark he transmitted his position again, so that base could judge his progress, and consulted his maps. He judged that he was within thirty miles, give or take a little, of the *hacienda*.

He used the machete to hack his way into a clump of thorn and make a bed. As he washed more food pills down with water he heard a plane.

Eagle crawled out of his thorn and tried to get a fix on the sound. He could see nothing, no lights or landing strip, but the sound appeared to come from the northeast. It figured. If he was on course the *hacienda* must be in that direction. He wriggled back into his barricade of thorn.

Before he slept, he lay for a time thinking and listening to the night sounds. A far off troop of nighthowling monkeys sensed his presence and resented it. A big cat coughed not far away and he wondered—puma, jaguar, ocelot? Eagle pulled the carbine a little closer to him.

A wild dog howled mournfully and was answered by another. Eagle thought of Emile Ortega and the guerrillas. The Wild Dog and his nasty pups. Eagle did not want any part of Ortega. He hoped to get through to the *hacienda* without encountering the guerrillas. Just as he hoped to avoid the Indians. Eagle unholstered the Colt revolver and slept, with it in his hand, on safety.

The next day, about mid-morning, he got into jungle. This, as he knew from his maps, was a freakish triangle of dense growth that pushed north from the Orinoco. Beyond the apex of the triangle there was again llano and gravel mesa—and Sir Rodney Hamilton's *hacienda*. An enclave of money and sophistication in a Stone Age culture. If Merlin's maps were right, and they usually were, the nearest village with a white policeman was a hundred miles away. Sir Rod liked his privacy.

Eagle grinned. In this case he might just be trapped by it.

The jungle slowed him, but not as much as expected. He found well worn paths and, always alert, used every Apache skill he possessed, sensing no danger. Now and then, after chopping his way through a tangled growth of vine, he stopped to pluck leeches off his arms and neck. Still no sign of the danger he feared—other human beings.

Suddenly Eagle did not like it. The jungle was too quiet. For hours he had been casting for danger, using his eyes, ears and nose, and there had been nothing. Monkeys overhead, an occasional sloth slung from a tree viewing the world upside down. Once he nearly walked into an anaconda digesting a wild pig, but his Apache eyes penetrated the protective coloration in time. A striped rattlesnake warned him and Eagle gave it the right of way. He watched a great lizard, the savage jacare, eat another lizard. All this was normal, nature as it was and should be, but now he grew increasingly uneasy. Where *were* the people? According to his briefing, and Jim Darby had been thorough, this region was fairly well populated.

He came to a grassy campo made into a greenish cathedral by tall trees that met and interlocked a hundred feet up. There was a small muddy pool and, after poking around with a stick for stingrays, he filled his canteen.

Eagle was squatting on his heels, Apache fashion, when he heard the two separate and distinct sounds. A spatter of gunfire from the north, like firecrackers, and a slithering in the jungle near him. He remained motionless, squatting, drinking the muddy water, every finely tuned sense alert.

Indians. All his instinct told him that. How long had they been watching him, following him? He was careful to keep his hand away from the carbine. They hadn't decided about him yet. It was in balance and could go either way.

A tangle of vine parted and an Indian child leaped into the campo. Maybe six years old and armed with a tiny bow and arrow. The boy laughed at Eagle and drew his little bow. He discharged the slim whittled stick that was his arrow. The arrow wobbled slowly at Eagle and struck him lightly in the chest.

Eagle was alive because he could think fast. He thought fast now and, as he glimpsed a painted face and feathered headdress behind the boy, he went into

148

his act. With great gusto, overacting, he stood up and grabbed at his chest, feigning injury. The boy laughed.

Eagle fell to the ground and kicked in a ludicrous death scene, the drawn-out antics of an arrow-shot man. He clenched his teeth into a rictus and groaned. He kept his eyes on the jungle fringe and spotted more painted faces.

The little boy chortled in glee and ran forward. He stood over Eagle, threatening him with another stick fitted to his small bow. Eagle clasped his hands in prayer; then he smiled and said, "Please don't kill me."

The boy released another harmless arrow. Eagle kicked and thrashed about. He picked up the stick and thrust it under his left armpit, near his heart, and pretended to pull it out. He groaned. The little boy was laughing and bouncing, beside himself with glee, chanting something in his thin child's voice. Eagle had not a word of Motilone.

He timed it exactly. He laughed and snatched for the boy, caught him up and whirled him about, laughing and grinning for his life. He held the small body between himself and the jungle fringe. The shield wouldn't work for long. He could hear them moving and knew they were surrounding his campo.

Eagle tousled the boy's head, grinning. "What's your name, son? What are you doing out here all alone? A big hunter like you! You sure did fool me."

Darby had told him that some of the Motilones spoke a little Spanish and English. Especially the chiefs. He hoped a chief was listening and that he understood.

Before the boy could panic Eagle put him down and slapped his little ass lightly. "You better run along home now. Your mother will be worried."

The child ran into the jungle. Eagle waited. This was it. They had him cold. If they wanted him.

The Indian did not so much step from the jungle as materialize. One moment he was not there, the next he was. Eagle knew all the tricks of moving silently and unseen, but he had met his match. He looked at the Indian, smiled, raised his right hand and said all there was to say. "Hello."

The Indian watched him with dark eyes. He was naked but for a twist of bark about his genitals. His

149

short, powerfully muscled body was painted in patterns of vermilion and black and he wore a flat-feathered headdress. The arrow fitted to his bow was five feet long, a fishing arrow, and it did not make the slightest difference. Fishing arrow, war arrow, at that range the man could not miss. Nor could his friends moving in the jungle.

Eagle showed all his teeth in the friendliest grin he ever gave. He held out his hand. "Hello. I am a friend. I am here looking for oil. You understand oil?"

The Indian nodded. "Understand oil. Not like. Much trouble. Understand road. Not like. Bad. You name?"

"Eagle." The Indian looked puzzled. Eagle repeated it. "Eagle."

"Hagle."

Eagle let it go at that. His luck was holding. So far. Gunfire sounded again from the north.

He gestured toward the sound. "Trouble?"

The Indian's stare was unwavering, the dark eyes opaque. He nodded. "White man trouble." He held out a hand. "You present me. Me chief."

A demand. Not a question. Eagle had brought along no trading goods. He slipped off his wristwatch. It was a Patek Bushmaster, custom made and paid for by Merlin. Water and shock-proof and accurate to within a second a month. He extended it.

The Indian came close, warily, and took the watch. He inspected it, shook it, held it to his ear. "Time good?"

This was a pretty sophisticated Indian. Eagle smiled and said, "Time best. You take. We friends."

The Indian slipped the Patek on his wrist and stepped back. He unnotched the fishing arrow. He made a sign and his friends oozed from the jungle into the campo. They were all around him; Eagle guessed at fifty or sixty. All men, all painted, all heavily armed—with bows, spears, knives and hatchets. No guns.

The Indians stopped at the jungle edge, ringing him. Eagle still had a tight stomach. He'd passed the first test but there was more to come.

The chief held out his hand. "Me Rauni. Chief. One time work for white man. Go to school. Learn much good white talk."

Eagle smiled and played along. "Very good English you talk."

Rauni puffed himself up, but before he could brag again the little boy came running back into the campo. He ran at Eagle and grabbed his leg and hugged it. Eagle blessed all little boys.

Rauni laughed and pointed to the boy. "Sister boy. Some day big warrior."

Eagle ruffled the dark hair. The boy was a plump coffee bean with a black thatch. Missing his two front teeth.

"What's your name, mighty warrior?"

The boy went from laughter to solemnity, as children will, and stared at Eagle. He sucked a thumb and was suddenly shy. He moved to his uncle and clasped his hand.

The chief said, "Him Tot. Sister boy. Come. Go now. *Meemee.*"

The boy laughed and clapped his hands. *"Meemee— meemee."*

They made no attempt to search him or to take his guns. Possibly they couldn't shoot. There was a good deal of whispering and giggling among the other Indians, but the concensus appeared to be that if Rauni accepted him, everything was okay. Still they were careful to place him between two groups of warriors as they filed into the jungle and along a well defined path. Eagle did not want to show his compass, lest Rauni demand it, so he waited for a glimpse of the sun through the jungle roof. They were going northeast. Toward the *hacienda.*

Rauni and the boy walked at Eagle's side. Rauni was proud of his English and talked constantly. Tot lost his shyness again, took Eagle's hand and chattered like a macaw. Eagle did not understand a word. He had gum in his pack and was tempted to give the boy some, but did not want to encourage the chief's greed. Rauni had been displaying increasing interest in the pack. Meantime Eagle garnered what he could from the chief's "English."

Rauni had lived for three years at the Capuchin Mission, had run away and worked on cattle ranches

151

and oil roads and, when smallpox and alcoholism decimated his tribe, including the ruling family, he had returned and taken over.

"Fight for chief," he told Eagle. "Kill three mens, make boss."

Quite an achievement, Eagle acknowledged. Rauni had ordered the old village burnt and had taken his people deeper into the jungle. He permitted quarterly visits by medical missionaries, but did not allow proselytism.

"Boss on cross no good my people," he told Eagle. He did not elaborate.

Anyone caught with alcohol in any form was executed at once. The black and vermilion paint on Rauni's face creased hideously as he laughed. "Give to fish. They eat fast."

Piranha.

Eagle had a bottle of scotch in his pack.

They trekked for two hours. Now and then, with great ostentation, Rauni would consult his new watch. Eagle, checking against occasional glimpses of the sun, decided that Rauni could actually tell time.

From time to time there came the sound of gunfire. Rauni and the other Indians ignored it. They might not have heard it. To Eagle it sounded like rifle and small arms, with now and again the riffle of a machine pistol. It came always from the northeast.

By now Eagle knew that *meemee* meant eat. Evidently they were headed for a feast. From somewhere Tot had come up with a bunch of tiny bananas and was popping them into his mouth whole. He did not offer Eagle any.

The jungle petered out. The village clearing lay just ahead, a circle of haystack huts surrounding the *bohio,* the communal house. The women paid them no great attention. Tot found playmates and ran off. A young girl, braless, pounded manico in a wooden bowl. She wore a necklace of beetle wing-covers and waved at clusters of flies with a turkey wing.

Before Eagle could note much of this, and file it for possible use in future, his attention was riveted by the tripod in the center of the clearing. Beneath it a fire of green wood smoked heavily. Over the fire, dangling from the tripod, hung a human head.

Rauni was watching him closely. Eagle, feigning great calm, as if this were an everyday experience, nodded at the head and said, "You take?"

Rauni shook his head. "No take. My people not do. Other bad peoples do. Come here from south, do, go."

Jivaro. Darby had mentioned them. But the head was still here. That meant they would be coming back for it. Heads were greatly prized by the Jivaro.

Eagle walked very carefully, on eggs. He knew nothing of the local taboos. He pointed to the head and then to himself. "Okay I look. See head?"

Rauni shrugged. "Look see okay. Not me. My people not do."

As he walked toward the tripod, Eagle thought of something else Darby had said. Cannibals. The Waimiri-Atraori. Darby's words came back to him. "The meanest Indians in Brazil and they've been moving north into Venezuela."

When he was within a dozen feet of the head he recognized it as that of a white man. The smoke had given it a cocoa color, but the thin features and petulant mouth were unmarred. The mustache was wispy. The long hair had been caught up and knotted and a vine looped through it to suspend it over the slow fire.

Eagle gave the head a name. No mistake possible. Don Simon had been explicit and had shown him a picture.

Carlos de Ojeda.

Rauni came to stand beside Eagle. He looked uneasy. He stared at the head, then at Eagle and touched his neck. "*Sashini.*"

Something to do with hurt or pain. Eagle nodded and touched his own neck. "Damn right *sashini.* Where body? Where rest of him?"

Rauni was definitely ill at ease. He did not want to answer that question. Eagle took a risk and persisted. He sensed that Rauni was off-balance, troubled, even afraid. Afraid of what? Eagle guessed the Jivaro and Waimiri-Atraori. So where were the bastards?

Rauni touched his mouth, and gestured toward the jungle. "Eat," he said. "Eat him."

CHAPTER 20

Having confessed so much, Rauni went the whole way. He beckoned Eagle to a path leading into the jungle, talking all the while. Eagle's respect for the chief's intelligence went up another notch—the wily bastard was trying to hedge against future trouble. This was possibly why he'd spared Eagle in the first place. He wanted a friend at court, a character witness in case of big trouble. He said as much.

"Soldiers come for punish you tell Rauni not do. Rauni and his people not kill white man, not eat, not take head. They do." He waved a hand to the northeast. At that moment came another splatter of far off gunfire.

Eagle had nothing to lose. He nodded solemnly. "I say. I tell you good people."

Then they moved into thick jungle for a time; this ended in another and much smaller clearing. On the far side a stream had been dammed to make a pool. In the center of the clearing was a long pit.

Rauni gestured at the pit. "They cook."

Eagle stood at the edge of the pit. It was about three feet deep and filled with the charred remains of old fires. Stout forked sticks were thrust into the ground. Eagle reckoned the distance between them at about six feet. For holding and turning the spit.

For barbecuing Carlos de Ojeda.

With his machete Eagle stirred around in the ashes. No bones. Cunning devils. Probably buried the evidence deep in the jungle.

"Bad," said Rauni. "Much bad. Bring big trouble."

Eagle agreed. And debated with himself. Some Indians changed their minds every two minutes, like children; at the moment Rauni was Christ-bitten and remorseful. Eagle had best take advantage of it.

Rauni was gabbling on. "Bad men think dead man's

154

important son. Much powerful. They eat and get power."

The cannibals had known who Carlos de Ojeda was. How in the hell could they have known that?

Eagle began to put something together in his mind. And was suddenly thirsty. He walked to the pool and was about to fill his canteen when Rauni stopped him. "Not do! Bad."

Rauni picked up a stick. "I show."

He thrust the stick into the pool. Instantly there was a flash of silver and buff as the water boiled. Rauni drew back the stick and showed Eagle a triangular slash the size of a dime. He laughed. "I fool piranha. They think food. Plenty mad now."

Eagle studied the pool. There must be hundreds of the tiny fish in there. Harmless-looking—except that they had a mouthful of teeth like sharks. Voracious. They could strip a man to bones in a matter of minutes. And this was where Rauni tossed those who transgressed the tribal laws.

No matter to Eagle, not his business. He left the piranha pool and walked back to the pit. He had a problem, or would have if he got out of here with his hide intact. To take the head back or not? Provided, of course, that he could *get* the head. That might take some doing.

Rauni touched Eagle's shoulder. He put a finger to his lips and pointed to the jungle beyond the pool, whispering, "Bad. Hide."

Eagle unslung the carbine as they raced noiselessly across the campo to shelter behind a tangle of jungle cactus. He went to his knees, poking about in the cactus until he had a firing coign, and thumbed the carbine to automatic fire. Rauni knelt at his side, eyes slitted in the grotesquely painted face, whispering.

"I think go. Maybe wrong. Maybe come back for head, maybe come back eat more mens."

Rauni had hit the nail on the head. The six Indians who filed out of the jungle on the far side of the campo were a different breed from the Motilone. Bigger. Taller and rangier. Naked but for paint and breechclouts; if Rauni was grotesque these men were hideous. Their bodies had been covered with mud, against insects; paint had been applied over the dried, caked mud. Terror paint. Yellow eye circles, black horns and scarlet bodies. Eagle slipped his finger into the trigger guard. Perfect targets.

Rauni saw the movement and nodded. Eagle shook his head.

The Indians had prisoners. Two men slung on poles, bound with tough liana and carried like pigs to market.

Sweat puddled on Eagle's forehead and ran down his face. More long pig? Stuffed with wild bananas and served a la carte?

He pushed the safety off. Rauni smiled. Eagle shook his head. Not yet. It was a minor dilemma. His sympathies were to a degree with the Indians. They were being harassed and murdered systematically to the south and so they'd emigrated north and struck back. Eagle did not blame them. Still he had a job to do and this was a rare opportunity. The prisoners were probably guerrillas, some of the Wild Dog's men, and he needed information. It was also a chance to get in solid with Rauni.

Eagle sighted. The problem was to catch them in a group. He debated whether rapid fire or single shots were best. A one-second burst and he would have to reload. He flicked the lever back to single shot. He handed Rauni a spare clip, motioning so the Indian would understand he was to hand it to Eagle on demand.

For the moment he lost his chance. The Indians flung the two prisoners to the ground and dispersed. Two of them went to gaze at the fire pit. Eagle, fifty yards away, could see the bone ornaments piercing their ears and noses. One Indian's mouth was distorted by a lip disc.

Another Indian stepped off to relieve himself. Two others were kneeling by the two bound prisoners, feeling their arms and legs, squeezing and pinching and chattering like women in a supermarket.

Appraising the merchandise. Determining which of the two would make the more succulent feast.

The two at the fire pit walked back. The absent one rejoined the group. They were now a group target and

156

Eagle curled his finger around the trigger. He began a long squeeze, just gentle pressure, when the target shattered. Laughing and jabbering, two of the Indians bent suddenly, seized one of the poles and trotted with it toward the piranha pool. Eagle released the trigger, swearing to himself. They had decided. One for the fish, and one for dinner.

There was no way he could save the man. With a dispersed target he could not use rapid fire and he could not be sure of getting them all with single shot. He would get only one chance and, ideally, he wanted them grouped about the fire pit.

It was over quickly. The man was gagged and could not scream. The Indians slid the pole out of the liana knots, picked up the bound man and flung him into the pool. There was an instant boil of water, a great thrashing, and the water began to turn red. The Indians did not stay to watch it. They went to join their companions at the fire pit.

Rauni shook his head in slow commiseration. Hypocrite! He did it to his own people.

Rauni touched Eagle's arm. He cocked his finger and pulled an imaginary trigger. Eagle was ready. The six Indians were grouped by the fire pit, three to a side, discussing some technicality, perhaps arguing about who was to gather the wood.

Eagle decided to go counter-clockwise. He zeroed in on the man who was at the moment speaking, gesticulating, giving orders. He squeezed off the first shot, thinking that if he made a clean sweep of it he would impress Rauni and help keep him in line.

He got six shots off in semi-rapid fire. No misses. Three of the Indians tumbled into the pit, their death throes sending clouds of ash into the air. Two more fell away from the pit and did not stir. Head shots. Luck. Eagle was going for gut shots.

The last Indian, drilled through the right chest, let out a wild cry and bounded for the jungle's edge. Eagle got off two more to make sure getting him in the head and spine. The man died with his head on an ant mound.

Rauni was laughing and chortling with joy. He slapped the spare clip into Eagle's hand and ran into the clearing, knife in hand. Eagle watched as Rauni cut six throats. Some of the bodies were still twitching.

Rauni approached the bound captive, still attached to his pole. Eagle called out. "No kill!"

Rauni, his knife dripping blood, turned to gaze at Eagle in puzzlement. "For why no kill? Bad mens."

Eagle pushed a fresh clip into the carbine, put the all but expended one into his pocket, and walked through the carnage to peer down at the prisoner.

"I need," he explained. He put out his tongue and waggled it. "Much talk. Tell me plenty he know."

Rauni got it. He didn't like it but he nodded and started cleaning his knife by thrusting it into the earth and wiping it with grass. Eagle let him sulk and turned his attention to the prisoner.

The guerrilla gazed back with terrified eyes. He wore a ragged uniform of sorts, Army fatigue pants and wornout combat boots, a faded blue denim jacket. A web belt and an empty holster. On his shoulders he wore homemade bars of bright tin. They looked as though made out of beer cans. Eagle knelt and tugged the gag from the man's mouth.

"Do you understand English?" He could handle it in Spanish if he must, but he preferred English. He was apt to miss nuances, subtleties, in Spanish.

The man nodded and gasped, "Water!"

Eagle slashed the liana binding the man's hands to the pole and gave him the canteen. The man tilted it and drank avidly. Eagle smiled at him.

"Good, eh. You might live to drink more if you talk to me and don't tell any lies."

The prisoner put down the canteen and stared at Eagle. "I will talk. I will tell you anything I know."

Eagle nodded at the piranha pool. "You saw what happened to your friend?"

The man shuddered. "I saw." He looked past Eagle at the squatting Rauni. "I beg you, *señor,* for the love of God do not give me to him. I will do anything, tell you anything, only do not—"

Eagle held up a soothing hand. "If you talk, and do not lie, I promise you will not be killed. That is the only bargain I make; you have no choice."

He hoped he could keep the promise. He glanced at

Rauni. "You understand? You are chief and I take your word. If this man does as I ask you will not kill?"

Rauni pouted for a moment and then nodded curtly. "Not kill. Make slave."

Eagle cut the man's feet loose from the pole. "That's the best you're going to get, pal. Take it or leave it. It sure as hell beats the fish or the fire."

The man huddled in abject fear and misery. "I will do anything."

Eagle touched one of the tin bars. "You are an officer in the rebel army of Emile Ortega? The one they call the Wild Dog."

The man raised himself on one elbow. He was desperately trying to summon some courage and dignity. "I am Lieutenant Francisco Vaquero. I am an officer in the FFF, the Fighters For Freedom against capitalistic oppression. My commanding officer is General Ortega."

Eagle grinned and let it go. Why crush the last of the man's self respect.

"Ok. Where is Ortega now?"

A vague wave to the northeast. "At the main camp, I suppose. I do not really know. I was on patrol with my men when we were ambushed by the savages." He grimaced. "There was no time. Five were dead of arrows before—"

"Never mind that. Where are the guns? The ones the Indians took from you." That had been puzzling Eagle.

"They hid them in the jungle. A cache." He shrugged. "Under leaves and brush. Perhaps I could find them, but—"

"I don't want the damned guns," Eagle said. "I want information. Up to now you're doing okay. Keep it up."

"Can I have more water, señor?"

Eagle gave him the canteen. "How many men does Ortega have?"

"A few over five hundred."

"All at this main camp?"

"No. Scattered at many places. Since the troubles with the Indians began."

"What started the trouble?"

The man handed back the canteen and wiped his mouth with a filthy hand. "Fools. Fools who would not listen or obey orders. Fools who murdered the Indians and raped their women."

Eagle nodded. That figured. He said, "Do you know of the *hacienda* that belongs to Sir Rodney Hamilton?"

A startled glance. "I know of it."

"How far is it from this place?"

After a moment of thought: "Twenty miles. Ten of jungle and the rest llano. The jungle is very bad."

"Is this Sir Rodney Hamilton at the *hacienda* now? Have you ever seen him or spoken with him?"

"He was there yesterday, *señor*. That I know. I saw him through field glasses."

"Why were you watching with field glasses?"

"I was so ordered, *señor*. There is trouble between this Hamilton and General Ortega. We were ordered to keep watch on the *hacienda* and the air strip. Planes are permitted in but none to take off. We were given orders to shoot down any plane taking off."

Eagle said, "I see. Why are General Ortega and Hamilton fighting?"

The prisoner spread his hands. "It is of a complicated nature, *señor*. I do not know all the facts. General Ortega does not confide everything to his officers. I tell you this so you will not think I am lying or being evasive." He glanced at the piranha pool and then at the squatting Rauni. Neither gave him much comfort.

Eagle nodded. "Try."

"There was a young man. A prisoner. We were told that he is the son of a very important man in the government."

"Was the son," said Eagle.

The prisoner shrugged. "He is dead? I am not surprised—the Indians ambushed one of our parties and took the boy, this Carlos de Ojeda, from them. Only one of our men survived, by feigning death, which is how I know of this thing."

Eagle thought about that for a moment. Rauni was now busy tossing bodies into the fire pit and raking ashes over them.

Eagle said, "Tell me about that. How did you people happen to have Carlos de Ojeda?"

The man reached for the canteen again and drank.

"I know only what I was told, which was not much, and the rumors. There are always rumors and—"

"Get on with it."

The man flinched at Eagle's tone. His life depended on Eagle and he became eager to please.

"The boy, this Carlos, was brought a prisoner to the *hacienda*. At this time General Ortega was very friendly with the *propietario,* this one who—"

"Sir Rodney Hamilton."

"As you say, *señor.* They were very thick, these two, and often the general would come back to camp drunk. *Muy borracio.*"

"Stick to English."

"Yes, *señor.* They were planning together, the general and this sir, what I do not know, and then the boy came and was given by this sir to the general for sale keeping. Or so it was said."

Eagle nodded slowly. That must have been the way of it. Sir Rod hadn't wanted to keep Carlos at the *hacienda.* What better than to turn him over to the Wild Dog. Hide him in the jungle. Government troops had never been able to pinpoint Ortega's hideout, so what chance would anyone else have?

Then it had gone sour. The Indians had ambushed the detail and taken the kid. End of friendship between Sir Rod and the general. Sir Rod would blame Ortega for fucking up. He might not even believe Ortega's story, might think he was holding the boy for his own purposes. Sir Rod must have been in a tearing rage. And still might try to bluff it through. As long as he claimed to have Carlos, and Don Simon did not know the truth, Sir Rod could hope to bring it off.

That settled one thing—Eagle had to take the head back with him. That meant a deal with Rauni. Which in turn meant walking a tight rope. Eagle set about it.

He continued to question the prisoner until Rauni, his task of hiding the bodies completed, showed signs of impatience. Then the man was bound again with liano and marched before them down the path to the Motilone Village. As they went Eagle made a deal with Rauni.

That night he feasted with the warriors and Rauni in the *bohio.* To avoid giving offense he stuffed himself

161

on pig and manioc and avocado until his belly swelled and he was uncomfortable. Later he was given a small hut to himself and Rauni sent him a young girl. While he waited for the girl to arrive—he dared not refuse—Tot came to see him and they played the game. Tot, giggling, shot Eagle dead with his tiny *tchee* and Eagle took five minutes to die. Tot was amused and joyous and Eagle hoped he was not acting out his future. When the girl arrived Tot grinned knowingly and took off.

The girl was about thirteen with sharp breasts; a pretty coffee-colored young thing. Eagle, who was exhausted and tense, was for a moment tempted, then decided no. He had enough trouble. For all he knew penetration meant marriage to the Motilone. All he needed was a thirteen-year-old Indian wife.

The girl was no problem. When she found that Eagle was not interested, she went to sleep. He lay awake, pondering and planning, and from time to time contemplating the palm leaf bag. Rauni had, after long palaver and many promises from Eagle, given him the head.

As he fought off sleep, with his revolver and carbine close at hand, Eagle debated his next move. His mission, strictly speaking, was over. He had accomplished what he came for—he had Carlos de Ojeda. What was left of him. The rest was littering the jungle. It was, Eagle conceded, a pretty terrible end. Carlos had been no prize, from all Eagle had been told, but still—

He knew he wasn't going to stop here. Call it thoroughness—he did not think of himself as an avenger—call it anything you liked, he still had a yen to see this Sir Rodney Hamilton. He must be quite a character. He would go on, then, and at least see what the situation was at the *hacienda*. A sort of war, if the prisoner was to be believed. Reinforcements had flown into the *hacienda* the day before—that would be Volkral and his men—and now they were pop-popping at each other whenever the mood took them. A seige.

Eagle found himself drowzing and pulled back just in time. Beside him the girl slept peacefully, curled up in a fetal position, smiling to herself.

When he was certain she was not feigning it, Eagle took off his shirt and assembled the little transmitter from the various pockets of the plastic body suit. He crept out of the hut—even the flimsy thatch would impede transmission—and sent a fast message to Darby, guessing at his position, because he had not had an opportunity for a compass or sun shot.

When he finished sending he lingered for a moment in the humid night. The moon was in its last quarter, shrouded now and then by clouds, but there was light enough to see the stake and the prisoner tied to it. The man slumped against the lianos which bound him upright. Eagle shook his head in sympathy. Lieutenant Francisco Vaquero. Lieutenant in a ragtag army that had no hope. Most of them would end up against a wall. There was not a goddamned thing Eagle could do about it.

There was one thing. He ducked back into the hut, checked the girl's breathing again, then picked up his canteen. He walked softly to the stake, lifted the man's head and poured water into him.

"*Gracias, señor.*"

"Keep your voice down." Eagle was whispering. He had been tempted to root the bottle of whisky from his pack and give the man a drink, but that was too much. Rauni was friendly now, but that could change in five minutes.

"What will happen to me, *señor?*"

Eagle glanced round. The village was sleeping off the feast. Still he did not want to linger.

The man whispered, "Cut me loose, *señor.* I beg of you. I will take my chances in the jungle."

The man would never make it. Rauni would be after him like a shot in the morning and there were still parties of Jivaro and Waimiri-Atraori drifting around.

And Rauni would know the liano had been cut. You could never fool an Indian on that. *And* the liano would have to be cut—the tough vine had been braided into a series of Gordian knots. It was too risky.

He patted the man's shoulder. "Keep your head. Keep your mouth shut and do what you're told. They value slaves and if you don't antagonize them you'll be all right. Sooner or later government troops will be in here; you can make a run for it then and surrender to them."

Across the campo a man stepped outside a hut to pee. Eagle whispered good luck and ducked back into his hut. It was cold comfort, but all he could do. He concentrated on staying awake.

CHAPTER 21

A last salient of jungle jutted like an arrow into the llano, level grassy plains dotted by pools and slashed by ditches. The jungle had thinned for the past few hours and Eagle and Rauni, with three Indians Rauni had brought along, had been hard put to remain under cover. As they reached the jungle fringe and wormed forward on their bellies Eagle glanced at his watch on Rauni's wrist. Just after three. The sun was blazing down and the llano was steaming. They were 8 degrees north of the equator and Eagle sweated heavily again. He had long ago turned on the cooling unit in his body suit, but sweat poured from his facial pores.

He lay prone in the last fringe of jungle and studied the terrain with field glasses, at the same time keeping a careful eye on Rauni and company. They had left the Indian village shortly after dawn, with Rauni agreeable as escort and guide, and Eagle did not want to risk a last minute change of mind by the chief. To this end he had now given Rauni his compass and a few packs of cigarettes.

Rauni was nervous and anxious to be gone. For the last hour they had been hearing gunfire from the direction of the *hacienda*. Now, as Eagle studied the llano with the glasses, there came a sudden spatter of light machine gun fire.

That did it. Rauni wriggled to Eagle and said, "Bad. Much gun. We go village now and wait—you keep promise. You do?"

Eagle nodded solemnly. "I do. Plane come and drop presents."

He had promised Rauni a shipment of knives and axes and other tools, a promise he meant to keep if he got out of this alive. Darby could get the stuff together and fly it in by helicopter.

Rauni stared at him for a long time, his muddy eyes opaque in the painted face, then thrust out his hand. Eagle shook hands. A moment later Rauni and his men disappeared silently into the jungle.

Eagle let out a sigh of relief. Life among stone-agers was chancy.

He moved out into the llano immediately, crawling through the tall grass, some of it as high as a man, and for half an hour watched his rear in case Rauni changed his mind and came back to chop him.

During the wait he divested himself of his outer clothing and pressed the switch that activated the chameleon unit. The body suit faded from white to the gray-green of the surrounding llano grass. Eagle made a bundle of his outer clothing and the pack and cached them in a ditch. He kept certain articles from the pack, along with the machete, the carbine and the Colt. Then he began to wriggle snake-like through the grass, heading for the crest of a ridge that sloped gently up half a mile ahead.

From time to time he heard more gunfire. Rifles. Machine pistols. The same light machine gun he'd heard before. He saw nothing and, though it was hard to pinpoint sound on this vast sea of grass, he knew it came from the northeast. From around the *hacienda*.

He elbowed his way up the *riso* and used the field glasses again. He was on the highest ground within miles; his view was unimpaired. He saw mown fields and grazing white-faced cattle and horses. The terrain had been checkerboarded, a field of grass mown and another left wild, with here and there a fence of white painted rails. Then he saw the *hacienda*.

At least two miles from where he lay. The powerful glasses pulled it to within half a mile. A rambling three story manor, flat-topped but for one soaring tower. At the distance he could not be certain, but it appeared to be built of stone and adobe and wood. The main house, and the many outbuildings, had been washed a faded dusky pink. The roofs were of blue tile.

The inner compound was large and square, judging from the configuration and the distance of the high wall from the house.

The wall. Eagle let out a sigh of annoyance. It was twenty feet high, of the same pink adobe brick as the house, and he could see only one gate. It was closed. From the north a narrow blacktopped lane led arrow straight to the gate.

The airstrip. Eagle focused the glasses on the far end of the blacktop lane. There it was—a half mile of tarmac, a Nissen hut and a wind sock on a pole. Nothing else. No sign of movement in the grass surrounding the strip. The sock fluttered for a moment as a vagrant breeze riffled the tall grass.

He switched the glasses back to the *hacienda*. Where in hell was the radio tower? Tower! He stared at the single tower pushing up from one corner of the house and saw a stubby mast. Probably retractable.

A burst of gunfire came from the far side of the house. Eagle crabbed along the ridge for an oblique view. His movement disturbed a snake that had been taking the sun within three feet of Eagle. Mutual unawareness. He waited until the snake slithered out of sight, then moved on. When he again used the glasses he had a fair view of the rear of the *hacienda*.

It was at the moment sporadic war. From clumps of palm and mango, breadfruit and banana, the terrain rose gently in graveled terraces. From the far side of these terraces a head popped up now and then to get off a shot at the house. There was a cluster of outbuildings, barns or workshops, and from these came the sudden stutter of the light machine gun Eagle had heard before. He swiveled the glasses and watched the burst pock the pink wall. Lousy shooting. Wasting bullets on a wall. He wondered just how serious the Wild Dog, Ortega, was about doing in his erstwhile friend, Sir Rod.

All this time he had seen no movement from the house or along the walls. No return fire. He let the glasses rove, wishing they were X-rays and he could see through the wall. Sir Rod could have an army in there. Eagle chuckled to himself. No army. What Sir Rod had was the Kraut, Volkral, and some hired gunmen. How many was a guess, but he doubted more than ten. Maybe a dozen. Enough to keep Ortega at bay.

Eagle flopped over on his back and relaxed. So it was currently a stalemate. The Dogs weren't about to lose men rushing that wall, trying to scale it in the face of concentrated fire now. And in the circumstances Sir Rod was unlikely to radio for help. Not to any government agency. But both might have reinforcements coming in.

Eagle regarded the bag, cleverly woven of palm leaf and vine, that contained the head of Carlos de Ojeda. He had made a sling for it out of woven grasses and now he sat up cautiously and put the glasses to his eyes, and once more studied the wall. Twenty feet. He had that much steel cored line.

From a long pocket of the body suit he took three strips of thin tungsten steel. One of Merlin's ideas. They could be bent and secured in place to make a grapnel. Eagle considered for a moment, then plucked one of his knives from its sheath and began to cut grass, moving to a spot where it grew as tall as himself. He had time to kill. He might need the line for something else.

He was cutting grass, slashing it off just above the roots, when he heard the patrol coming.

Eagle rolled into a ditch, leaving the bag with the head. He lay prone as they came swashing through the tall grass and passed within ten feet of him. He could not see but he could hear. And he grinned. They were feeling sorry for themselves, and each other, and griping in Spanish about the food and the lack of women and booze. Soldiers, even irregulars, never changed.

Eagle watched a lizard, the same color as himself, scuttle away to safety. So that was it—the main body of Ortega's men here was on the far side of the manor, dispersed about the cultivated enclave and the barns and garages, while patrols beat the llano to keep an eye on the front gate and the airstrip.

Eagle went back to cutting grass. When he judged he had enough he began to plait it into a rope. He had seen Apache women, working with poorer grass than this, weave a rope that would support a three-hundred pound man. Eagle, worn to a frazzle as he was by the past few days, would not go much over two hundred.

When the grass rope was finished he spent a great deal of time tying in the grapnel. When it was secured to his liking he moved again to his left, not forgetting the palm leaf bag, circling about to come up on the airstrip from the west. He was curious about the contents of the Nissen hut. Curious, and kicking an idea around in his head.

A verge had been mown around the airstrip and the Nissen hut. Eagle stopped in the tall grass at the edge of the mown strip, twenty feet from the Nissen hut. There were voices coming from the hut, speaking now and again in Spanish, but no sign of anyone. Armed men, of course, to greet any plane coming in. Taking it easy at the moment.

Stacked to one side of the Nissen hut stood a pile of gasoline barrels. Near them was a smaller pyramid of oil cans. At the base of both lay greasy puddles from spillage. Nearby there was a pile of scrap lumber.

Eagle slipped a flat object from a pocket of his body suit. It looked like an old-fashioned cigarette tin painted black. It was a phosphorous grenade. The casing was of phosphor bronze, meant to fragment and scatter, causing numerous small fires.

Eagle slipped the grenade back in its pocket. Come darkness he would start the home fires burning, create a little diversion. He snaked back into the grass, fifty yards from the airstrip, and prepared to doze a bit. Not to sleep, that was too risky, but to relax and hoard his strength for the night's ordeal. It was an Indian trick, keeping the mind alert while the body was comatose.

Wind stirred the grass over him and brought a sound of dogs barking from the house. Big dogs. That figured. Probably shepherds or Dobermans. Let loose at night. They probably had floodlights, too, but they wouldn't be using those now. That would give the guerrillas a fine target. Sir Rod and Volkral were too smart for that.

Eagle smiled to himself. Sir Rod was certainly in the thick of it here. He tried to put himself in the knight's place. What would he do if he were in the other man's shoes?

Joe Garm was dead. Or as good as dead for now. There had been no time to check his pulse. And Garm had been the big cheese in charge of dirty stuff. The Kraut might be a hard case, but Eagle doubted that he could adequately fill in for Garm. There was a security problem, too—Sir Rod couldn't let too many people know what he was up to. He'd bought Garm's gun and brains and experience—it must have cost him plenty—but he couldn't keep hiring murderous honchos forever.

According to Merlin the knight was down to his last million. He'd gambled and he was losing at the moment. Without Carlos he couldn't pressure Don Simon; he probably wasn't going to get those oil concessions. What did a man like Sir Rodney Hamilton do when he became desperate?

The far off buzz of a plane brought Eagle alert. He rolled over on his back to search the sky with his binoculars. Who the hell was that? It might be only a passing plane, oil men or freight, but he doubted it. He began to get a gut feeling; that plane was coming in here.

His vision was limited by the tall grass, but he dared not stand up, or disturb the grass too much. On his knees, craning, he swept the glasses around in an arc.

There. Off to the south and circling back loomed a small plane; it looked like a charter craft of some sort, and it was not making a landing approach. It was high. Far too high if it intended to land. And it was not a stray or passing plane. It was circling the airstrip purposefully—to what purpose?—and remaining high. Eagle estimated about three thousand feet. What the hell was going on?

Silence had fallen over the llano and the *hacienda*. No gunfire. All eyes were on the little plane buzzing like an angry mosquito.

Eagle began to get a hunch. He hoped he was wrong. He slipped the head bag over his shoulder, thumbed the safety off the carbine and made sure the revolver was loose in the holster. When he looked up again a dot was falling down the sky.

Eagle trained the glasses on the plunging dot. He

saw the pilot chute pop and then the main chute. The dot wore a white jumpsuit and a crash helmet. Goggles. Eagle swore softly to himself and the grass. There was something familiar about that swinging figure, arcing like a pendulum under the chute, spilling wind expertly and slanting for the airstrip.

She was an expert, just as she'd told him on the flight over from London, and she was going to land near the Nissen hut. Eagle ran, crouching, for the airstrip, still swearing. She was supposed to be out of the way in Caracas, safe in a safe house. A lever to bring pressure on Sir Rod. *That* little deal was sure shot to hell. She was here and she was in more trouble than she dreamed of. Unless—

Eagle crawled the last few yards on his belly. Jennifer Hamilton was a thousand feet over the airstrip. She must be aiming at the Nissen hut; she would land within fifty feet of it. Eagle moved rapidly to his left, to avoid the hut and get a clear field of fire. He was tempted to blow the stack of gas barrels, but decided not. He had only two grenades and he might need them later. What he needed was darkness, and that was at least two hours off.

From somewhere behind him he heard the sound of an engine. With it came a burst of firing from the house; he caught a glimpse of men on the walls. Trying to pin down the guerrillas *and* cover the girl; they weren't doing any good. The range was too far.

Eagle put the glasses on the parachutist again. No doubt about it now. The jumpsuit could not hide her figure and she had taken off the goggles. Her legs were close together—that was a switch—and she was coming down in the approved fashion. Another five hundred feet and she would land, roll, spill wind to keep from dragging—*and* the Dogs would have her. Eagle shook his head as he made a last check of the carbine. Let General Ortega get the girl and he had Sir Rod by the balls. If the father cared that much about the daughter. From what she'd told him—

He could see the men who had been sheltering in the Nissen hut. Three of them. In the same nondescript uniforms as the lieutenant, but heavily armed. The rifles looked like AR-16s. Mean. Eagle lay prone, at the very edge of the grass, inches from the mown strip. He zeroed the carbine in on the three men. Two of them were watching the girl descend, beginning to move in her direction, and a third was talking excitedly into a walkie-talkie.

First target. The man with the walkie-talkie. Eagle heard the engine sound again but had no time to look for the source. The girl was a hundred feet up and two of the guerrillas were running toward her. The man with the walkie-talkie lagged behind still talking.

Eagle squeezed off his first shot. The man with the walkie-talkie fell sprawling, the walkie-talkie skittering across the tarmac. Eagle swiveled the carbine and counting, *one, two,* headshot the two remaining guerrillas. The girl hit the tarmac at the same time, rolling, being dragged, boot toes scraping as the evening breeze caught the chute and bellied it. Eagle stood up in the waist high grass and shouted.

"Jennifer! Over here. RUN!"

She was on her feet and tugging at the shroud lines. She was frightened and totally confused. She saw him and her mouth opened.

Eagle waved frantically. "Come on. Run!"

She fumbled with the harness, trying to disengage. It jammed. She tugged at it, her fingers shaking and clumsy.

Gunfire rattled from the manor. The machine gun raved. Bullets snipped the grass near Eagle. He was spotted, there would be no more surprise element, and as he watched Jennifer finally disengage from the harness and run toward him, he saw the front gates of the manor crash open. A jeep full of armed men careened out, skidded, straightened and came roaring down the blacktop road toward the airstrip. Sir Rod was sending a rescue party.

The running girl stumbled and fell. Eagle cursed. She got up and came on. As Eagle ran to meet her, he heard the engine noise he'd heard before. Now he saw what caused it. A monster was lumbering at them across the llano, coming from the south.

Jennifer Hamilton fell into his arms. "My God! What is all this? Where is my father?"

"Later." He dragged her into the tall grass. Her

hands were bloody where she had scraped them on the tarmac. He gave her a shove. "Stay down. Catch your breath. We'll have to run for it."

She panted and gasped beside him, fighting for breath and words, and for the moment he paid her no attention. He focused on the weird machine rolling across the llano beyond the airstrip. It had altered course and was angling to intercept the jeep bearing Sir Rod's men. The men in the jeep, seeing Jennifer disappear into the high grass with Eagle, left off their shouting and began to fire at the strange vehicle. The jeep began to circle.

A moment of respite. Eagle glanced down at Jennifer. She was throwing up. Eagle patted her shoulder. "Get it out and get ready to go."

She nodded at him, unable to speak through her retching.

By this time Eagle knew what the monster was. A marsh or swamp buggy. Sir Rod must have brought it in to roam about the llano, in the shallow pools and marshes and ditches. The tires were enormous, ten feet high and of great width. It had a boat bottom and a truck top. The powerful snarl of the engine said diesel. An ideal vehicle for getting about the soggy llano.

Something had been added. The Wild Dog had armored the marsh buggy, welding steel plates in strategic places. Flaps of plate hung over the tires and a steel box had been built around the driver. Steel plates jutted upward along the sides of the passenger space. These plates were loopholed and men were firing through them at the jeep.

The jeep circled the swamp buggy at speed, skidding and sliding and tipping on two wheels, while the riders wasted their ammo on the steel plate. The gunners in the buggy were not such great marksmen, either. One man fell out of the jeep, the only casualty so far.

The resolution of this approached. The swamp buggy stopped and a side of steel plating fell away. Eagle saw the fifty caliber machine gun, its mount welded to the floor of the buggy. A fifty cal, at close range!

The fifty wasted the jeep in four short bursts. The jeep exploded in fiery wreckage and bodies sprawled in shattered debris, swimming in bloody pools of oil and gasoline. Eagle's nose, always sensitive, caught the stink of exploded bodies.

The swamp buggy came about in a slow full turn and headed for them. The big diesel chortled, spouting gouts of blue smoke as the vehicle, a malformed dragon, came to search them out. Whoever was directing the thing, maybe General Ortega himself, had guessed who the girl was. Ortega had binoculars. Ortega was after loot, loot and ransom, and he knew the girl was the key to the gates.

Eagle was ready. He slung his carbine and the bag with the head over his shoulder and told the girl: "Come on now. Run! On all fours. Watch me. Follow me. Save your breath."

He began to run on all fours through the grass, bearing to the right to escape the path of the swamp buggy. One thing—they wouldn't fire. Wouldn't use the fifty cal. They wanted the girl alive.

He bore a bit to the left to work deeper into the llano. They were out of the direct path of the buggy now and the grass was taller, but he could hear the roar of the diesel. The buggy, with those huge tires, was crashing over the llano, through the thick grass, like a tank taking down a picket fence. Eagle glanced at the sky. Not much help there. Still an hour, more like an hour and a half, until dark.

He heard Jennifer cry out. "John! I—can't—"

He turned. She was on her face in the soggy grass, her shoulders heaving. He crawled back. The diesel was off to the left and behind them. They had gained, perhaps, a hundred yards.

He shook her roughly. "Come on. You've got to. If we can make it till dark we've got a chance."

Jennifer had thrown away the crash helmet. She was livid, her lips dry and split, her eyes wild. Her red-gold hair tumbled down on the shoulders of the jumpsuit.

"I can't. I just can't. I'm dead. You go on. Leave me."

He shook his head. "No deal." He listened, his ear an inch off the ground. He could barely hear the panting of the diesel—it seemed to have stopped—but another sound, a combination of sounds, worried him.

Voices, very faint, and the *swish-swash-swish* of men moving through high grass. Patrols.

Eagle lay beside the girl and considered. Of course. A radio in the marsh buggy and the patrols would have walkie-talkies. Ortega wasn't dumb. He could sit in the buggy, using it as a command post, and direct the circle of patrols gradually closing in on Eagle and the girl. Ortega would know, too, that he had to catch them before dark.

Jennifer was still breathing painfully, great rasping breaths, but the look of panic was gone and she appeared a bit stronger. Eagle saw a glint of black water ahead and made up his mind. This was a losing game. If they kept running before the hunter they would eventually be snared. He would try an Apache trick. Go to ground and let the hunters pass them by. Then double back. It might just work one more time.

He touched her arm and pointed to the pool of black water. "Come on. Crawl slowly and don't disturb the grass. We're going to take a bath."

Her look said he was insane.

As they crawled he whispered. "This is the oldest trick in the book. So old that they may have forgotten it."

They reached the edge of the pool. It was shallow; he guessed it was nowhere more than four feet deep, and it spread over an acre or so. Shallow ditches connected it with other pools.

As Eagle plucked reeds he told her, "This might work because the water is so dark. Opaque. The trick is to lie on your back, with the reed in your mouth, and breathe. Keep your nose closed off and don't move a muscle. No matter what you hear, or what disturbance you feel, don't move!"

Jennifer looked at the black water and shivered. "I can't. I'm afraid. I'll drown."

"You won't. Not if you do it properly." He gave her a push. "I'll show you."

He lay supine beside her and put one of the long reeds in his mouth. He used his heels to push himself out into the water, sliding easily in the mud. As he went under he began breathing through the reed. He kept pushing out until there was a foot of water over him.

He opened his eyes and could see only darkness. Thank God for the opacity of the water.

Eagle crawled out, dripping, and said, "It's simple. Just don't panic. Hold your nose if you have to. But don't move. Once you're under don't move a muscle. Just breathe. Now go on. If you're okay I'll nudge you with my foot."

The diesel roared again. He could hear men calling back and forth. He chose a reed, blew through it to make sure it was clear and handed it to her. "Hurry. They'll be here in a minute or two."

"I'll have to tie up my hair. It'll float." She fumbled in the pockets of the jump suit.

Eagle threw a handkerchief at her. "Here, for Christ's sake. Get in there!" The swamp buggy was moving toward them.

Hastily she tied up her hair and slid into the water on her back. She held her nose. He grabbed her feet and pushed. She slid out of sight. Okay so far. He could not see her and the reed was only one of many. He fumbled about with his feet and nudged her.

A man was speaking into a walkie-talkie not fifty yards away. He said in Spanish: "No sign of them here. Continue searching." A metallic garble came back.

Eagle worked like a fiend. He tossed all his gear, including the head, into a ditch running into the pool. He pulled grass and spread it over the gear. He was conscious for the first time that the head was beginning to stink in the heat and humidity. And he had interrupted the curing process.

Eagle slid into the dark water on his back. His reed worked well, bringing down a plentiful supply of air. He inched his hand to the gas pistol and drew it from the holster, careful not to roil the water. Moisture did not affect the gas pistol.

It was hard to lie there unmoving, helpless, and put your faith in luck. He stared up into the water. Waiting. Everything depended on how brainy they were, how thorough their searching.

Near him the water riffled. Someone had stepped into the pool. He heard the diesel snorting nearby. Voices and sounds came to him, but the water distorted them and he caught no meaning. He began to count the seconds. If they gave the pool only a cursory glance, he and Jennifer had a chance.

A minute passed. The patrol was lingering on the bank. A gabble of voices, and the diesel roar became increasingly loud as the seconds ticked away. Eagle breathed slowly and easily through the reed, but his heart swelled and raced. That damned marsh buggy. It could crush them!

The dark water swirled and built into miniature waves as the buggy, its diesel roaring like a demon, plunged into the pool. The huge tires found traction on the muddy bottom and pulled it ahead. Water roiled about Eagle and the girl.

The swamp buggy was within ten feet of them.

It passed, and the voices and other sounds began to recede. Eagle sucked in a long breath through his reed. Close. And they were not out of the woods, or the reeds, yet. Luck could change. It was a long time until darkness.

He gave it five minutes. Then he cautiously brought his eyes to water level. Nothing. Nothing but the deep imprint of the buggy's tires in the soggy earth at the pool's edge. Dinosaur tracks, but the creature had not found them.

Eagle crawled out of the water and glanced at the spot where the girl still lay hidden. No sign of her. He could not even determine her reed. He grinned. She'd done okay. Been up to it. He waded out and nudged her with his foot. She came up slowly, her hair sodden and streaming, her eyes wide on him. He patted her shoulder and whispered. "Good girl. You did fine. Now if we can find a hole and go to ground we might make it. I don't think they'll search the same area again—"

Her mouth opened in a silent scream and she pointed behind him. Eagle spun around, the Lugersque gas pistol in his hand. A guerrilla was staring at them in open-mouthed astonishment.

Eagle never knew if it was bad luck or a calculated guess; if the man was a straggler, trying to catch up with his companions, or if he had gotten suspicious and come back to check the pool again.

Eagle moved fast and first. If the man got off a shot—

He did not. The steel fletchette blossomed from the man's forehead. He dropped his rifle without a sound and fell forward; his head slid into the pool. A stream of slow bubbles surfaced and broke.

Jennifer Hamilton, sitting in two feet of water, let out a strangled cry. Eagle sloshed to her and pulled her erect, whispering fiercely. "Okay—okay. Don't crack now. He's dead. Keep quiet, for God's sake."

After a moment she nodded. She pushed back her hair and began to wring the water out of it.

"You're okay?"

Again she nodded. Eagle went to uncover his cache. Nothing had been disturbed, but there was a footprint, not his own, within a foot of the cache. As he was assembling his gear, he noted a ditch leading into the pool, and out of it, about six feet to his left. It looked deeper than the other ditches and the grass grew tall along the edges. He motioned to Jennifer to follow and imitate him.

Eagle crawled into the ditch. He was impeded by the carbine, the machete, and the head bag—again he caught the stench of carrion—and the going was awkward and slow. But the ditch was a refuge—it was three to four feet deep and during the rainy season the water had scooped out hollows in the bank. Eagle crawled until he found a recess, a burrow extending into the bank, with an overhang of thick tall grass. It would hold both of them. He motioned the girl in before him, then he squeezed in beside her. He arranged his gear as a barricade across the entrance to the tiny cave and carefully arranged such grass as he could reach as a thin camouflage.

They lay side by side, face to face, a tight fit with her body pressed to him, her mouth no more than an inch or two from his. He kissed her lightly and she clung to him, trembling and sobbing quietly. He patted her between the shoulders and lightly stroked her damp hair. For a time neither of them spoke.

At last she whispered, "Is it all right to talk?"

"If you whisper. Just barely whisper."

"What do we do now? What's going to happen to us?"

Eagle shrugged. He could hear the diesel roar of the swamp buggy far north of them.

"We'll wait till dark and get the hell out of here."

"How?"

"Walk." He tapped his body suit. "I've got a little transmitter. I can call in someone to pick up us. But not here. We'll have to put some distance between us and this place."

He had already determined to go north, to stick to the llano and avoid the jungle. She would travel better on the llano and he still had to consider the Jivaro and the Waimiri-Atraoro, the latter of the cannibal persuasion when they could get away with it. Not to mention Rauni and the Motilones. Rauni had a short fuse and probably a shorter memory. No way was Eagle going back into the jungle.

Gunfire again from the direction of the manor house. It appeared that Sir Rod and Volkral, et al, were still holding out.

"What's that all about, John? What is this, anyway? What's going on? Why are they fighting?"

He shook his head. "It would take a month of Sundays to explain all the angles. Very briefly it goes something like this—this is guerrilla country and the guerrillas, namely a self-styled General Ortega, have been working together with your Dad on a certain project."

"The thing you told me about? The kidnapping? The de Ojeda boy?"

"Partly. Some of it. There must be more. Anyway the partners have fallen out. My guess is that Ortega's idea now is wipe out your Dad and his gang, then loot the place and take off in a hurry. Guerrillas don't like to stay in one place too long."

She breathed in his face. "Can't my father use his radio to call in help?"

"He could. If he wants to do all that explaining. Pop is not in much of a position to ask the Venezuelan government for help just now. I told you about the oil scam he's been trying to pull."

"Scam?"

"Con game. Whatever."

She put her dry lips against his and moved her body.

178

"This would be pretty cozy under different circumstances."

Never in his life had Eagle felt less like sex. This was some hot pants kid. Or was she trying to con him into something?

After a moment she said, "I'm not going with you. I have to get in there and see my father."

Eagle affected indifference. It did not take much acting. He'd done his job and he was getting pretty sick of the Hamiltons.

"You're out of your skull. You'll get yourself killed. At the very least gang raped over a long period. These guerrillas are very short on women. They've been stealing Indian women, and getting in trouble over it, and they would just love to see a dish like you. But it's your funeral."

Jennifer sighed and drew her face from his as far as she could. She stared into his eyes. "That wouldn't be exactly novel. I must be just about the easiest rape in the world. How long did it take you—five minutes or ten?" He could hear the self hatred in her words.

Eagle shook his head. "You've never been screwed by a hundred rough bastards in a day. That's what will happen."

"I still have to stay. I have to see my father. I have to try once more."

"Try what?"

She put her cheek against his. "Hold me, John." He put his arms around her. After a moment she began to weep. So softly that had not he felt her tears on his own flesh he would not have known.

"I've always hated him, and loved him," she said. "Hated him for the way he's treated my mother. He's a dirty old bastard, I know that, and he wants to sleep with me. I've known that for a long time, too. There's nothing admirable about him, nothing to love and everything to hate, but still I just can't give up without one more try."

Eagle repeated, "Try what?"

"To straighten him out. Get him to see the right doctors. Go into a sanitarium or a hospital, something. Anything so he can be treated. I think he's really mad.

That he doesn't know half the time what he's doing, or realize the consequences. That terrible silver plate, for one thing. His accident. It must have done something to his brain!"

She had a point. A board of psychiatrists might very well concur. Eagle did not bother to point out that it was a little late for all that now. Sir Rod was in too deep.

When he was silent she pulled away and squinted at him. Gunfire still exploded near the manor; the diesel snorted and growled like a distant giant.

Jennifer whispered: "You think *I'm* mad, don't you?"

He was noncommittal.

She went on. "Or you think I'm worried about his money. That's true, in a way. I've never been poor and I don't want to be. But it isn't only that. I wouldn't feel right, I could never live with myself, if I don't do this last thing. Try to sort things out. For one thing —I want him to go see my mother before she dies."

Eagle was examining the quality of the light. "About an hour to sunset," he told her. "After that we wait another hour or two and we can start."

"You haven't been listening. I told you. I have to stay."

"We'll see." He was pissed off with her. If she stayed he would have to stay. And it made no sense now. But he couldn't let the lovely imbecile wander around by herself and get killed. Or raped to death.

To change the subject he said, "How did you get away from my people in Caracas?" Merlin would be in a rage about that.

Jennifer patted his cheek and grazed his lips with hers. "Easy. A trick even older than the one with the reeds. I surrendered my lovely creamy white ass."

Eagle believed it. It happened. All the time. And she was right—the sex ploy was older than the reed trick.

"I screwed the hell out of him and he left a window unlocked. I went out the back way, climbed over some fences, found a taxi, went to a bank and cashed some travelers' checks. I found a charter service in the yellow pages, rented the plane, a chute and everything else I needed. That was after I called the island and they said my father was here at the *hacienda*. Simple as that."

Eagle did not bother to ask the man's name. Merlin would know soon enough. There would be a trial and the man would be punished. Eagle hoped the man thought the piece of ass was worth it.

Jennifer wrinkled her nose. "What's that smell? That stink? I've been noticing it for a long time now."

He glanced at the palm leaf bag and decided against telling her or showing her. No point to it; she might go over the edge. He sluffed it off.

"I don't know. Maybe some animal dead around here. Maybe the mud or rotten vegetation. You get a lot of smells in marshes. Don't let it worry you. I think you had better try and—"

The word 'sleep' was interrupted by the rush of delta winged jets. They came in low from the north, skimming the llano, their shadows distorted by the westing sun. Banshee fighters, eight of them in perfect formation, bearing the Venezuelan roundel and the insignia of the prancing Horse of Freedom.

The Air Force was in.

CHAPTER 22

The sky exploded. The Banshees struck like vengeful Furies, dragging their thunder behind them. They flashed in at Mach 2, stealthy as the death they carried, stood on their tails and clawed for the sky like lonesome angels.

Eagle and Jennifer rolled into the ditch and stared upward as the jet sound shattered the evening. Both spoke and neither could hear over the ear shattering din. Eagle got it at once. Simon Carlos y Garcia de Ojeda. The Don. Eagle had transmitted to Darby and Darby had passed on to Merlin and Merlin had gotten the word to Don Simon. Carlos was dead. The Don must have picked up a phone, spoken a few words and here were the planes. It must have been all laid on, plans for the strike made; only Carlos' kidnapping had delayed matters. The Venezuelan government had known all along where the guerrillas were concentrated.

Jennifer pointed. "Look!"

Six fat transports followed the Banshees in. They spilled paratroopers from their bellies. This was no half-ass effort. This time the government meant to finish off the Wild Dog and his pups.

Eagle slung his carbine and the head bag, arranged his other gear and grabbed the girl's hand. "Come on. This is our chance."

She hung back. "Where are we going?"

"Come *on!*" He tugged at her hand. "We'll cut west across the llano until we're out of the combat zone."

He was screaming over the sound of the planes. "I'll call my people in and they'll pick us up."

"No! I'm going to my father." She fought to break loose from him.

Five miles to the east a Banshee made a tight turn and came back to strafe the llano. It streaked in low, hammering the llano with cannon and machine guns. Eagle dived for the ditch, pressing his face and body into the muddy bottom, his back cringing. Water spurted and grass and mud exploded as the Banshee worked the llano over. A series of water spouts erupted in the pool. When Eagle looked up the girl was gone.

Damned little fool.

The temptation was great to let her take her chances. All his work, his success, was predicated on secrecy. On not breaking his cover. He had taken chances, gone unarmed, to avoid a Venezuelan slammer. What he ought to do now, if he had any brains at all, was to fade quietly out of the picture.

Eagle crowded out of the ditch, carbine at the ready, and began to run, crouching through the tall grass. In the direction of the house.

He stumbled over a man and went sprawling. The guerrilla was dead, a gaping hole in his back from machine gun fire. Eagle ran on. He neared the close mown strip, got to his knees and crawled. A drift of oily smoke, carrying the smell of burnt flesh, came from the airstrip. The jeep still burned.

Beyond the manor, four Banshees winged over and came in low to sweep the llano with cannon and machine gun fire. Eagle cringed. They were coming directly at him. He was scared shitless, but could only duck. He lay at the fringe of the strip and watched the .50s rip the tarmac, shred the Nissen hut and zoom out across the llano, tracers glowing in the fading light.

No sign of Jennifer. The blacktop leading to the manor gate lay empty. At the far end of the tarmac, a quarter of a mile away, the first paratroopers were assembling. Eagle put the binoculars on them for a second—armed to the teeth; grenades, grease guns, automatic rifles. A light machine gun was being set up.

From behind and beyond the manor there came a spattering of machine gun fire. The guerrillas were fighting back. Not for long. They would break and scatter soon—this was not their kind of fighting—and the troopers would hunt them down like rats.

Eagle, still in the protection of the tall grass, scanned the mown strip with the glasses. Where the hell had she gotten to?

Behind him two of the Banshees came screaming in to attack the manor. Eagle watched with stupefaction followed immediately by understanding. Don Simon's fine hand. A misunderstood briefing, gung-ho young pilots exceeding orders? A routine fuckup? Some such excuse would be used in the official version.

Eagle's smile was grim. He wasn't buying it. The old Don knew his son was dead, that he had failed in his promise to his dead wife, and he was out for Sir Rod's skin. He remembered the glint of cruelty he had noted in those old eyes. This was revenge for a dead son.

He could only lie and watch. The two jet fighters assigned to the manor knew their business. On their first pass they worked it over with cannon and machine gun fire. Chunks of pink adobe brick exploded and the tower was suddenly pitted and windowless. The front gate burst open and men ran out, white men, Volkral's ruffians, to try for cover in the tall grass. Another Banshee came flashing in and scythed them down. Two made it into the grass. Panic. They would have been safer in the manor.

Eagle watched them. The grass was shoulder high. He saw the men stop and shout, dive out of sight, and a moment later reappear with Jennifer Hamilton. A hostage. Jennifer was struggling and screaming as they dragged her, each one twisting an arm, deeper into the grass. Eagle began to run toward them, stepping out of shelter onto the grass verge for speed. He checked the carbine as he ran.

Machine gun slugs drummed along the tarmac behind him, moved onto the mown strip, passed him and moved on. The Banshee whipped over him at better than Mach 1, slow for them, and concussed air knocked him flat. He dropped the carbine. It skittered into the tall grass. No time to look for it. He drew the revolver and ran on. As he ran he also drew the gas pistol. With one in either hand he ran into the grass where he had last seen the girl and the two men.

They were pinned down. Banshees criss-crossed the llano, gridding it, gutting and destroying it. These were young pilots, fire eaters, and they were having a ball.

A line of flaming tracer severed the grass just ahead of Eagle. He saw the two men, still clutching the girl, huddled on the damp ground in a small concavity left by cannon fire. For a moment the Banshees turned elsewhere and Eagle ran toward the group. Jennifer saw him and wrenched away from the men with a scream. One of the men tripped her.

Eagle had one second of opportunity. He fired both his guns, the revolver and the gas pistol. One of the men took the steel fletchette in his gut and collapsed with a scream, rolling and thrashing about. The other man, his kneecap smashed, fired once at Eagle, missed and scrabbled into the grass.

Jennifer ran to Eagle sobbing, her face smeared with dirt and grass stain. "My God! My God! Get me out of this."

He glanced up. The sky was full of parachutes. Six

184

of the Banshees had abandoned the near llano and moved out to look for quarry in the far reaches. A dozen fire fights were raging around the perimeter as small groups of Ortega's men tried to organize and fight back. Eagle didn't give them much chance.

Or himself, for that matter. He wasn't going to make it across the llano now. There was a chance, but it was slim and he had a better idea. He caught the girl's arm and hustled her back toward the manor. They dropped on their bellies at the fringe of the mown strip. Jennifer was sobbing and crying, clutching at him, near hysterics.

Transports were passing over the airstrip in a steady procession, dropping heavy equipment. A lot of oil money was being spent. Eagle eyed the stuff as it came down—light trucks and jeeps, an armored car, smaller and more conventional swamp buggies. The Wild Dog had had it.

Eagle began to divest himself of his equipment, weapons, transmitter, tools and gimmicks, all of it. He told Jennifer, "Listen carefully to what I tell you. I've got to have a story for these people and you'll have to back me up."

She nodded. "Yes. Yes, of course. Anything—" She broke off and ducked, trembling, as a Banshee came in to blast the house again. They were using rockets now, methodically taking the manor apart, enormous bit by shattered enormous bit. The two Banshees had it well worked out between them—one slashed in to blast while the other one was turning and coming back. They alternated from different directions. Eagle's suspicions were now certainties. The two pilots had been especially trained and briefed for this. Sir Rodney's manor was their baby and they were doing a job.

Eagle hurriedly covered his gear with grass, tearing it up by the roots. As he worked, he explained to the girl that there was not much time left.

"You know me as Jerome Peabody. I've got papers to prove that. We met on the plane, liked each other, drank too much, and you invited me out here to the ranch to meet your father. It's weak and full of holes, but it might get by. I'll try to clue you as we go along.

You know nothing about Carlos de Ojeda. You never heard of him."

The Banshees came in for a final pass at the manor, hammering and blasting, and they huddled close together. Firing from the llano around them was tapering off. Eagle held her close and yelled into her ear over the shriek of the planes.

"Forget everything that happened in England. Forget everything, period. We met on the plane, got drunk together and here we are. In the middle of hell and we don't know why. Let me do most of the talking."

Eagle didn't like it. Merlin wouldn't like it. Too bad. No help for it. Paratroopers were ringing the house now, beginning to move in for the final mopping up, and Eagle had to work with what he had. He might get by. Long enough to get the word to Don Simon. The old man had a lot of grease, more than he admitted to, and he would use it to get Eagle off the hook.

Jennifer said, "There's that horrible smell again."

The bag was at Eagle's feet. He had been unable to make up his mind about it. But if she could spot it, even in this chaos, the men who questioned him sure as hell would smell it.

He nudged the bag aside with his foot and took her hand. "Come on. The safest place right now is in the house. We're going to walk over there and through that gate. Nonchalantly. Hand in hand. As though nothing has happened and all this has nothing to do with us."

She let out a wild scream of laughter. "As though nothing has happened! My God! The world just blew up and we act as though nothing has happened?"

"Try," said Eagle. "Let's go."

It was eerie. They left the tall grass and sauntered up the blacktop toward the smashed gate. The house was a pile of rubble, a smoking ruin; he would never have to use his grass rope. Cannon fire had ripped the wall into leaning segments.

They walked slowly. Nobody paid any attention to them. There were troopers on the tarmac and around behind the manor, but the couple was ignored. They stepped around the bodies of the men who had attempted the sortie, and kept going.

Eagle talked. The Banshees had gone and the only gunfire was from far out on the llano. A weird near silence descended on the shattered manor and environs. Men called to each other outside, there were sounds of engines, troops moving and shouting, curses, orders being given, but no one bothered Jennifer and Eagle.

"I don't believe this," said Jennifer.

"They'll get to us."

They were nearly at the gate. "They'll separate us," he told her. "Probably confine us. Me, at least, until they can check with Caracas. Stick to the story I gave you. Ask for drinks. Let them think you're a bit of a lush. And/or a nympho. It won't hurt."

Jennifer nodded. "I have got a bit of a reputation that way."

"Use it. And remember—you don't know a damned thing about me. I'm just a pickup."

"In a way you are."

As they walked through the gate, splintered and blasted from its hinges, someone shouted at them. They kept going. Nobody fired. Eagle breathed easier for the moment.

They were in a paved courtyard. A shambles. Bodies lay around in pools of already blackening blood. A doberman pinscher, degutted, trailed a pink ribbon of intestine. Eagle stopped and looked around. Jennifer clung to him.

"Where do you suppose—he would have taken cover, don't you think. He isn't stupid. He would have run to the basement or something. Do you see—?"

What Eagle saw was Hans Volkral. The Kraut had taken a burst in the chest. Eagle bent to make sure and straightened with a sigh of relief. Volkral could have tied him into all this. He turned to Jennifer, about to make some encouraging remark about her father, when he saw the body.

Jennifer saw it at the same time. She gave a muffled cry and ran. Eagle followed slowly.

A last ray of sun glinted from the silver skull. Jennifer was kneeling by the body as Eagle approached.

She did not touch the body of her father and Eagle saw that she was dry-eyed.

The top of the silver skull was pierced in the exact center. The hole was near, but blackened and blood stained at the edges. A bit of brain matter had leaked and was smeared on the silver.

After contemplating it for a moment Eagle said, "A fifty caliber through the top of the head will do it. But I wonder why he didn't take cover?" He gazed at the reeking, shattered, burning structure.

"A place like this must have deep basements. Even dungeons. Why did he die out here?"

Jennifer got off her knees. She had not touched the corpse. She looked at Eagle and her eyes were wet at last.

"He was a lot of things," she told him. "None of them very nice. But he wasn't a coward. I think he knew what he was doing."

Eagle nodded and turned to face the troopers pouring in through the gate. An officer was striding toward them, revolver in hand.

"Put up your hands," Eagle told the girl as he raised his own. Just before the officer reached them, he whispered. "Keep your cool and stick to your story."

CHAPTER 23

Merlin did not like loose ends. Before he filed a case away he liked everything tidy and tucked into place. He sat at his desk now, surveying the litter of Caracas newspapers just flown in. He had read the shouting headlines and now he turned to the obituaries.

General Alonza Lopez Venecia, age 99, a former President of Venezuela . . . to lie in state at the Capitolio . . . all military honors . . .

Merlin clipped the obit with a pair of gold scissors. He had paid his debt. It was somehow fitting, Merlin thought, that the old man's death should put a period to the carnage.

And such carnage. Merlin was not easily shaken, but this affair had fazed him a bit. Polly had been grim-lipped ever since the reports began to come in from Eagle.

Polly was right, in a way—Merlin *had* been judge, jury and executioner. Had pulled a D file and meddled. He, personally, thought the result worth it. Don Simon had given assurances that so long as he was in power the United States would get its fair share of oil at a fair price.

Sir Rodney Hamilton lay in a grave on his *hacienda*. Merlin put down the scissors and lit a cigar. The knight had gambled and lost and paid the price. An exorbitant price, to be sure, but he had been shooting for the moon. Had he won the concessions on the new Orinoco fields he would have had prime collateral for the banks, could have borrowed enough to ride out the storm, squeezed the world for top dollar.

Polly was in her chair working with papers on a clip-board, going over John Eagle's final report. She said, "John's idea is that Sir Rod deliberately exposed himself to gunfire. A kind of suicide."

Merlin spun his wheelchair about and stared at the volcano. "Yes. I think it very possible. Hell is a private place, you can't share it, and he must have been a very lonely man."

"Jennifer Hamilton told John that she thought her father was mentally unbalanced."

The volcano puffed smoke. Merlin puffed back at it with his Havana. "We'll never know for sure. Especially is such a matter—who *is* sane and who *is* crazy."

Polly got on with her work. Eagle had a tendency to write with flair; his reports had to be carefully edited.

Merlin stared at Makaluha and thought: The old Don used us, once we were into the thing, just as Garm used the Wild Dog and Sir Rod used Garm. And now they were all dead but Simon Carlos y Garcia de Ojeda. An old fox. He had known more than he had ever admitted to Eagle, had been on top of the situation and ready to strike when the kidnapping of young Carlos stymied him. But how beautifully he had coped, how quickly adjusted. Yet in the end he had failed to save his son. The *coup* had been smashed, the Army and Air Force rebels rounded up and jailed, but the Don had failed in his promise to a dead wife.

Polly glanced up from her work. "You know that John buried the boy's head after Don Simon ordered his release?"

"I read the report, Polly. Our John Eagle, as tough as he is, is a compassionate man."

"I know. I love him."

Eagle had never told Don Simon the complete truth about his son's death, or the manner of it. Just that he'd found the boy's body, badly decomposed, and buried it in the jungle. No need, Eagle had written in his report, for the old man to know the grisly details.

The Venezuelan authorities had moved onto the island of La Blanca in force, had seized everything in sight and were in the process of sorting matters out. Merlin considered the move of doubtful legality but thought they would get away with it. Just as the stories in the newspapers, on his desk now, had been heavily censored. The printed version was what the government wanted printed and no more.

Polly said, "John has submitted a voucher for five thousand dollars. For tools dropped to some Indian tribe—the Motilones?"

Merlin had been doing his homework. He nodded. "Yes. A promise he made their chief, one Rauni. For saws and hammers, chisels, the like—honor the voucher."

He chuckled. "John may have to go back into that jungle someday."

Polly riffled through her papers. "Not for a long time, if the tone of this report is any indication. He says he is going to put a DO NOT DISTURB sign on his ranch in Arizona and shoot the first bastard, I quote, who bothers him for two months. Including Samson. Especially Samson. And he is not answering his phone."

Merlin wheeled back to his desk. "He deserves a

long rest. I hope it works out for him. But in this world who knows?"

Who indeed?

Homo Homini Lupus.

Man is a wolf to man.